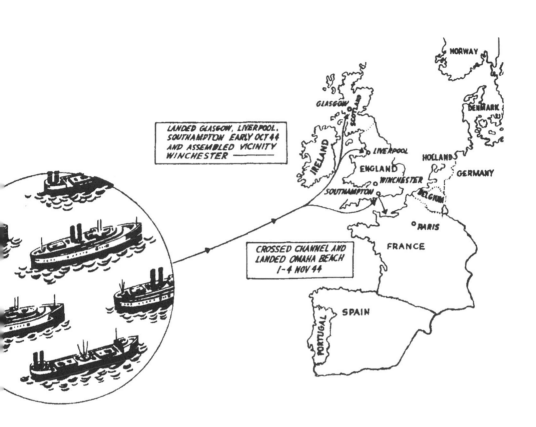

LANDED GLASGOW, LIVERPOOL,
SOUTHAMPTON EARLY OCT 44
AND ASSEMBLED VICINITY
WINCHESTER

CROSSED CHANNEL AND
LANDED OMAHA BEACH
1-4 NOV 44

NORWAY

GLASGOW

SCOTLAND

DENMARK

IRELAND

LIVERPOOL

HOLLAND

ENGLAND

GERMANY

WINCHESTER

BELGIUM

SOUTHAMPTON

PARIS

FRANCE

PORTUGAL SPAIN

IE WAR ZONE

WAR CLASS

A NOVEL

BY

JACK COBB

Quotations used by permission of:
Pat Conroy for quote from *Lords of Discipline*.

Putnam for quote from *Fools Die* by Mario Puzo.

Printed in the United States
by
Palmetto Bookworks
P.O. Box 2105
Lexington, SC 29071

Library of Congress Preassigned Control Number
2002107209

ISBN 1-887301-18-6

TO
The 2d Lts, "The 90-Day Wonders"
and the Enlisted Men who fought the
good fight in the combat infantry
platoons
of the 84th Division
against the
invincible Armies of the
Third Reich in the
Mother of All Wars.

These unsung heroes:

Went where others feared
to go, and did what
others did not want to do.

Saw the face of terror;
felt, and at times enjoyed the
bittersweet taste of victory.

Cried, suffered pain, and
lived lives that some would say
should best be forgotten.

Yet, they cannot, for
once bloodied, they will never view
the world quite the same.

And, in memory of Charles J. Coakley 01326154,
2d Lt AUS, Sgt. RA, CIB, SS, BS, PH,
trusted friend and fellow graduate of
OCS Class 323A, Fort Benning, GA 2 May 1944.
Charlie was killed on Christmas Day, 1944, while
leading a rifle platoon of L Company, 333rd Infantry
Regiment. He embodied the best of the Irish: the
love of good ale, the company of friends,
the sound of music, and courage in battle.

Other Books by Jack Cobb

Cobb and Cobbs- Early Virginians

The Complete Book for Doing the Family History

Cobb Chronicles

House Spouse- Man in a Woman's World

AUTHOR'S NOTE

This novel is based on the author's research, personal experience, and interviews with former officers and men who served in rifle companies at the front. Any similarity to persons living or dead in this work is coincidental, and exists only in the mind of the reader.

It is about college students from a military college, mostly teenagers born in 1923 or 1924. They were called-up a year short of graduation to fight as infantry in the most costly of all wars. Their friends and brothers of the classes of 1942 and 1943 drove the enemy from the beaches of Normandy back to his borders. Now it was the turn for the class of 1944—"The Class That Never Was"—to carry the battle to the heart of Northwestern Europe.

The largest group of this military college war-class of '44 experienced war at its ugliest with the 84th Infantry Division, a division of citizen soldiers. Nearly all of the group were killed, wounded, or captured.

Members from a number of other college classes of '44 also carried a disproportionate share of the burden of the war. One university built a monument to its war class of '44 with the inscription:

"We were just boys, pure boys, and then there was the war and half of us were dead or wounded."

But wait, I am moving too fast. I must be careful or I will get to the end before the beginning. Be patient with me. For I have waited a long time to tell this story. It is not just about young men dying for God and country. It is also about the love of women and bonding of men.

So let's begin in September 1940. It was a year of challenges, happiness, and innocence. The flames of war had been lit in Europe—but Europe was of no concern. It was far away!

I want to tell you how it was. I want precision. I want a murderous, stunning truthfulness. I want to find my own singular voice for the first time. I want you to understand why I hate the school with all of my power and passion. Then I want you to forgive me for loving the school. Some of the boys of the Institute and the men who are their sons will hate me for the rest of their lives. But that will be all right. You see I wear the ring.

Pat Conroy
The Lords of Discipline

CONTENTS

ILLUSTRATIONS

WAR CLASS

THE CLASS THAT NEVER WAS

PROLOGUE

The entrance to The Military College (TMC) was impressive. The ostentatious wrought iron gate, embellished with state and college crests, reflected a sense of pride and orderliness. The whole scene, the oversized gate and the suddenly rising white towers beyond, were a bit intimidating to the 16 year-old Ashley. But it was too late to turn back; this, after all, had been his choice. He was entering an institution known for making men out of boys.

Ashley lifted his heavy, shop-worn leather suitcase and with a sigh of relief passed through the gate. Suddenly, a cadet appeared. He was not much older or larger than Ashley, but it was obvious from his bearing and command voice that he was a more mature, self confident individual.

"Mister, where the hell do you think you are going?" he said in an unmistakable southern drawl.

"I'm reporting in for freshman registration," Ashley answered, startled and annoyed at the intrusion.

"Who in the hell are you? You are 48 hours late!"

"I'm Brett Ashley. My father died last week. I attended his funeral yesterday," Ashley replied, pulling himself up to an erect position and looking his inquisitor in the eye.

"Mister Ashley," the cadet gate guard yelled. "There are no excuses allowed here. Do you know who you are talking to?"

"Nope," Ashley replied.

"Take a good look, mister, I'm a cadet corporal. I have been assigned to this gate to keep riffraff like you out. Now try `sir' and get used to it."

"Sorry, Sir," Ashley acknowledged

"Ashley, go to the second building on the left. It's called Byrd Hall. You can register there. After that, walk to the last building on the left beyond the parade field. It's called the Armory. They are issuing uniforms there now. By the way I suggest you burn those God awful, green trousers you are wearing as soon as possible.

"The `Rat', Cadet Platoon Sergeant Ratkowski, will spot you right away and you will be in big trouble. The Rat is a big, mean guy from somewhere in Ohio. He came here on a boxing scholarship and to no one's surprise he has become the Southern Conference heavy weight champion. The Rat tries to run off those that he considers unfit. He thinks of it as purifying the Corps. So be on the lookout for him and a few others like him who feel that time is too short to try to make `silk purses out of sows' ears. So get moving Mister Ashley—you got a lot of catching up to do. By the way, sincerely sorry to hear about your dad. Good luck," and with this the corporal smiled for the first time.

"Thanks, I appreciate your advice. I'll remember it well, Sir," Ashley called out while moving on the double toward Byrd Hall and registration.

It came as no surprise to Ashley that the name on the door of the Registrar's Office was French Huguenot. He knew that they were among the earliest and most prolific immigrants in the old port city. However, it was a surprise that the registrar was a woman.

An extraordinarily attractive young woman in the registrar's office gave Ashley an appreciative smile in response to his eyes, which did little to disguise his thoughts. The self confident lady sitting behind the masculine, oversized desk across from him was gorgeous, and it was obvious that she knew it.

"Welcome to TMC, Mr. Ashley. Have a seat please. I'm Kit Montague, the acting registrar today. My father, Major Montague, is the registrar. He thought that all students would be in by now, so he took a day off. This has been a busy week; he needed the rest. So it will just be the two of us."

"Thank you Miss Montague," Ashley responded, taking his seat nervously. The thought of just the two of them being together for any period was enough to generate all sorts of imaginative fantasies. The colored rays of the late afternoon sun that filtered through the ancient lead glass windows gave a reddish tint to her blond, shoulder length hair. Although no authority on the subject, Ashley thought her clear fair skin, perfectly shaped nose and full mouth were too perfect. At first he thought the face lacked character, a face of someone who could easily trade on her good looks to get ahead. But then he looked again. The first impression was quickly discarded once he discovered the highly intelligent look in her mischievous, dark blue eyes.

"Mr. Ashley," she continued. "I note from your application that you have not selected a major. Although there is no requirement that you do so at this time, there are some things you should think about. There are a number of liberal arts as well as scientific majors available. The most popular are political science, business administration, and civil engineering. The poly sci majors often go into the military, to law school or graduate school. Some of the business majors go back home to run the family's business in dirt-farmer towns in the South or tired, depressing cities in the northeast, and get rich. The higher starting salaries are usually found in engineering and other scientific fields but these programs are the most difficult. And there are really not too many wealthy alumni among the group. This evaluation is my own and off the record. You see, my dad has been here more than 20 years. I was born on campus. Now having said that, there are a number of documents that I must have you sign before joining the Corps."

It was a day of many surprises for the last entrant of the Class of '44. It occurred to him that this girl, this woman, was no more than a year or two older than he was. Yet, she had the manner and sophistication of a 30-year old.

Kit Montague moved from the oversized desk across the room with the dexterity and poise of a fashion model. Ashley watched her every move. For the first time he saw her full figure. "My God, how beautiful," he thought. There was something strange, something mesmerizing about her. Her silk-like dress was a blue floral print, a color that complimented her eyes. The square neckline was cut just low enough to provide a slight but titillating view of her small breasts. The hot humid air moved only with the aid of a single ceiling fan. She wiped the perspiration from her arms and face. Her damp, thin dress found its way into every crevice of her perfectly shaped body.

Ashley's opened mouth expression of astonishment was readily transparent even to an amateur. She had seen that Anglo-Saxon, slack-jaw look many times before. She enjoyed the attention within the protected environment of the stone walls and wrought iron gates.

"Mr. Ashley, "I'm a psych major. I am also a student of body language, and mind reading. I find the mind a magical universe. By the way, if you behave yourself and they let you outside the iron gates in a couple of months, you might sit in on one of my classes. It would be useful. You know if the war comes, you might end up in the infantry. Just think what it would be like to feel the enemy watching you, when they can't see you. That's possible, you know."

Miss Montague took a chair across from Ashley and handed him copies of the processing documents. She then proceeded to meticulously advise him on how to find the next orientation station. He listened intently to her instructions for the next processing step, which turned out to be the same as the gate-corporal had given him, but he enjoyed having her repeat them.

"By the way," Miss Montague continued, "I almost forgot, your assigned roommate's name is Cal Sinclair. He's from California. It's school policy to mix Carolinians with Yankees and Westerners. That way, by the time they graduate their "hominy grits" accent is not so pronounced. It makes it easier for their would-be employers outside the state to understand them."

Before rising to say good-bye and good luck, she crossed her legs. Kit Montague smiled devilishly as she watched the blood rush to his sun burnt face. Ashley had a sudden need for air, even sweltering humid air.

"I have to leave now, Miss Montague, thanks for your orientation," he said as he quickly moved for the exit. He bumped headlong into the door, turned back to smile sheepishly, leaving her with her hand cupped to her mouth like a Japanese Geisha trying to conceal her laughter.

"Mr. Brett Ashley, I hope I see you again," she called after him, but he was gone. For some inexplicable reason she was drawn to him. Was it his innocence or his awkwardness that attracted her? She didn't have the answer, but she would find out. Time was on her side.

PART ONE

THE THIN GRAY LINE

September 1940-May 1943

1

The line of cadets at the armory waiting for issue of uniforms extended beyond the entrance and halfway around the building. Ashley took his place at the end of the line of a group of nervously chattering high-school graduates. Like him, they too wondered what the next few days and weeks would bring. For Ashley, misfortune would not wait for the next day, there were no trousers left in his size. The Army supply clerk told him to stop by in a week to see if they were in. My God, he thought, the cadet corporal at the gate had warned him to avoid being conspicuous. As he looked around at the field of gray, he knew the "Rat" could not miss him in his colorful pants—trousers. Upper classmen would remind him that the girls at the local finishing school for proper young ladies wore pants—cadets wore trousers.

Ashley walked alone along the river's edge in a circuitous route toward Lee-Thomas Barracks, his new home. He had had an inauspicious day: he had been chewed-out by an arrogant little corporal, flashed by a local beauty, and now he would join the Corps out of uniform. For a brief moment, he had an opportunity to take in his surroundings and take stock of himself for the first time. He thought of quitting, but he couldn't do that. To go back home and face his family and local cronies would be even worse. Ashley's father's long bout with cancer left his family little money except for the college education for him and his two sisters. His options were limited.

Reality had now begun. He turned back towards his assigned barracks with determined resignation. He entered through another impressive wrought-iron gate; passed a guard room on his left and a large, open quadrangle (quad) to his front. The rectangular shaped "quad" was surrounded by a four-decked structure connected by circular towers at the corners. Ashley cautiously turned left past the first tower room, reserved for ranking upper classmen, and finally located his smaller room two doors beyond. His roommate was sitting at a table under a single window poring over a small red book—the cadet bible that contained the honor code, customs, courtesies and traditions, rules, regulations, punishments, and cadet activities.

"You know how this little bastard of a book says we rank?" his roommate asked.

"No, how do we?" Ashley answered.

"Below the president's dog, the commandant's cat and all the waiters in the mess hall. How do you like that? Hi, I'm Cal Sinclair. Welcome to your new home."

"Hello, I'm Brett Ashley. Sorry I'm little late."

After looking each other over for a moment, Ashley gave a brief summary of his personal problems to his newly found and, hopefully, compatible friend. It was obvious that any other situation could be a drag in space no larger than an oversized closet. And it was an arrangement that could last at least a year.

From a first impression, Brett was satisfied that he and Cal Sinclair would get along. He could see already that Sinclair had a sense of humor, and he figured he would be the kind of guy who wouldn't sweat the small stuff.

Sinclair was taller and thinner than his Carolina roommate. His features were small and regular and his hair light brown with blond sun-burnt tips. From the movies he had seen, Sinclair fit the California stereotype perfectly. Ashley decided then and there that he had better never introduce his girl friend to this guy, unless he wanted to lose her.

"Where do you come from, Brett?"

"Stevensville," Ashley said

"Where in the hell is that?"

"Go out the main gate a couple of blocks, hit Rutledge Avenue, turn left, go about 50 miles or so west and you got it. Where are you from?" Ashley asked.

"Newport Beach, just south of LA but, for me, a little too far from San Francisco—a great place to eat, drink and have fun.

"Brett," Sinclair continued. "I was one of the first here, so I'll tell you a little bit about what I've found out. Outside the barracks may look like a movie set for 'Ivanhoe', but inside these rooms there are not too many luxuries. You can see we've got an non-air conditioned room furnished in early military—an oak table, two chairs and one lamp between us—and something called a "press". That's this monster here, an oversized wardrobe. It almost touches the nine-foot ceiling. We have individual shelves on each side of this thing where we display our socks, shirts, underwear, etc., for daily inspection. In between the shelves are rods for hanging our uniforms. And this space underneath is for storing our folding cots and mattresses each morning before we go to classes. And an important item—the open toilets and showers are a short walk down the gallery. Over there in the corner is the wash basin we both use. They tell me that anyone caught pissing in it is confined to campus for a month. And you are required to walk tours. One tour equates to a fast walk on the quad for an hour carrying a ten-pound rifle. That's about it for now. I'm glad to have company.

"Oh," Sinclair continued. "There is one other thing."

"What's that?" Ashley asked.

"In the Red Book, among other things, there is the honor code. I understand that at the other real military college in Virginia they call it the Gentleman's Code. The honor code recognizes that we come from a world where it is commonplace to lie, cheat, steal and cover up for those that do. Not here. You get caught breaking the code and you are out on your ass. The tough part of the code is the requirement to inform on those who break the code. In effect, we become snitches—truth before loyalty. This place is up to its rear with the subject of duty too. Did you see that bronze plaque at the entrance when you came in?" Sinclair asked.

"No, I missed it," Ashley said, finally getting a word in.

"You gotta read it. It's by somebody called Robert Edward Lee. It says— 'Duty is the sublimest word in the English language.' I remember it because I plan to be an English major. I thought that 'most sublime' would have been a better choice of words than 'sublimest'," Sinclair joked.

"Cal, better watch the not so subtle humor involving General Lee. To people in these parts he ranks just below Jesus Christ," Ashley cautioned his talkative roommate.

"Yeah, Brett, I think you might be right."

The evening meal was informal. The high school kids with cropped haircuts chatted easily around rectangular tables as though they were in their chosen fraternity house, and being waited on by smiling, black waiters. But this would be their last such supper for the year.

The next day began with the reveille bugle at 6:15. Doors opened and piercing screams of the "elite cadet cadre" filled the air. The rebel yells of General Pickett's fateful charge at Gettysburg could not have been more bone-chilling. Hell week had begun! And with it the proven metamorphosis of converting recruits to cadets and boys to men was underway.

"Hit the quad on the double, move it, line up, dress right dress, suck up your fat gut, roll your butt forward, rap your neck back, pull your shoulders back, eyes straight ahead you dumb squat, etc., etc." the cadre yelled endlessly.

After three or four days of running around, Ashley and Sinclair began to get the hang of it all, and were able to see a little humor in the suffering. But this introduction to the system was too good to be true.

"Mister, you duck butt in the green trousers, get in step." It was a high-pitched, but effective command voice.

"Sir, do you mean me?" Ashley said, knowing full well that the command was in his direction.

"You bet your sweet ass I'm talking to you, you dumb squat—get in step!" the big sergeant yelled.

"Sorry, Sir, I didn't know you were talking to me, you see my pants, I mean my trousers, are teal blue," Ashley mumbled, realizing too late that the sergeant found no humor in his remark.

"Squad, halt," the sergeant commanded. "You wise ass, your trousers are green, do you read me?"

"Yes, Sir, they are green, Sir."

"Ashley, you and your roommate, that ding-bat Sinclair have been on my shit list since I saw the two of you talking in ranks yesterday when you were supposed to be at attention. You two are the sorriest excuse for recruits that I have ever seen since I've been at this institution. I'm putting both of you in the awkward squad until further notice. Mr. Sinclair, did you hear what I had to say to Mr. Ashley?"

"Yes, Sir, Sergeant Ratkowski, I understand, Sir!" Sinclair had learned the right verbiage in military prep school.

"Good, both of you drive by my room now, I need to teach you two pieces of shit a few things," the sergeant growled.

Sergeant "Rat" was physically intimidating. He was about six feet two, and easily weighed 200 pounds, fat free. He was slightly below the average size for a division one college boxing competitor but he was the current Southern Conference heavy weight champion. From his excessively muscled body and thick neck, it was obvious that he spent all of his free waking hours pumping iron and admiring himself in multi-view mirrors. The overdeveloped chest muscles caused his long arms to swing out from his body like an ape.

The Rat was pacing the floor of his room when the two recruits arrived.

"Welcome to my cozy place, said the spider to the fly," he snarled.

Ashley and Sinclair took their position a few feet within Cadet Sergeant Ratkowski's room as instructed and stood at rigid attention. They soon came to realize that the early reports on the fury of the Rat were grossly understated. They both immediately concluded that the monster looking down on them, with the angered expression of a pit bull, was a sadistic son of a bitch.

"Now both of you stand against that wall over there at the position of a cadet at attention—chin rapped back, butt forward, eyes straight to the front.

When I release you, I want to see the outline of sweat from your flabby bodies on my nice clean wall. Got it?" the Rat said.

"Yes, Sir," they responded in unison.

The Rat checked his cheap watch and took a seat at his desk and began reading the training schedule for the next week. Either he was a slow reader or was purposely allowing his "captives" to melt in their own sweat. After precisely 15 minutes, he stood up from his desk and made an inspection of the wall for perspiration marks. His expression showed no displeasure, which led the two recruits to assume his torture-project was going as planned. Ashley, however, noted out of the corner of his eyes that his roommate had become pale and was unsteady on his feet.

"Now, I need a volunteer for the next series—a strength test, which I am convinced both of you slobs will fail miserably. I will demonstrate each of them once. Clear?"

"Clear, I volunteer, Sir," Ashley responded, realizing his new friend was too sick to continue much longer.

"All right, watch closely—the first test: Grab this heavy, 1903 bolt-action Springfield rifle by the small of the stock. Hold it straight out from your body, with your arm parallel to my spotless floor, turn the rifle to your left a 90 degree angle and return it to the original upright position. Do you think you can handle that Mr. Dumb Squat?" the Rat inquired.

"I think so, Sir," Ashley answered, in a less than assured voice. He then took the old weapon precisely as the big sergeant had demonstrated. To his surprise and without too much difficulty, Ashley completed the maneuver that could have easily torn the tendon connecting his elbow to his wrist. Ratkowski was visibly disturbed at the outcome of his first test.

"All right, we will now test your back as well as your arm strength. This oak chair weighs 50 pounds. Watch how I lift it." Speaking now from his hands and knees, the upper classman selected a specific leg of the chair and lifted it from the floor with one hand as though it was a feather. Ashley, sensing the test was one of balance as well as strength, watched closely which leg was chosen as a lift point. He asked for a repeat of the demonstration. The Rat reluctantly obliged.

It was now Ashley's turn. From all fours, he took hold of the lift point and lifted straight upward. Nothing happened. Hot sweat turned to cold at the thought of verbal abuse he would receive should he fail. He shifted his position slightly and with a new surge of adrenaline, he lifted again. This time the heavy chair slowly cleared the floor. Ratkowski stood with mouth wide open in disbelief.

"How in the hell did you little shit do that?" he fumed. "Do you realize that except for jocks on scholarship like me, you are probably one of a dozen freshman who can do both of those on the first try. How did you learn to do that?" he roared.

"For two summers I worked in a lumber yard with a bunch of big, strong colored guys. They taught me a few things about strength and balance. But they also cautioned me to remember that, 'he who brags of his strength acknowledges that the mule is his superior,'" Ashley said, returning promptly to his position of attention against the wall.

At that unpredictable moment, Sinclair sprayed a gusher of vomit striking the invincible Rat in the chest. It slowly oozed down his once starched shirt, down his perfectly pressed trousers into his shoes. Then without warning, Sinclair fell forward in a semi-unconscious state. His head struck the edge of the solid oak press, causing an ugly gash above his right eye. Blood and vomit intermingled on the floor as he struggled to regain consciousness.

Ratkowski roared like the wounded animal that he was—"Get this man to the cadet hospital, now!" This was an order that Ashley had no problem with. Using a cold wet towel as a compress, the bleeding was slowed. Sinclair's color was nearly back to normal by the time they reached the small hospital. He was rushed into the emergency room with a doctor and a nurse at his side. It was an hour later when he waddled back to the waiting room.

"Brett, how do you like those twelve little stitches and the shiner?. I told them I fainted and took a little fall. They want to keep me overnight for observation. Thanks for your help. By the way, as God is my witness, that big bastard is going to pay in a way that he will never forget."

"OK, Cal, mum is the word," Ashley said. "See you in the morning after breakfast."

Brett left his roommate at the hospital and stopped at the canteen soda shop for a chocolate milkshake. He decided to check his post office box next door for the first time for word from home or elsewhere. After several tries at the combination it opened. The news from home was that all was well and the envelope included money—not much, but enough under the circumstances. Then he discovered an envelope, a pink one seductively perfumed. He looked about to see that he wasn't being watched and carefully opened it. The hand writing was unfamiliar, as was the tone. He read it over and over again and again and inhaled the perfume until dizzy from the sweet fragrance. It read:

Dear Brett,
By now you will have finished 'hell

week'. The worst is over, and like most of the others you will grudgingly learn to love this place as much as I do. I wish you the best. I care what happens to you. Strange of me to say that, since I spoke with you for only a few minutes in my dad's office your first day here.

K.M.

Ashley couldn't believe his good fortune. Where there was only despair, there was now hope. He immediately returned a note on the most expensive stationary that he could find in the canteen:

Dear Kit,

Your note of encouragement could not have come at a better time. I had begun to get the feeling that I was in the camp of the enemy and there was no route of escape. Now I realize that it was only my imagination. There is at least one friendly within the fortress.

Thanks for caring.

B.A.

Ashley retrieved his roommate from the hospital the next morning. His prognosis was excellent. There would be minimum scarring of his handsome face.

"What are you smiling about Brett, you look like you figured an honorable way out of here?"

"Not that lucky, Cal, but almost. I had a nice letter from a newly found friend. In your condition I'm afraid you would frighten her if I introduced her to you. Someday I will."

2

Except for a small article in the Charleston News and Courier, hardly anyone would have known that a new class of cadet recruits had begun their school year at TMC, the premier Military College of the South. It was a special day for the new cadets. Hell week was over. General Mark Pealot, TMC's President, would now welcome them. The Class of '44 was assembled in the large armory after a short march from near by Lee-Thomas barracks. They waited quietly and anxiously for the arrival of the general.

Brett Caldwell Ashley had never seen a military officer before, but he would this day—four stars and all and one of most respected military men of his time. The highest ranking and only military man Ashley could recall in his one horse town was a Marine Corps lance corporal. He was a handsome devil in his dress blue and red uniform. Just the sight of him turned the head of many a young lady. But the corporal's good looks proved to be his downfall. He was doing well until his last hitch. It was during this fateful period that he was posted to some God-forsaken, south sea island where he had an inappropriate relationship with a raven-haired, Eurasian beauty. And, as was the custom of the natives, a "shot gun" wedding followed. That ended the corporal's promising career. He returned home to his old job as a used car salesman, and reared a bevy of handsome, black-eyed kids.

The fresh-faced recruits stood at something that resembled attention until a striking cadet figure gave the commands: "At ease. Take your seats."

Cal Sinclair nudged him and asked, "Do you know who that cadet is?"

"No, do you?" Ashley said, mesmerized by it all.

"Yeah, he is the cadet colonel for the entire Cadet Corps. At West Point they call him the first captain. Look at him standing there. He's General Pealot's fair-haired boy. Take a good look and you can see why. He is ramrod straight. He has wire-like red hair, and midnight blue eyes that look past you in search of something more important. Note his straight teeth and a slightly crooked smile; that alone will make him a prime Army Air Corps candidate. Check out the gold stars he wears on his collar. That's the military version of Phi Beta Kappa. You can be sure this guy will never have long hair or a tattoo on his ass, like my beach buddies in California. He is what every mother would like her son to be—Jack Armstrong, the All American Boy."

"Sinclair, how in the hell do you know all this? We have been here less than a week," Ashley whispered, being careful not to get an unsolicited glare from the cadet colonel.

"I spent a couple of years in a military prep school in California before my parents sent me east to keep me from becoming a beach bum. I read up on this place as soon as I got the word that they had accepted me. I had the grades and my dad had the political connections to get me an appointment to the `Point'. But I chose this mosquito swamp instead. I may have made a bad mistake. These damn rebels down here take this military crap seriously," Sinclair lectured his roommate.

Ashley and Sinclair would soon realize that the top cadet and his cadre of cadet officers, not the president, or the academic colonels, would decide who would measure up to the disciplinary standards of the Corps, and who at the end of four long years would be deemed fit to wear the RING. It was not the commission or the degree that was the ultimate prize, but the ring—the ever-present reminder of having met the standards of an institution dedicated to making honorable men from a few good boys.

Suddenly, there was a sound of movement and muted voices from the side entrance of the armory. General Pealot had arrived exactly at the scheduled time. As he proceeded to take his predetermined position, the cadet commander turned to the new freshman class and roared: "Tench hut" (attention) and then calmly, as if in a trance, made a smart about face and raised his hand in a perfect salute.

"General, the 550 members of the Class of '44 are all present or accounted for, Sir," the cadet colonel reported to the college president.

The general looked out over the perspiring group of young men standing rigidly before him for several long seconds before returning the cadet commander's salute. He stood alone in the center of the stage, without a note or a prop. It was as if he were an actor playing to first nighters. It was a role he knew well, for he had been the star performer at the institution for ten years.

"Thank you, Colonel. Gentlemen, please take your seats."

It was a rich voice, with a soft nasal resonance common to Southern preachers. He was the first southerner since the Civil War to be nominated by the President for the army's top job—the chief of staff.

The general was bigger than life. Not physically, he was less than six feet tall, somewhat overweight. His shoulders sloped slightly, giving the appearance that they did not exceed the width of his hips. But his bearing and manner was that of a Prussian. His thick wavy gray hair was parted so as to be perfectly aligned with the nose of his strong, chiseled face. His dress blue uniform was a show piece of ribbons, sashes, and badges for his service as an artillery officer in the Philippine Insurrection, the China Relief Expedition, and WWI. Only General Douglas MacArthur had a more distinguished career.

The Board of Visitors brought him in as the college president to add to the prestige of the institution. He did not disappoint them. He kept the old school alive and well, even during the great depression. The public had the impression over the years that he and the institution were one. The college had become, in the view of some, the West Point of the South. If this were considered an asset, then the credit belonged to General Pealot.

There was a feeling at times, however, that the years had taken its toll on the military college head master. He had begun to think of himself as King Arthur and his cadets as Knights of the Round Table.

"Gentleman of the Class of '44, I wish to take this opportunity to welcome you to the proud city of Charleston and this great institution. You have chosen well. And we believe in your acceptance, so have we. There is something in training for the profession of arms that takes on a mystic form in the lives of men. Our college has it. It was established to train youth for soldiers in the defense of this great city. Its founders followed the inspiration of the code of arms handed down to us from knighthood, teaching men to do worthy deeds, teaching service in keeping with the best and noblest traditions.

"We produce soldiers, scholars, and gentlemen here at the college. We look for those who grow in

mind, body, and spirit. *The words of the inscription over the entrance of the chapel: 'Remember thy creator in the days of thy youth', are not the words of a fool. Heed them. I do not need to belabor the subject of Duty and Honor, for here they are taken for granted.*

"*I'm reminded of Teddy Roosevelt's counsel to young men of his day when he said: 'I want to see you game, boys. I want to see you brave and manly. Keep your eyes on the stars, but remember to keep your feet on the ground. Courage, hard work, self-mastery, and intelligent effort are all essential to success in life. Alike for the nation and the individual, the one indispensable requisite is character.'*

"*Gentlemen, I sense that your Class of '44 will have a rendezvous with destiny in the not too distant future. There are strong winds of war spreading through out Europe and Great Britain. At about this time last year, a dangerous war began with the German invasion of Poland. By June of 1940, the mighty German Army under the control of a madman overran France and the Low Countries. As I speak to you today, the battle for Great Britain between the Royal Air Force and the Luftwaffe has begun. Our Congress has responded, thank God, and approved the first peacetime draft. I pray that your class will not be called upon to serve until you have completed your chosen fields of study. However, if this war involves our country, this may not be possible. You could well be called upon to do the most difficult of jobs—to lead infantry platoons in the thick of battle. God forbid, but if that day should come, you will be ready to answer the call to duty. God bless you all.*"

The cadet commander, on cue, called the class to attention and closed the ceremony with: "Company Commanders, take charge of your companies." Ashley and his classmates had had a full day. They had seen a great General and a great showman at his best.

3

After seven days and nights the cadet cadre was satisfied that they had done their job. The Class of '44 was told that it would be the best class ever, and oddly enough they believed it. They learned to stand up straight, to walk square corners, and eat square meals for the pure entertainment of upper classmen. They also learned to tuck their shirts with the use of coat hangers, not only giving them a neat appearance but the illusion that their shoulders were broader than their butts.

The new and eager members of the class were now able to march in a manner that resembled close order drill. They marched everywhere—to mess, to classes, to chapel side by side with the Agnostic, Protestant, Catholic, and Jew.

The day that began at 6:15AM ended with lights out at 11:00PM. After taps, the cadet duty officer never failed to make his check with a firm knock on the door and with not always a cheery—"All present in there?" To which the occupants dutifully responded—"All present and accounted for, Sir!"

No one was permitted to study after lights-out even using concealed light sources. Nor was there time for self-pity. There was no time left in the day for it. Once the indoctrination week was over, the day began with classes followed by physical training. Much of the afternoon was spent in classrooms or laboratories. The college curriculum of the forties, like the Ivy League colleges, required credits in math, chemistry, physics, history, English, and a foreign language as a graduation prerequisite. It was a demanding curriculum for the likes of Ashley who had come from rural schools of 11 grades with few college preparatory courses. Students from 12-year city schools with good academic programs had a much easier time of it.

It came as no surprise that the highest attrition rate came in the first few weeks, when the unsuited and unmotivated went back home to mama mumbling that life was unfair. For those of the Class of '44 who stayed, it was for the badge of honor, the ring—the precious piece of gold—that kept them in the Corps.

At the end of the military indoctrination week, the cadet recruits were assigned to lettered companies of infantry and coast artillery. Ashley and Sinclair were asked to volunteer for the infantry. The upper class recruiters told them that only the best soldiers were chosen for the infantry—"The Queen of Battle." Of course they wondered how they could have made such an impression from the awkward squad. They were told that if they chose infantry they would be able to continue to room together. With that, they took a step that they would live to regret. But for the short time it had its advantages, they would be able to distance themselves from the Rat since he was an artilleryman. They would meet a nasty little corporal, called "Puppy Dog" because of his incessant barking of orders and yapping in general, but he was basically harmless. Then there was Cadet Sergeant "Gump" who played the military game as though he were the commandant's personal representative. The "Gump" was a tough and demanding one, but he never required his charges to do anything that he wouldn't do and couldn't do better himself.

There was no shortage of rank on the campus.

General Mark Pealot, the retired four-star regular officer, was the top dog and the highly respected president of the college. Next in line was the rather strange Colonel Peter McNutt. McNutt was the senior regular army officer on the faculty. As such, he was the personal representative of the War Department with the title Commandant and P.M.S. & T., the head of the Department of Military Science and Tactics. Among the cadets he was referred to as "Panama Pete." When the heat approached a hundred degrees, he would breakout his tropical uniform, khaki shirt and shorts with a sun hat not unlike the type worn by the British in India. The problem with McNutt was that he took his job too seriously. Most regular officers knew the assignment was a career sidetrack for those nearing retirement, and one with little potential for further advancement. For lack of enough to do, McNutt meddled in the area of cadet senior officer prerogatives, making life miserable for the Corps as a whole.

It was rumored that Panama Pete had the "chef" put saltpetre (potassium nitrate) in the food to keep cadet libido in bounds. When string beans turned yellow—"look out for salt peter," the saying went. Old Pete didn't hesitate to resort to mass punishment either when a confession to a violation of rules was not forthcoming. Once a battalion of the Corps was marched half the night to uncover the culprit who tossed a garbage can down a connecting concrete stairwell, but to no avail.

In addition to the few regular officers on the faculty, there were others: reserve and national guard officers, and officers of "local rank" including the academic faculty who held military grades appropriate to their seniority and professional level. Members of the Board of Visitors were appointed to the rank of colonel.

Ashley thrived in the structured military environment. Having met and been befriended by the beautiful Kit Montague, his adjustment was a lot easier. On the other hand, his roommate was not nearly as enthusiastic. But he was determined to stay with it, at least long enough to repay the Rat in kind for the sadistic treatment he had received during hell week.

During the first year Ashley and Sinclair became inseparable. They made a vow to return the next year, and continue as roommates if at all possible. Life as upper classman would be more civilized. It was a "stick and carrot" disciplinary system. They had had the stick. They were now ready to try the carrot.

4

Brett Ashley and Cal Sinclair returned to the institution for their second year as they had agreed to do. But the long gray line was thinner now. Nearly a fourth of the class was absent for roll call in September 1941. The roommates each had achieved some measure of success. Ashley had been promoted to corporal and selected to be a part of the cadre, the group responsible for the indoctrination of the incoming freshman class. He was also chosen to be commander of the awkward squad, of which he was an alumnus. Sinclair, though still a private, had earned gold stars for the highest academic achievement.

The 1941-42 school year was not exactly an average year for college students. Off American shores a World War was in the making. Germany was in control of France, Belgium, Denmark, and Norway, and had begun its futile invasion of Russia. Japan had joined the Berlin-Rome Axis. The world crisis still seemed a long way from the peaceful campus until the Japanese Air Armada sank the American Pacific Fleet on 7 December 1941. By the end of May 1942, the Class of '44 was inducted into the Enlisted Reserve Corps (ERC). A similar action was taken at all federally funded Reserve Officer Training Corps (ROTC) programs. World turbulence was now a serious issue within the administration and the Corps of Cadets. General Pealot was very much concerned that his students would be sent off to the war and his college shut down.

Cadet Corporal/Army Reservist Ashley's immediate problem, however, was learning to adjust to his newly discovered authority and responsibility. He was ordered to report to a board of military officers to answer to a charge of hazing. He confessed to the officers that he had requested that as a favor a freshman put down his and his roommate's bed in the evenings.

"Corporal Ashley, why do you think that anyone would want to put your bed down at night?" the board president asked.

"Sir, it is the custom for fourth classmen to take care of small tasks for upperclassman. It is not a demeaning requirement. My roommate and I took care of the beds for two sophomores last year. It was not considered irregular. We in turn received some reciprocal protection and guidance from them. They were our mentors—they knew the ropes."

Ashley fully expected to be stripped of his rank and confined to the campus for an indefinite period of time. But he wasn't. He was given a verbal reprimand, and the Red Book of regulations was revised to prevent reoccurrence.

Then there was the "Garfield caper". Sergeant Gump, Ashley's superior, held his corporals responsible for the appearance, order and discipline of members of their respective squads. Garfield, a member of Ashley's squad, presented his new leader with a sizeable challenge. He was a street-wise kid from an affluent, Long Island family. He had obviously been sent to TMC by his naive parents to get him straightened out. Garfield had one goal—get the hell out at all cost. He presented an unbelievable appearance at formations: his shoes were seldom shined, his brass never polished, and his uniform a rumpled mess. The poor guy was born with a large gut, curved back and arms that nearly reached his knees. When he was told to pull in his gut his butt popped out, and vice versa. He was not exactly reserve officer material; but he had a plan. One night he sneaked out of his room, found his way to his chemistry professor's office, climbed over the door transom, and stole a major chemistry exam. The little weasel was caught a few days later selling the exam at an exorbitant price.

It was moonless night when Ashley and Sinclair got a final glimpse of the stooped figure being marched toward the main gate. The drummer was on his left and the Corporal of the Guard on his right. The drummer beat the slow cadence of the funeral march.

"Hey Brett, there goes one of yours. Look, he's in step. You finally taught him how to march," Sinclair said, needling his roommate.

"Yeah, I bet the little bastard has a smile on his face. His plan of escape is complete," Ashley said with a sigh of relief.

"Brett, you are not getting to be one of those hard asses, drunk with power, are you? Some freshman are beginning to refer to you as 'The Rock'. This is the second guy from your squad that you have sent home mumbling to mama about their mean little corporal. What he told his mama about you would probably not be fit to print. Tell me you are not getting to be another "Rat"—a cleanser of the Corps."

"Damnit Cal, give your roommate some credit. Garfield was a crook. The other kid was a wimp. Everytime I told the weakling to clean himself up and stand up straight, he'd start crying. Neither of the two were exactly destined to be future leaders of the nation."

"OK, roommate, you are right," Sinclair said. "They were not fit to wear the ring. By the way, I have not forgotten to do unto Ratkowski what he hath done unto me. I still have a scar above my right eye as a reminder. The day of retribution is near."

5

"Ashley, you've got a telephone call in the guard room. Nice female voice. How'd you get to know someone with a voice like that?" yelled the cadet sergeant of the guard.

"Irresistible, sergeant, irresistible. That's how I made corporal. I'll take the call."

"Hello!"

"Brett, It's you, I'm glad to hear your voice. This is Kit. How are you?"

"Couldn't be better under the circumstances. Great to hear from you," a happy Ashley replied.

"How would you and Cal like a tour of the town this weekend?" Kit continued. "I have a friend who would like to meet him. I told her he is not only good looking, but that he also comes from a rich California family with Hollywood connections."

"Right you are, I'll say yes for both of us."

"Good, Brett, we will meet you at noon in front of the Calhoun monument across from the Francis Marion Hotel. By the way, her name is Liz Rutledge. Does that name mean anything to you?"

"No, should it?"

"I've got to give you a history lesson—she's a direct descendent of Edward Rutledge, signer of the Declaration of Independence."

"Great, but Cal would be more impressed if she were a surfer," Ashley joked.

"He can teach her, see the two of you Saturday at noon," Kit said, signing off.

"Cal Sinclair, have I got a deal for you, and me

of course," chirped Brett to his roommate on return to the room.

"What's up Brett? What kind of deal?"

"I've got you a `hot date' with a beautiful, local blueblood this Saturday for lunch, and a historical tour of Charleston."

"How do you know she's beautiful?" Sinclair asked his roommate.

"All southern girls are beautiful, you know that. With the new convertible your dad gave you for getting through your first year, you will be a winner. Any woman in town would love that car of yours. Who wouldn't flip over a 1942 Mercury, taffy tan with a khaki top, 120-horse power and just enough room for four to sit close together. I know more about this town than even Kit gives me credit for. I came here many times with my dad on business trips. I know most of the nooks and crannies. I will correct our tour guide's version of history if she rewrites it," Ashley explained, hoping for a positive response.

"What's her name?" Sinclair asked.

"Liz Rutledge, a direct descendant of Edward Rutledge, one of those who signed the Declaration of Independence."

"Brett, that sounds interesting. I'll even buy the lunch."

Brett Caldwell Ashley III was not exactly a stranger to Charleston, South Carolina. He lived somewhere between the low country and the up country northwest of the city in a place called Stevensville, an hour-plus drive from the city. Stevensville would be just another road junction were it not the homeplace of the powerful Chairman of the House Armed Services Committee. He was noted for his competence in the political arena as well his affinity for warm women and cold beer. There was also another notable and eccentric native of the town—Ralph "Ace" Warton, a sometime pilot and confidant of the congressman. Warton, a graduate of TMC was one of America's first war aces and nationally recognized heroes. The major downed more than a dozen German aircraft and was shot down three times himself—but always managed to escape and fight again. By 1943 he had become a national treasure, well known in the highest political and military circles. He traveled around the country with celebrities selling war bonds and giving patriotic speeches. But once the days of glory passed, he lost a final battle—a battle with depression. He took his own life in a rented airplane.

Although not a Charlestonian, Ashley shared a common Caldwell ancestor with one of South Carolina's most honored sons—John Caldwell Calhoun (1782-1850). Even so, Ashley knew of the rigid social order of the local aristocracy, and that he would always be considered an outsider. A good pedigree was not enough. He was neither born in the city nor did he have a distinguished family member buried in St. Phillip's or St. Michael's Episcopal cemetery. Thus it was with some anticipation that he would by chance meet the beautiful Liz Rutledge, the state debutante chairman who lived on the proper side of Broad Street.

Ashley knew Charleston as a place that one could come to love or hate, but never completely forget. He could almost predict Liz Rutledge's city orientation speech. She would likely begin by saying:

"This city is the civilized centerpiece of the Carolina Low Country, wonderfully rich in history and folklore. It is at the confluence of the Ashley and Cooper Rivers, where the land and sea embrace, that one has the strange feeling that it was here that the Atlantic was formed. From the city's edge south to the Sea Islands, ringed with white sand beaches, it is difficult to determine where the ocean ends and the Carolina Low Country begins. The majestic palmettos and ancient live oaks that line the streets of the historic area are monuments to the city's durability through the worst of hurricanes, wars, and depressions."

Cal parked in the Francis Marion parking lot adjoining the hotel. It was a few minutes after twelve when they arrived to meet their guests. Kit Montague, with a mischievous smile, made the introductions. Kit did not exaggerate. Liz Rutledge was most attractive—great figure, auburn hair, hazel, all knowing eyes, and a dusting touch of freckles over a thin nose. Her feet were a little large, but who was going to look at her feet except other women, and then only to check the shoes she was wearing.

"Sinclair, what a nice name, as in Sinclair Lewis. Are you in someway related?"

"Unfortunately not, Miss Rutledge, I never had the pleasure of meeting the gentleman. But I read his American classic, *Main Street*, while in high school. You must have too. The book came out in 1920 as I recall, long before any of us here were born, I would hope," Sinclair responded, playing along with her game of one upmanship.

Liz Rutledge took her historical tour seriously. Since they were standing in front of the large, dark Calhoun monument, she began with his story. She had a nice voice, without a heavily affected southern accent.

"This is one of the largest and most prominent monuments in the city. It is no surprise, since he was one of South Carolina's most distinguished citizens. As a senator from South Carolina, he was a strong supporter of states rights as we were during the War Between the States, and still are. He was also Secretary of State, Secretary of War and Vice President under Presidents Adams and Jackson."

"Miss Rutledge, why is it so prominent a Carolinian was not permitted to be buried in St. Phillips cemetery?" Ashley asked, to check her spirit and sense of humor.

"How did you know that, Mr. Ashley?" she asked, with somewhat less confidence.

"Well, I've studied some things about him since we share a common Caldwell ancestor. He was Scotch-Irish, not English as you are. Our Caldwell ancestors were exported to Ireland by James I to neutralize and civilize the Irish. They of course failed and so they immigrated to Pennsylvania, Delaware, and then down the Appalachian trail into the South Carolina foothills. So as you know, not being a real Charlestonian he was not allowed to be buried beside your Rutledge ancestor."

"In view of your enlightening information, Mr. Ashley, may I call you Brett?" she asked and at the same time giving Cal a smile reassuring him that she was not about to jump ship for Scoth-Irish blood. Even if Ashley was good looking—he lacked money and transportation. She had done her homework.

"Yes, by all means, if I may call you Liz."

The Rutledge-Ashley exchange broke the ice; the city tour went well. Lunch at Henry's near the old slave market was equally successful. With the she crab soup, local shrimp, fresh okra, stewed tomatoes, rice, and blackeyed peas, it was a win-win situation.

This was the beginning of a long and lasting friendship for the two couples, but then there was still the dark cloud of the war.

6

Sinclair turned his new convertible south on Rutledge Avenue. Spring had arrived in Charleston. Azaleas and dogwoods were in full bloom. With his top down, he inhaled the seductive sweetness of the honeysuckle. It was his favorite season here. He was beginning to enjoy the old city, something Californians were reluctant to admit. But today was a day he couldn't fully enjoy. He had become deeply immersed in a plan to punish Cadet Ratkowski, now a staff lieutenant, for the pain he had caused him his freshman year.

He turned left on Calhoun Street and after a few blocks right on King. This was not the shortest route to his destination but the most familiar. His head was spinning with thoughts of the risk of his plan, and the consequences should it fail. He thought of Kit Montague and Brett enjoying their boat ride to Fort Sumter and the picnic they had planned later.

Liz Rutledge was spending the weekend with her brother at New Haven, and had a blind date with his roommate. Her mother was pleased about her daughter's trip. She assumed that if the young man were at Yale, he would be upper class. She wasn't as sure about the pretty boy from California.

Even if his friends were here, he couldn't review the plan with them for fear they could become involved and be held jointly liable if things got out of hand. As a minimum, he could visualize he and his roommate being booted out of school. And as a worst case scenario, he could see them both being jailed for assault.

Continuing on his mission he turned left on Broad, Charleston's Wall Street, left on Meeting, a right past the old slave market and finally north on East Bay. There he spotted the bar—Hangovers, a watering hole of the college jocks. The two-story brick building was favored by an alley on one side and a street on the other, offering good escape routes if needed. The soot and deterioration of the bricks was indicative of at least a hundred years of life. But the building was still full of life. Last year a drunken sailor at the bar made the mistake of calling a football lineman a bellhop, the local name bestowed upon cadets by local, envious ruffians. The lineman responded as expected—"Boy, the only belle I've hopped lately was your sister," and promptly threw the fat sailor thorough the plate glass window into the street. The sailor hit the ground running and never returned.

This was the place where justice would be served. The place where the Rat would finally be trapped. Sinclair had begun to have some second thoughts about the whole operation but it now involved too many people—dangerous people who enjoyed breaking a pretty face or any face if the price was right. Sinclair had worked out the plan with his dad during the summer break. It seemed simple enough: recruit a big street fighter to give Cadet Ratkowski the deserved beating of his life.

The elder Sinclair had done well for himself. He and his devoted family lived among California's rich and famous in a mansion on Newport Beach. After graduation from Stanford's business school, Sinclair tried the banking and brokerage businesses with some success. But he found his niche as a venture capitalist—a deal maker using somebody else's money.

He followed the money trail wherever it took him. The original source of the money was of no concern to him. His view was that the responsibility for policing the financial system was a problem for the federal agencies, not him. Thus operating under this philosophy, he was able to conduct business with impunity in a manner that a lawyer uses to defend a guilty client. In both professions, he had learned the hard way that one comes in contact with some unsavory characters of questionable ethics and backgrounds.

So it was with the elder Sinclair. The Mafia had money, lots of it for investment in legitimate businesses. They had legitimate enterprises in Chicago, New York, Hollywood, and Las Vegas. They particularly favored the entertainment business—gambling and movies. There were deals to be made, deals in cash. Sinclair felt comfortable enough in the environment to ask for a favor, a favor his friends were happy to grant. Between them they set up a "rat trap." The deal had been made. There was no turning back.

"Cal, you look like you are carrying the world on your shoulders, what's the problem?" Brett asked, still in a good mood himself after an enjoyable sojourn with Kit Montague.

"Brett, I have to see someone down town next Saturday early in the afternoon. I may need your help. Can you break away from your beautiful Huguenot to go with me? I know just the spot where they serve fresh boiled shrimp, chilled in their shells, a whole plate for 25 cents and a draft michelob for 10 cents in a frosty glass."

"Sure, I'll go. At those prices, I think I can even treat," Ashley said.

"Good, it's a deal," Cal said in a voice that was

more upbeat.

After the usual Saturday morning inspection, and the colorful parade for parents and tourists, the old friends began their unforgettable adventure. In route to Hangovers, Sinclair gave Ashley the whole story of the Mafia connection and the plan that was now underway to witness a big Mafia plant, a ruthless street fighter, kick the shit out of the Rat.

"Brett, have you ever been to Hangovers?" Sinclair asked.

"Yeah, but it is not exactly a place we would take Kit and Liz for cocktails," Ashley said.

Sinclair had studied the plan well. He parked the car around the corner from the bar and closed his convertible top. He wanted to draw as little attention as possible, and to be able to make a quick get away. He began to feel the rush of excitement that he experienced riding his surfboard atop a billowing wave speeding toward some remote California beach. The earlier fears of failure were history.

"Brett, before we go in this place, I want to tell you something about this guy we are going to see in a few minutes. He is called Rocko `The Brute' Cobolino. I've never seen him nor him me. That's the way it has to be, for obvious reasons. I've been told that he is a big swarthy guy, about six foot four and weighing in at over 300 pounds. Maybe that's the reason they call him The Brute. He is from Las Vegas and likes young boys. I have had to deal with him by telephone using a code name."

"My God, Cal, you have got yourself a live one going here. When we finish with this caper, and we are still alive you ought to be able to get a job with J. Edgar Hoover. Let me see if I understand this, you've got a big Sicilian Mafioso, with strange sexual habits, on your payroll—a guy that you have never even seen.

Cal, one other thing before we go in. I've heard that
odd balls like your employee don't fight. This means
the Rat will kill him."

"Brett, don't worry about that, this guy is a professional wrestler. He is probably a `switch hitter'.
Now, we will look for a booth out of plain view to watch
the show. If Rocko approaches us, he will probably
try to make a hit on me since my hair is lighter than
yours. But I want you to do the talking. The bastard
might recognize my voice, and that would be curtains
for the both of us. Got it?" Sinclair asked.

"Yep!"

"Let's go. Stay cool." Sinclair said, with a forced
smile.

The roommates passed the long, well used
mahogany bar to their left and plastic covered booths
on the right, without making eye or body contact with
the rowdy cadets at the bar or the hired help. They
luckily found a booth out of the way in the rear with
a good view of the action at the bar.

"What would you gentlemen like this afternoon?" the waiter asked in an easily recognizable
Gullah/Geechee accent.

"Two shrimp plates, two micks, and a big bowel
of oyster crackers," Ashley replied, carrying out his
assigned role as speaker.

"OK, I think I've spotted Rocko. Brett, do you
see that big monster standing at the end of bar looking around like he owns the place?"

"Yeah, you had him pegged right, the name
"Brute" becomes him," Ashley said.

"I don't see the Rat yet, but my source says the
lieutenant will make it. Let's eat while we can,"
Sinclair assured his roommate.

The two had just finished their shrimp and were
sipping the superior michelobs, when the Rat with a

couple of his boxing buddies swaggered up to the bar.

"The shrimp and beer are great. I'd forgotten how good they really are. Look there's our target at 2 o'clock." Ashley whispered. "You got him, Cal?"

"Yeah, don't let him see you make eye contact?"

"How's Rocko gonna recognize him?" Ashley asked.

"I sent a him photo. Look at Rocko now. He's looking at the photo and at the subject. He is smiling. He has made an ID and is beginning to make his move. Wow! This operation is moving into high gear. The show begins," Sinclair said.

Rocko moved to the barstool next to the Rat and warmed up the prey with—"How you guys doing?"

The boxers pretended they didn't hear the unsolicited greeting and continued sipping their draft.

"Bartender, give these three friends of mine another beer," Rocko Cobolino directed.

"Yes Sir, Mr. Cobolino, coming up," the bartender said.

The cadets accepted the drinks, thinking that would be the end of it, but it was only the beginning. The drinks kept coming and the conversation came easier.

"Understand you boys do a little boxing out at the college," Rocko said continuing his mission.

"How did you know that?" the Rat responded, a little pleased at being recognized as something of a local celebrity, but uncomfortable with the attention received from an odd-looking stranger.

"Used to do a little fighting myself?" beamed Rocko with his hand now moving along the inside of the Rat's leg.

"Hey, mister, keep your God damned hands to yourself, what the hell are you doing?" the Rat growled.

"I like good looking young boys," grinned Rocko with his beefy hand now well into the Rat's crotch.

"You are a fat bastard that only a mother could love," the Rat said. "I'm going to kick your ass."

"That would be nice, I'll see you in the alley in two minutes. I'm so excited, I have to take a nervous pee," Rocko said, playing a perfect role.

The boxers roared. They couldn't believe the sequence of events. It was as though the whole situation was contrived. They would not be laughing if they had known that indeed it had been.

"Hey, Ratkowski, you wanted a warm-up fight before your big fight next week. Looks like you got one," one of the Rat's boxing buddies said.

The Rat laughed with his buddies, but beneath the laugh there was anxiety. Had he pushed his luck too far?

The Brute appeared, squinting into the setting afternoon sun. Ratkowski now saw for the first time the full silhouette of his gorilla-like opponent—long thick arms, and a beefy middle.

The Brute, half blinded by the sun, charged recklessly toward the trim figure in the boxer stance. The Rat, with the grace of a Barcelonian matador, stepped aside allowing the enemy to plow headlong into the side of the brick wall to his rear.

The Brute, now with blood streaming from a broken nose and deep gash in his lower lip, clambered to a standing position. Never once did he raise his hands to defend himself, a technique he often used to intimidate the opponent.

"Come get me, you little prick," he yelled at the Rat, waving his hands towards himself.

The Rat gave no response, but moved in closer circling for the right position to unleash his power. He found the right side and easy target for his left jab. He jabbed the ugly, laughing face time and time again with no results. He then tried his best right to the jaw, which moved the large head no more than a couple of inches. Desperately now, the Rat moved closer to his target and pounded away at the midsection with well delivered lefts and rights. On each occasion, the blows struck deep into soft gut of the incredible giant with no effect.

The time had now arrived for the Brute to make his move. He grabbed the Rat around the waist like an angry grizzly, and squeezed him until his face turned into various shades of crimson and purple. He then adroitly spun the hapless Rat around and tossed him face-forward into the wall that he himself had so abruptly rammed a few minutes earlier. The Rat bounced off the wall, bleeding profusely from cuts above his eyes and mouth, and fell to his knees facing the Brute. In a position for the *coupe de grace*— a knee to the face. To make sure it was over, Rocko now jumped on top of the now helpless Rat, and continued pounding away at his face and body.

"Cal, call an ambulance, I'll try to get this thing stopped," Ashley said, pointing to the telephone booth outside the bar.

"OK, Brett, I'll be back in a minute to help."

Ashley jumped on the back of the hired wrestler yelling—-"Enough, enough, the police are coming, the police are coming, you're gonna kill him!" Now out of control and barely aware of his surroundings, Rocko whirled his body about tossing Brett off of his back like a rag doll. "Rat" Ratkowski's boxing pals, finally getting over their shock, joined the fray and pulled the giant beast off of their friend.

Brett spotted the arriving ambulance, as Cal waved to him from the group of cadets who now began to empty the bar. According to the plan, they made their escape hardly noticed. Even Ratkowski's friends didn't recognize them. The two retreated to the restaurant at the Fort Sumter Hotel. To recover their strength, they ordered two rare steaks and two cold beers. Mission accomplished, next stop Lee-Thomas Barracks for a shower and studies. All was well, except for Cadet Lieutenant Ratkowski. He would spend the night at the city hospital. His roommate reported him not accounted for at bedcheck. The Rat's problems had just begun. As for Rocko Cobolino, he had seized the day. From this time on, he would be known as the—"Fighting Fag" of East Bay Street. He loved the title.

Ratkowski stayed overnight in the city hospital and two days and nights at the hospital on campus. His debt settled, Sinclair visited the cadet hospital with Ashley to see the fallen warrior. They were shocked at what they saw: his eyes were blue-black and nearly closed, ugly stitches in both eyes and upper lip, and a chipped front tooth. Sinclair's injuries caused by Ratkowski paled in comparison.

"Glad you guys could come to see me. Ashley, thanks for helping pull that monster off me. I'm in pretty bad shape. That damn crazy fool caught me by surprise," the Rat said.

"No problem, Lieutenant, under the circumstances I think you would have done the same," Ashley said uncomfortably.

"If you had him in a ring with gloves on, I think you could have taken him," Sinclair said, genuinely trying to build up his spirit and secretly wishing him a speedy recovery.

"That might have leveled the playing field, but I sure as hell don't want to see him in an alley again unless I am the only one with a baseball bat," Ratkowski said emphatically.

The roommates had done their good deeds, said their good-byes and retired to the canteen to check their mail and pick up a local city newspaper. There was always a chance that a reporter would make a head-line story of the disturbance.

In the privacy of their room, Sinclair and Ashley had a chance to take stock of the situation.

"Brett, I think you will agree with me that the Rat got more than he really had coming. If he had been permanently disabled, there would have been a hell of an investigation. No telling where that would have led."

"Right you are, Cal, right you are. Hold it a minute there is an interesting article buried in the middle of the newspaper."

"What does it say, read it, read it!" Sinclair said in a concerned voice.

"Date line 13 March 1942, Charleston, S.C.: Mr. Rocko Cobolino, formerly of Las Vegas and an employee of the Hangover Bar and Grill, was brutally assaulted by several hoodlums last night as he was leaving his place of employment. He is being treated at city hospital for a broken arm and collar bone and numerous facial cuts and bruises. Cobolino believes the assailants were homophobics, who randomly cruised bars in search of those whose sexual habits differed from their own. As soon as he is able to travel, Cobolino plans to return to Nevada. He reports that he has enjoyed his work at Hangovers, and wishes to thank all of his many young friends whom he met there. He particularly wants to thank Ralph for paying his hospital expenses and giving him a bus ticket home."

"Ralph, you son of a gun. So that was the code name you used. You were very generous," Ashley whispered.

"Ashley, my good friend you don't want to know any more for your own sake. Let's let this dog sleep. If we don't, he could jump up again somewhere down the road, and bite us both in the ass. It suffices to say that Cobolino is a good Mafioso soldier. You can be sure that he will have his old job back in a casino, and no one in Vegas will give two hoots in hell about this small affair," Sinclair cautioned.

"Agreed. Cal, I have some inside information on the Ratkowski situation. He will be charged with disturbing the peace, absent without leave, and conduct unbecoming a cadet officer of the Corps. His sentence which was posted on all cadet company bulletin boards called for the Southern Conference boxing champion to be reduced in rank from lieutenant to senior private, one month confinement and 30 walking tours."

Post script. Ratkowski would box again and retain his Heavyweight Championship in the Southern Conference. He would graduate with his class, be called to active duty as a reserve officer in the coast artillery and stationed in Hawaii. He never heard a shot fired in anger during the entire war.

7

Sinclair and Ashley returned to Charleston for their junior year at TMC. Ashley was promoted to platoon sergeant. Sinclair who had been a private for two years was finally promoted to sergeant and the platoon guide in his roommate's platoon. They both felt that their chances of finishing four years at the institution were slim. They read the newspapers and saw the newsreels in the movie theaters.

Most of Western Europe was now under German control. On the Eastern Front, the German Army had penetrated deep into the Russian heartland to within a hundred miles of Moscow. The Japanese had captured the Philippines and much of Southeast Asia. In the early going in North Africa, American armored forces in the battle for Kasserine pass suffered an embarrassing defeat at the hands of General Rommel's Afrika Corps. It was not a pretty picture for any college student, particularly students in ROTC programs. It was now payback time to Uncle Sam.

Before the end of first semester, Ashley received his greetings and introduction to the draft selection process. He dutifully responded to the board, reminding them that he was already a member of the enlisted reserve and that he expected to be called to active duty whenever the War Department required his services. Unimpressed with his rhetoric, the board responded that until such time as they received official notification of his status, Mr. Brett Caldwell Ashley III would continue to be property of the board.

"Brett, you sure know how to piss-off a draft board," Sinclair said in uncontrolled laughter.

"OK, Sinclair, laugh, you son of a gun; you are going to miss me, good buddy. Who is going to get you dates with all these good looking, Charleston blue bloods when I'm gone?"

"Oh, I think I'll make out."

"Cal, you know," Ashley said. "I think you will. I think you will!"

The matter of the draft would take care of itself. At the end of their junior year, the entire class of '44 was marched to the Charleston train station, entrained and transported to Fort Jackson, SC. Here within the shadows of the State Capital, they were inducted into the armed services of the United States. The process was routine: physicals, immunizations, and issue of minimum necessities. They were then returned by train to the college for a meeting with their president.

"Gentleman of the Class of '44," the General began his speech to the group assembled and seated on the parade field.

"Three years ago when I welcomed you to our college, I said that your class had a rendezvous with destiny. Gentleman, that time is here and now. I have just returned from Washington where I spoke to the Army Chief of Staff, the officer who has the job that I once held. I urged him to allow you to finish your last year at our military institution. I suggested to him that the training that you are now receiving would be better than the training you would receive in the Armed Forces. Moreover, I told him you would be entering the service as commissioned officers, and as such be of more value than enlisted reservists. The Chief of Staff declined my request that you be permitted to remain with us. He pointed out that there are eight military colleges and

numerous universities that operate under one ROTC charter with one set of rules. He said it would unfair to give preferential treatment to military colleges. Frankly, gentlemen, I was surprised and even amused to hear that there were eight colleges who called themselves military institutions. I only know of two or three whom I consider to be in the same category as our college.

"So be it. The decision is final—there is nothing more that I can do. You have been a good class. The Class of `43 has recommended to me, that as special tribute to your class, that you be given your class rings. I have considered their recommendation and have approved it." With that the class came to it's feet, and cheered the near broken man who stood before them.

"Gentlemen, Gentlemen, your attention once more for a final word. When you go into the service, do not be overly concerned about being promoted for that will come in due time. All we ask and your country asks is that you do your duty. And I have no doubt that you will. God be with you, farewell."

On the parade field that day in May 1943, there were two hundred fewer young men than began this less traveled road in 1940. By the spring of '44, there were only three. Then there were none. The Class of '44 was then and now—The Class That Never Was!

PART TWO

THE MAKING OF 90-DAY WONDERS

1943-1944

8

The Department of the Army allowed General Pealot a few concessions affecting the status of the now US Army Class of '44. The class would be allowed three weeks to complete their junior-year academics and final exams before being ordered to basic training at the end of May 1943. They would also be allowed to wear their cadet uniforms until departing for their training centers. These were seemingly small, but to the future soldiers they were important exceptions. They would be able to participate in the graduation farewells of the Class of '43, who had so generously supported the early award of their class rings. Normally, the coveted ring would be awarded during the fall of their senior year. For Sinclair and Ashley, it also gave them a chance for lingering farewells with Liz Rutledge and Kit Montague, with whom they had become inseparable during the past year.

The time was especially critical for Sinclair. He had been in contact with the Canadian Military Attaché at the Canadian Embassy in Washington concerning the possibility of joining the Royal Canadian Air Force (RCAF). To his amazement, not only had he been favorably considered, but the Canadians had gotten permission from the Department of the Army personnel for his transfer, subject to the approval of Col. McNutt, the cadet commandant.

"Brett, I've got good news and bad news," Sinclair reported joyfully to his roommate after picking up a special delivery letter from the post office.

"Ok, give me the good news first," Brett tuned

in, looking up from his homework scattered about on the ancient oak table in front of him.

"I'm going to fly for the RCAF. They have accepted me for flight school."

"Congratulations, you bastard," Ashley said. "You've been holding out on me."

"Didn't mean to. I did it as a kind of a lark. Who the hell would have thought that it would have come through? I was afraid to let you in on it for fear you would talk me out of it. You know I don't like mud on my boots and dirt under my finger nails," Sinclair explained.

"You did all right, now what's the bad news?" Ashley asked.

"Well, I had to stop by to see Colonel McNutt to get his approval."

"Yeah, go on—I can hear it coming," Ashley said laughing.

"You remember the time he was so pissed-off with the whole battalion over the garbage-can caper, that he marched us half the night around the park. Well, this was worse. He nearly went off his rocker. You would have thought the world was coming to an end. He told me that for the past three years, I had wasted the army's money, brought discredit upon the institution, and that I was looking for the easy war— scotch whiskey, clean sheets, and English broads. He had me at attention for 10 minutes burning me a new rear end. He finally let me speak my piece. I think I convinced him that we were in the same war as our Canadian allies, and that I would be in the war sooner than if I stayed with the current infantry program. I finally appealed to his professional pride— I told him that the infantry was the "Queen of Battle", and that I was not a good enough soldier to be in the infantry. With that last remark, I think I saw a smug smile come over his face. Then amazingly he stood up, held out his and said, `You may be a sorry soldier, Sinclair, but we taught you something here—honesty!' And with that he said, `I'll let you go. Good luck. Kick the Luftwaffe's ass'. For the first time, I saw another side of this rough old man. Maybe we have misjudged him all this time."

"Cal Sinclair, that was a super sales job. Congratulations! Now, all we have got to do is pass these damned final exams. We have dates with Kit and Liz for the special ring hop (formal dance with a big-name band). We will have a farewell party all night, or as long as the army will let us stay out. Deal?"

"Brett, you got a deal."

It was a good deal, a memorable time, and the beginning of many memorable times. Their dates were beautiful in formal satin gowns. The roommates wore cadet formal dress for the last time. The couples passed arm and arm through the big ring replica. The dates slipped the rings on their fingers, and were rewarded with a kiss in return. The lights dimmed, the big band played softly, and the vocalist warbled appropriately—"Will we be sweethearts aftcr graduation day?" Kit whispered in Brett's ear—"Yes, yes!" Cal could be seen lifting Liz off her feet, and simultaneously kissing her on receptive lips.

"Why, Mr. Sinclair, I declare. You are certainly flirtatious tonight," Liz Rutledge said, in her best Scarlet O'Hara voice.

"Brett, this is getting to be too much. Let's go have dinner as a start."

"OK, if the girls are willing," Ashley said with a wink.

They chose the restaurant at the Fort Sumter Hotel. Not that it was noted for great cuisine, but because of the location along the south battery wall with a beautiful view of the harbor. And it was within walking distance of Liz's home, where the evening began. Her mother had champagne and hors d'oeuvres waiting for them.

The meal at the Ft. Sumter was decent enough, but the unaccustomed, additional bottle of champagne was a little too much. The alcohol hastened the replacement of joy with melancholy. They sadly strolled along the battery wall, bathed in the reflected light of a full moon. Two young men in Confederate gray walked their best girls to the Rutledge house, where Kit Montague would be the guest for the night. They made promises to return as a foursome at war's end. Yet, they all knew that it would be promises over which only time and destiny could control. Tears came easily and without shame.

It was after midnight, when Sinclair and Ashley, in the silence of their own thoughts, were stopped by the guard at Ravanel Gate. Already, there was a changing of the guard. A regular army private, not a fresh-faced cadet, asked for identification.

"Soldiers of the Class of `44, you are cleared to pass," the guard said, rendering a respectful salute.

9

Fort McClellan, Alabama was an ideal area for basic training. The town of Anniston adjacent to the fort was a quiet, peaceful family town before the war. It was nestled in a valley surrounded by the picturesque foothills of the Talladega Mountains. Although the days were hot and humid in the summer, thermal breezes cooled the nights.

Atlanta was where the city boys went when they wanted more excitement than bucolic Anniston could provide. The Georgia State Capital was within a two-hour drive to the east. The historical city had risen from the ashes of the Civil War, survived the post-war depression and the Wall Street crash of '29. When General Sherman burned and sacked it near the end of the war, it was merely a railroad junction of some 12,000 souls. Now it had become a thriving metropolis—a pool of economic activity in an otherwise calm sea. To the liking of both soldiers and merchants the cafes, bars, and clubs along Peachtree Street were bustling with activity. But for many basic trainees there was too little money and too little energy left by the weekend to make the excursion. An occasional milk shake at the snack bar, watered-down beer at the EM club, and the company of local Anniston girls were good enough.

The tough Army cadre was determined to make citizen soldiers out of the OCS-bound ROTC cadets. The environment provided a first hand look at how the war-army went about its business of preparing young men for the fight of their lives. ROTC students from various colleges and universities were trained in special units of about 200 men, separated from other enlisted training companies. Ashley and his friends were also surprised how little contact they had with the command group—the company officers and the first sergeant. The officers showed up occasionally for Saturday morning inspections. The first sergeant was relegated to administrative functions. It was a place where the field first sergeant was God, and the platoon sergeants his lords of discipline. Even the autocratic little corporals were kings of small fiefdoms. The field group ran the show. They con ducted the classes, led the long marches, and kept a close watch on every recruit.

Obedience to orders was absolute. Reprimand and restriction were the price of failure. For the former cadets of TMC, this was normal procedure. For ROTC students from some relaxed university programs, it was a different matter. While at TMC, in a visit to a local college, Ashley and Sinclair had found their opposite numbers living in unsightly quarters, drinking beer, and in serious discussions among fraternity brothers as to whether or not they would attend the next parade formation.

For Ashley and his classmates the training was a "no brainer." They knew the routine in spades. But it was the first and last time for them to be kids. And occasionally, they tested the system. It was unforgivable to answer your name other than—"here!" when responding to the never-ending head counts.

The sun had barely come up at one reveille formation when Private Ashley decided to become a member of the infamous.

"Sound-off when your name is called—Ashley, Brett C.," bellowed the Field First Sergeant.

"Ho!" Ashley yelled in an equally loud voice.

"Get that man's name. You can bet your ass, he'll get no pass, not even to Anniston! Platoon Sergeant, see to it that that idiot gets a big, browning automatic rifle to clean this weekend while he is confined to the post."

It was an intense 17-week, basic training period. Infantry weapons instruction and qualification, map reading, customs of the service, small unit tactics, etc. Physical training was second to none—calisthenics, tumbling drills, bayonet practice, obstacles courses, and forced marches. The final phases of training included a 25-mile march with pack and rifle through Bains Gap, the highest area in Alabama, into the Talladega National Forest. At the end of the day's march, there was the requirement to dig-in and prepare for an attack by "enemy forces," which came at the predictable hour, first morning light. Next came the requirement to fill the foxholes dug the day before, police the area, and march back to the barracks. And as always within minutes after returning from field exercises, the cadet-soldiers were assembled in the company street for a weapon's inspection.

Ashley soon realized that the test of the system, which began at roll call a few days back, had not been a good idea. He had gotten the attention of his little regular army corporal. He now spent more than his share of time on K.P. But he soon learned that it had decided advantages. He ate well, and missed the long marches in the hot sun. And then there were the enjoyable bull sessions, while sitting in the shade with his classmates peeling potatoes. Ashley also learned that if you impressed the mess sergeant, you could get the special job—"cleaner of the grease pit", the collecting point for all the week's grease and other contaminants. Ashley discovered that this too had its advantage—you could finish the filthy task early, and if the little corporal didn't find you, you could enjoy a good nap in the barracks.

However, avoiding his corporal was not so easy.

"Private Ashley, I'm looking for a volunteer. I think you're the man I'm looking for."

"Corporal, what would I volunteer for?" Ashley inquired.

"The company boxing team."

"The what? Corporal, I've never boxed," Ashley countered, hoping he'd forget the whole thing.

"Don't worry, we will teach you. And one other thing you ought to know, every one who has made the boxing team went on to OCS," the corporal boasted.

The training consisted of running a mile or two for a few days in your underwear covered with an impermeable, rubber-like, GI raincoat. The theory for the training was that if you lost five or ten pounds you could fight in a lower weight class, and enjoy a big advantage. The fallacy of the theory, as Ashley learned, was that the trainee was lighter but weaker.

The gladiators entered the ring on a warm night under hot lights and a roaring crowd of nearly 500 "Government Issues." In the opposite corner, there was a wiry, redheaded kid from West Virginia who the referee introduced as Killer McCoy. Ashley figured his daddy must have run a moonshine still somewhere in the Appalachian hills. However, he wouldn't have much time to contemplate the social and ethnic background of his opponent. As soon as gloves were touched, a little redheaded bastard with an insane look in his eyes charged in his direction at the only speed he apparently knew, full! Ashley stepped aside. The wild one missed him, bounced off the ropes, and charged again. This time he tried to box him, but Killer McCoy wanted none of that. McCoy swung wildly in the air, and charged time and time again. In the third round, Ashley could hardly hold his arms above his waist from fatigue. Pushing off his opponent had taken its toll. He was about to lose the fight to the more aggressive bull. His only chance was to trick McCoy into charging through the ropes into the crowd, and perhaps not be able to get back in the ring before the referee counted him out. Killer made one final charge. Once more Ashley stepped aside, but this time he lifted his right glove, and in a desperate hammer-like blow struck the charging bull in the back of his neck just below his big, protruding ears. This time McCoy missed the ropes, and plummeted headlong into a corner post. He lay motionless on the floor for a long time, too long a time. Finally, the medics arrived with a stretcher, and carried the near lifeless creature away. The crowd loved the mayhem. Ashley finally met his company commander who shook his hand, and greeted him with "Good show, Ashley, good show."

When in competition with other basic training units, the OCS-bound company won all the contests including field exercises and parades. The enlisted cadre was proud of the unit, and to a man the recruits held their enlisted leaders in the highest esteem. It had been a good and thorough 17-week basic training course. It ended with a final winning parade and farewells.

The Captain made one of his few appearances, but with appropriate final remarks:

"Men, we are—as I am sure you are—proud of your accomplishments here. We have prepared you for combat as infantry rifleman. You have excelled in every area. Most of you will go on to Infantry OCS at Fort Benning and then on to combat theaters. It is the mission of the infantry in battle to break things and to

kill the enemy, not to be killed! Don't forget the last part. The German soldier has been at war for many years. He has become mentally tough. He says philosophically—"Es ist du oder ich," It is you or me, and he has learned to do his job very well. So have the Japanese. I wish you the best, and when the war is over I hope that, God willing, we will meet again."

Some members of the unit maintained contact with the enlisted cadre. Within a few weeks after Ashley and his classmates returned to their college Army Special Training Program (ASTP) studies, they learned that the field first sergeant—the best soldier of them all—had been killed in North Africa.

10

Returning to TMC for continued college work as ASTP students was not a popular option. General Pealot wished the men in khaki would go away, but he was a pragmatist. He needed the government revenue to support ever increasing operating costs, despite a decreasing student population. The academic program was changed from a semester to a quarterly system because of the uncertain tenure of the military students.

Intelligence test requirements for ASTP students were higher than those for ROTC students earmarked for OCS, 115 versus 110 minimums. How the Department of the Army, came up with these magic standards was the subject of much discussion and ridicule in all the ranks.

Life for Ashley and his classmates, now privates first class, went on. They lived in barracks separated from the younger cadets. The controls were now in the hands of an army cadre. It was a much easier and less structured routine. They attended classes, ate, slept, and kept their rooms reasonably neat. If there was a problem, it was boredom and difficulty in maintaining focus on the class work at hand. There was need for all to move on to OCS, get a commission, win the war, and get on with life. And no small point for Ashley. He missed his roommate Sinclair, who was now in the Canadian flight program.

The Class of '42 received commissions upon graduation, but the Class of '43 was required to complete OCS after graduation. In contrast, the West

Point Class of '43 was treated differently: They were graduated early—in January 1943. They received their commissions upon graduation, adding to the mystique of the West Point Protective Association.

Finally, the Class of '44 got its wish. In December of '43, after a few days home-leave, they were on to OCS. Fort Benning was no Fort McClellan. Benning is located along the Chattahoochee River near Columbus, Georgia. Across the river was Phenix City, Alabama, the sin city of the time. The Alabama town was a place where bad women, bad soldiers, and bad booze mixed like boiling oil and cold water. Military police were on constant patrol trying to keep GIs out of off-limit gin joints.

Inside the gates OCS candidates found a more pristine, orderly environment, freshly painted tempo buildings and Quonset huts row on row. Clean-shaven officers and men in heavily starched uniforms moved about from place to place with a sense of purpose.

Candidates were billeted in two story, temporary buildings common to all military bases in the '40s and '50s. Twenty-two men were "bunked" on each floor, in two rows of 11 each. Open showers and toilets at the end of each floor served the group. In addition, there was one private squad room for use of the non-commissioned officer in charge of the contingent.

The program was an advanced basic training course with emphasis on hands-on leadership. Each candidate was required to lead sections, squads and/ or platoons in assimilated combat conditions. The purpose was to test the reaction of young, potential officers under stressful conditions second only to combat itself. Close supervision was present in every activity and the candidate was rated on his every move. The future officers were even required to rate classmates on their floors. This worked against those who lived near by and occasionally visited their parents and girl friends. They missed the bonding with their peers, which often resulted in low peer ratings. In one instance, a competent TMC candidate who frequently visited home was an early program "washout." He would later be killed as a enlisted leader in the Normandy invasion.

"What are you going to do now, candidate? Do something, even if it's wrong!" was heard frequently. The latter guidance was obviously dangerous. The guidance should have been: "Do something, but don't do anything stupid, stupid." It was a stress factory— pressure-cooker environment. Ashley and classmates would come back to their barracks at the end of the day and often find their good friends missing and their bunks empty. It was if they never existed. They would never see them again. They had failed to make the cut. Although there was never a day that wasn't a high anxiety day, Ashley had a relatively easy time of it.

During one of the first few days at an obstacle course, he was chosen to clear an eight-foot wall after a single demonstration by an enlisted instructor.

"You there, avoiding eye contact for fear of being called on. Stand up! Who are you?" yelled the lieutenant in charge.

"Candidate Ashley, Sir," Ashley responded in an acquired bravado voice.

"Do you think you can get over that wall?"

"Don't know, Sir, but I'll try," Ashley said, giving the typical TMC taught response.

To the amazement of the tactical officer and himself, Ashley negotiated the wall as easily as the instructor had done in demonstration. As a result of his athletic ability or good luck, he gained a strong supporter in the tactical officer. He didn't realize it, but from then on his graduation was assured. Of the 200 who began the course in December of '43, only 128 received their gold bars in May of '44. Brett Ashley graduated in the upper echelons of the class. Sergeant Gump, his cadet squad leader, and later his cadet first sergeant at TMC, probably would have predicted it.

To call these new second lieutenants "ninety-day wonders" would be a misnomer, for it had taken them four years to be entitled to wear the shiny gold bars. They began their quest in 1940. They had been ROTC cadets, enlisted reservists, ASTP students, active duty privates, corporals as OCS candidates, and now lieutenants in the Army of the United States. They were not officers in the United States Army. That classification was reserved for the regulars.

The next stop for Ashley and 62 other members of his OCS class, nearly half of whom were from TMC, was Camp Claiborne, Louisiana with assignment to the 84th Infantry Division.

Camp Claiborne, named for the first elected Governor of Louisiana, was located near the middle of the state within a few miles of Alexandria. The division had been at Claiborne since December 1943 for completion of predeployment training. The division, regiments, and battalions were for the most part commanded by regular army officers. Reservists, national guardsmen, and OCS graduates commanded the companies and the platoons.

By the time Ashley and his OCS group arrived, there was little left to do except participate in a field exercise, pack up, and move out. They could just as well have joined the unit overseas. The old timers had been working together for nearly two years.

Cliques and powerful, unofficial organizations were well entrenched.

Ashley's first assignment was with a rifle company. However, within a few days he and several other new arrivals were interviewed for the Second Battalion supply officer job, the S-4. For some reason unknown to him, Ashley got the job. It was a thankless position with an awkward command relationship. When in the field, he worked for the battalion commander. In garrison, he worked for the Regimental S-4, the regimental supply officer. There were no standing operating procedures or training manuals available. If anyone, including his supply sergeant, knew what they were supposed to do in combat they kept it to themselves. Ashley realized too late that he had become the commissioned battalion gofer.

Colonel Meddler, the regimental commander, had a reputation as an "autocratic terror"—a man to be avoided at all costs. He was commissioned from OCS during WW I. There was a record of his college attendance, but no record of his graduation. Between the wars, he found a home in the regular army. However, Meddler had not been selected for any significant command position, as he moved up the peacetime chain of command. Unless an officer was earmarked for greatness, there was little opportunity for command. General Eisenhower himself had only commanded a battalion before the war.

Colonel Meddler was fundamentally an honorable man, but his age, background, and temperament made him a poor choice for one of the army's most important combat commands. Like many senior officers, he ruled by creating an atmosphere of fear, fear of making a mistake. The result was the stifling of individual initiative.

The colonel used the "I gotcha" command technique. For lack of something better to do, Ashley frequently enjoyed a piece of cake and coffee with the regimental service company mess sergeant. But this small pleasure would soon be denied him. One morning, he abruptly encountered Meddler and his inspection retinue. Recognizing danger, Ashley began a rapid retreat through the mess rear exit.

"Sergeant," the Colonel screamed. "Stop that man!"

Ashley returned to the scene to face the music. Saluting respectfully from the position of attention, he reported to his regimental commander. The old man would not pause long enough from the ass chewing of the new lieutenant to let him explain who he was, and what he was doing there. He proceeded to give him an inspection tour of the mess hall, holding him responsible for every flaw. He even found fault with the caps on the mustard and catsup containers, and wanted to know how many ounces of salt were required for a gallon of coffee. Before it was over, he had almost convinced Ashley that he was the service company mess officer, and a very poor one at that. Finally, the colonel took out his black book and wrote down the shocked lieutenant's name. Six months later, when the list of second lieutenants selected for promotion came out, Ashley's name was missing from the list.

This was the man who was going to lead the regiment in a few weeks in one of the bloodiest campaigns of the war. It was Ashley's good fortune that once the shooting started, he never saw the old gentleman again.

PART THREE

THE SIEGFRIED LINE

1944

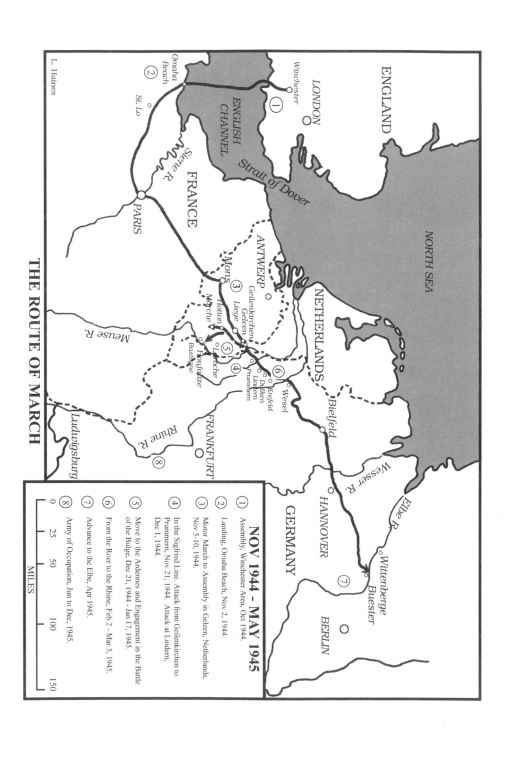

THE ROUTE OF MARCH

L. Haines

NOV 1944 - MAY 1945

① Assembly, Winchester Area, Oct 1944.

② Landing, Omaha Beach, Nov 2, 1944.

③ Motor March to Assembly in Geleen, Netherlands, Nov 5-10, 1944.

④ In the Sigfried Line. Attack from Geilenkirchen to Prummern, Nov 21, 1944. Attack at Lindern, Dec 1, 1944.

⑤ Move to the Ardennes and Engagement in the Battle of the Bulge, Dec 21, 1944 - Jan 17, 1945.

⑥ From the Roer to the Rhine, Feb 2 - Mar 5, 1945.

⑦ Advance to the Elbe, Apr 1945.

⑧ Army of Occupation, Jun to Dec, 1945.

MILES
0   25   50   100   150

I am always alert for death. He doesn't fool me. I spot him right away. He loves to come in his country-bumpkin disguise; a comical wart that suddenly sends its roots to the very bone; or hiding behind a pretty little fever blush. Then suddenly that grinning skull appears to take the victim by surprise. But never me. I'm waiting for him. I take my precautions.

Mario Puzo
Fools Die

11

On the 4th of September 1944, the 84th Division entrained for Camp Kilmer, New Jersey, the staging area for the New York Port of Embarkation. Ashley had made the usual high school senior trip to Washington. But like most of his friends, he had never been to New York. So he made sure this time that his battalion gofer duties didn't prevent him, along with two other lieutenants, from enjoying a night in the bright lights. If they could have foreseen the future, however, and taken action to change the course of events, how wonderful life would have been. Two of the three would never live long enough to celebrate the New Year.

Boarding of the troopship, *Edmond B. Alexander*, commenced on 20 September 1944. It was a festive atmosphere, the division band played martial music and other patriotic songs such as "Over There." Families and friends waved their final goodbyes. Ashley and his supply sergeant lugged their duffel bags up the gangplank, when suddenly he saw a familiar and beautiful face throwing him a kiss.

"Sergeant, hold my bag please. I see someone I know, back in a minute," Ashley yelled, half way back down the ramp.

"Got it, Lieutenant, take your time. I'll hold the ship."

"Kit Montague, are you for real?"

"Yes, very real, I wish I could have gotten here earlier. This strange place is a long way from Charleston," she said, giving him a hug and kiss simultaneously.

"God knows I've missed you. Why did this war have to come along? As if I didn't know the answer," Ashley said, still in shock at seeing Kit.

"How's Liz Rutledge doing? What has she heard from Cal?"

"Liz is at the hotel in Manhattan," Kit said, hurriedly responding to his rapid-fire questions. "We came up together. She didn't come here, said that she didn't want to interrupt our short reunion. Yes, she heard from Cal Sinclair. He's now flying for a Canadian unit that is attached to the Eighth Air Force somewhere in England."

"Great, please send me his address when you can," Ashley said.

"OK," Kit answered excitedly.

The ship's crew began to sound the all aboard, and his sergeant waved the on-the-double sign.

"Gotta go, Kit. Thanks for coming. One more kiss."

"Brett, there is a little present in this box for you. Don't open it until you are in your bunk to-night. I'm lucky to have met you," she said.

"Kit, loving you is going to keep me alive."

"Goodbye, darling, I'm counting on it," she said, throwing him a goodbye kiss.

Back aboard the *Alexandria*, Ashley had an unobstructed view of the harbor for the first time. The great commercial ships of the day were there in all their glistening glory: The *Queen Mary*, *Queen Elizabeth* and even the great *Normandie*, all waiting to load men and machines of war. The *E.B. Alexander* at 20,000 displacement tons was a boat in comparison. Even Navy seaplane tenders weighed nearly 50,000 tons. Whatever the size, the *Alexander*, protected from German submarines by American ships of the line, would hopefully take the division elements safely to their scheduled destination—Cherbourg, France. Better that Ashley didn't know that a TMC classmate with another division had gone down on a troop ship sunk by a German sub in the English Channel.

It had been an exciting day. Ashley had sailed a number of times on a friend's sailboat in the Charleston harbor, but this was his first night ever at sea. The evening meal in the officer's wardroom was excellent. After dinner he strolled along the deck. The air was cool and crisp. And as far as he could see there was a never-ending moonlit ocean. It all seemed incredibly surreal. For a moment he forgot that he was on the way to a war.

Quarters for second lieutenants were not exactly staterooms. They were more like sailor-bunks, canvas hammocks suspended from the ship's steel-walled partitions. Compared to standard infantry pup tents, however, they were a welcome improvement. Ashley found his lower bunk, bid goodnight to his newly found friends and crawled in for an overdue good night's rest. He remembered the present in the small box that Kit Montague had given him at the dock and her instructions to open it before going to sleep.

To his surprise it was a gold medallion and chain of the Virgin Mary and Child. It was a thoughtful gift but an unusual one from one whose ancestor's were among the founders of Charleston's 17th century Huguenot church. With the present there was a simple note:

Dear Brett.

Wear this during the dangerous journey that you are beginning. It will bring you comfort, as it has for me for many years. You will always be in my thoughts and prayers. I love you.

Kit

Soldiers don't cry, he said to himself, brushing a tear off his cheek. He turned toward the steel-walled bulkhead in silence, and with the help of the rolling motion of the ship fell soundly asleep.

Time aboard the troop ship moved quickly, too quickly. The master of the vessel and his crew were relaxed and helpful. The protective umbrella of the navy obviously made a difference. There were a number of make-work jobs such as duty officer and mess officer. But there was little seasickness, unless too much time was spent below deck near the kitchen with the ever-present odor of cooking beef and pork.

After 13 days at sea, the beautiful coast of eastern Ireland came into view. There had been a change of plans. There would be no landing at Cherbourg. The damage to the port could not be repaired in time to accommodate the *Alexander* and other ships scheduled for debarkation there. The fine old ship made its way up the sea between England and Ireland and finally docked at Greenock, Scotland. From there the unit was put aboard a train to Newbury, England for a temporary stay. After a few days, it was on to Barton Stacey Air Base where final preparations were made for movement to France.

The stay at Barton Stacey seemed pleasant enough, at least on the surface of things. Units found billets where they could. Ashley's group was billeted in a barn and slept on straw not needed by the animals. As the battalion supply officer, Ashley wondered why he had had little or no contact with the new battalion commander and his staff. To his surprise, he learned that the battalion commander who hired him for the job was fired shortly before sailing. He never met the battalion executive officer who, on being issued live ammunition at Barton Stacey before departing for France, shot himself in the foot.

The situation did not lend for itself to smooth staff operations, despite the competency of the new, but inexperienced, battalion commander.

But there were some light moments. Lieutenant Jeb Carrington, a friend of Ashley from Camp Claiborne, needed help in escorting a young English lady to a dance for officers at Andover, a nearby village. The requirement seemed simple enough at first:

"Brett, I need a favor. As I recall, you owe me one from Claiborne," Carrington said, patting his old friend on the back.

"Uh oh, uh oh! I'm afraid to ask whose husband is after you now," Ashley responded with a smile. Carrington had the good looks of a Robert Redford of his day and the charm of a rich Mississippi planter, which his father was, and he would also be if he lived long enough. His problem was that women of all categories fell in love with him on sight.

"Ashley, no big problem this time. A lovely woman that I met the other day asked me to join her at the Andover dance this Saturday. The problem is I'm the duty officer Saturday night, and I can't make it," Carrington said.

"God damn it, Jeb," Ashley complained. "Playing the role of John Alden for Miles Standish has gotten me into deep trouble in the past."

"Don't worry, Brett," Carrington continued with his sales pitch. "She's good looking, she's horny, and she will be nice even to you. You can use my jeep, too."

"Hey, I don't need this problem. What's her name? How will I recognize her?" Ashley asked.

"Susan Wiley, her looks—English, sad hazel eyes, brown hair, average height, and great legs."

"OK, Jeb, If you weren't a front line rifle platoon leader, and I wasn't `a rear echeloner', I wouldn't do it," Ashley acquiesced.

Ashley took the John Alden assignment with reluctance, but once at the dance hall he began to enjoy it. Carrington's description of Susan Wiley was perfect. He had only one Black Guinness' Ale at the bar before he spotted her. She was at the welcome desk, good looking—really, with a seductive smile. Carrington, it seemed, had found a treasure!

"Miss Wiley, My name is Brett Ashley. I regret to inform you that `Left-tenant' Carrington has the duty this evening and will be unable to attend this wonderful affair. He sends his apologies, and requests that I act as his replacement and assist you in any way that I can under the circumstances," Ashley said in a put-on English accent.

"How charming, Brett Ashley you say. English blood, I presume."

"Of course, one of your colonists at your service, madam."

From that point on, Ashley could do no wrong. She loved his sense of humor and affected accent. They both knew full well that within two weeks he could be dead. Susan Wiley came on to him as though he were the great Carrington himself.

The band played endlessly. The young girls and mature housewives never seemed to tire of dancing the fox trot. Some old Brit "with a snoot full" took the stage frequently and sang: "It's a long way to Tipperary; it's a long way to go." And from the bar, an overly endowed "lady" would tune in with: "Roll me over Yankee soldier, roll me over, lay me down and do it again."

"Miss Wiley, it's getting late. Maybe we should be getting you home," Ashley reminded her.

"One more dance before we go, Brett. Why not call me Susan. I feel that I've known you for some time," she said with a mischievous smile.

Ashley was beginning to see the direction the situation was going, and was glad that he hadn't overly imbibed. He helped his companion into the hard, cold seat of Carrington's jeep, and they were on their way. It was late October 1944, and true to form English nights were cold. Their heavy woolen overcoats gave them some but not enough protection from the cold wind that poured through the unsealed, fabric doors of the vehicle.

"Brett, I want to thank you very much for filling in for Jeb. He is such a dear boy. I can't wait to get him in my bed and fuck him until he asks for mercy. Our boys have a saying: `There is nothing wrong with the bloody Yanks, except that they are over paid, over sexed, and over here'. To tell you the truth. I don't subscribe to that. There is a war going on, you know—you've got to have a little fun!"

With that clarification of her motives, Susan Wiley slipped her hand under her surprised driver's coat and kissed him on the lobe of his ear, and said: "Make a turn to the right at the next small road that we come to. There is a beautiful little spot where we can stop for a moment."

"Miss Wiley, I don't think Jeb would like our getting too familiar," Ashley said, making the right turn as directed.

"Susan, not Miss Wiley," she said, enjoying the game she had obviously played many times before.

"There, park over there." Her hands skillfully unbuttoned his coat and teasingly each button of his fly.

"Brett," she said, "there is something I have to say. I have been cursed."

"You what?" Ashley said.

"Cursed, I've made mad passionate love to four

infantry platoon leaders since D-Day. And they all have been killed——two on landing at Omaha Beach and two—at the battle for St. Lo." Tears now slowly moved down her lovely finely sculptured English face.

"My God, Susan Wiley, you are like the female praying mantis. You know, the stalk-like, little green creature. The one that entices her lover bug to `roll her over' for a quickie, as you say, and he then dies almost immediately. It is as if breeding is his only purpose for living."

"Well," she said, "my palmist told me that if I make love to one more American stranger, I will be free of the curse."

"What if the palmist is wrong?" Ashley asked.

Wiley didn't have a chance to respond. The next voice was that of a military policeman from his own division.

"Lieutenant, I gotcha," the MP corporal chirped as though pleased with his catch for the day.

"I've been following you for awhile Lieutenant, you weren't driving very straight."

"Yeah, you can see I had a few problems," Ashley said, unhappy with the situation he had gotten himself into.

"I could book you for a number of things—indiscretion with a female of an allied nation, driving while intoxicated, or transporting a foreigner in an army vehicle, all of which are pretty serious. You going into combat pretty soon, lieutenant?" the MP asked.

"Yeah, in a couple of days," Ashley answered.

"Well, in that case I'll just write you up for having a female in the vehicle. That's the least serious charge. And if you don't mind, Sir, I suggest that you take the lady home now, before you get into deeper trouble," the MP warned.

"OK, Corporal, I'm on my way. You may have saved my life."

Carrington was in the guard tent listening to the BBC on his new long-range radio when Ashley arrived.

"Lieutenant Jeb Carrington, you bastard, you've gotten me into big trouble," Ashley said interrupting.

"What happened?"

"Your girl friend made a move on me, and I got so excited I almost ran off the road. Then a God damned MP gave me a ticket for giving a foreign female, as he called her, a ride home."

"Is that right?" Carrington asked smiling.

"Yep!" Ashley answered. "That's right. One more thing, stay away from her! She's worried about a curse. Since D-Day, she has screwed four lieutenants and they are all dead. Now get this, her shrink is a palmist, who tells her she's got to make it with one more infantry lieutenant in order to break the curse."

"Brett, that sounds like a lot of bull shit. What can I do to help?" Carrington asked.

"Go with me to see the provost marshal in the morning, and use your charm to help me get that ticket fixed. If Colonel Meddler gets a hold of that report, I'm dead meat. You know from your own experience with him, he's the meanest man on the planet," Ashley said.

Captain Schultz, the division provost marshal, was not particularly happy to see a couple of second lieutenants with personal problems. He was busy assisting the division operations officer, the G-3, in planning the move from England to France and from France through Belgium to the Holland-German border, where the major battles were about to begin. The captain's job would be the security and traffic control at key intersections, with the assistance of local police.

Schultz was West Point Class of '42, but he looked older. Maybe the good life of a military police officer in the rear was beginning to show. His hair was thinner and his waistline larger than the typical infantry commander. His round, ruddy face and red eyes were indicative of long hours and a generous supply of Kentucky bourbon.

"What can I do for you `Shave Tails' on this nice gray English day?" Schultz asked in a caustic tone that matched his body language.

"Sir, I'm Lieutenant Brett Ashley. One of your corporals gave me a ticket last night that could cause me a great deal of trouble if Colonel Meddler, my regimental commander, were to get a hold of it. Knowing something of our past relationship, I'm convinced he would transfer me out of the division and leave me here in England to twiddle my thumbs. Not to be able to go into combat with my unit would be an embarrassment to me, and would make me the butt of jokes of my cadet class." Ashley continued, giving the circumstances of the charge and the nobility of his mission—to assist a maiden in distress.

"Lieutenant, I'm glad I've got my boots on or that romantic shit you are putting out would dampen my socks. Who's the silent one with you?" Schultz asked.

"Captain, I'm Lieutenant Carrington. I'm here to support my friend and corroborate his story. As a friend from our days at Camp Claiborne, he was doing me a favor. The vehicle in the incident was actually mine."

"Not yours, Lieutenant! That vehicle, which should have been impounded by my corporal, belongs to the United States Army."

"I stand corrected, Sir," Carrington responded nervously, now unsure of what the outcome of the hearing might be.

"I've wasted too much time since I have been in England with you damn guys wearing those crossed rifles—those crossed idiot sticks. You live the life of cockroaches. You eat! You keep from being eaten! You sleep! And you have sex when and wherever the situation permits! Now, having gotten that off my chest, I'm tearing up the ticket. A lot of people in your regiment have bigger social problems than yours. Go on into the fight in Germany, and shoot those fucking Nazis. Good luck. Be careful. Now get the hell out of my office. I've got more important things to do," Captain Schultz growled.

"Thanks, Captain," they said in unison, while making a quick retreat.

"Whew, that was close. We had both better behave ourselves until we get out of this country," Ashley said, taking a deep breath.

"Brett, I know how I can pay you back. I had a letter from my Dad today. He said this year's cotton crop was the best he has had in years, due to sales to the government. He also enclosed five, one hundred dollar bills, and told me to have a good time while I could. We both know we will crossing the channel in about three days, so why don't we spend a weekend in London on me?" Carrington suggested.

They did. It was a short train-trip into the city, by reputation the most civilized in the world. They took it all in—Big Ben, The Tower of London, Buckingham Palace, Westminster, Piccadilly Circus, etc., etc. They toured the pubs, and topped off the weekend with afternoon tea and a dance at the Savoy with upper crust, city girls, who made them feel as if they were Knights of the Garter. But this would be their last laugh for many months to come.

12

On the first of November 1944, the battalion troops moved by truck from their Barton Stacy base to the port of Southampton, where they were herded aboard a transport ship. It was a short, but exciting trip across the English Channel. The sun was bright, the sea calm, and morale high. The rising cliffs of Normandy's Omaha Beach lay ahead.

The skipper's commanding voice over the loud speakers broke the silence:

"Hear this, hear this! Men of the 84th Division. This is your captain speaking. The land you see ahead is Omaha Beach. Here on 6 June 1944, the famous 29th Infantry Division and British units made the initial Allied landing to restore freedom to the people of Europe. Within one week of D-day, more than 325,000 American and British troops were landed in France. They caught the Germans by surprise, and rapidly established a continuous, 65-mile beachhead along the Normandy coast. Now, prepare to disembark. Good luck and good hunting."

Ashley and members of his battalion made the exchange by ropes and ladders from their anchored transport to LSTs, used as ship-to-shore lighters. The destroyed implements of war—tanks, vehicles, and weapons—got their immediate attention. Damaged homes and a relieved, but still desperate, look on the faces of the French could not be missed. Yet to Ashley's surprise, there was an occasional sighting of an English sparrow and even the remains of a single-pump Shell station. Things weren't too different from home, he thought.

For three days the battalion moved by foot and truck in cold rain and mud through France and Belgium to Geleen, Holland. The route included sightings of St. Lo, Paris, Liege and Aachen. Ashley found out later that a battalion commander of the division that captured St. Lo was a graduate of The Military College. The French are not known to honor many heroes other than their own. But in the case of this officer, they made an exception. During the bloody battle to take the city, the major challenged his men to be the first to enter the city. He didn't make it, but his battalion did. His soldiers fittingly saw to it that their commander would be the first. They covered his body in an American flag, placed it in on the hood of his jeep, and drove him at the head of the first column that entered the city. It was a noble act that made a deep and lasting impression on the French people. The French built a monument, and named a square to honor the man they call—"The Major of St. Lo."

At Geleen, Holland the battalion camped in an apple orchard, surrounded by smiling faces and happy kids. The kids naturally gathered around the soldiers during meals, where they were given generous handouts. Ashley practiced his sophomore German with the kids, and accepted an invitation from their parents for an evening at their home. A night in a warm featherbed was a great experience for the battalion S-4, but it didn't endear him to his new battalion commander, who slept in a sleeping bag on the cold, damp ground in the apple orchard.

The division was initially assigned to the XIII Corps of the Ninth US Army, but for their first action against the Siegfried Line they were attached to the XXX Corps of the British Second Army. Except for a daily ration of black, British rum, strong enough to burn the bottom out of a canteen cup and tough odorous mutton, it didn't mean a lot of difference to those down the ranks. The attachment, however, offered the Americans a chance to see how the British fought their war their way. The Brits were a different looking bunch. Their flat steel helmets looked like reissues of the pancake-type they used in the trenches in WWI. They had no use for blackout conditions or stealth in battle. Their enlisted men bitched loudly and constantly as they went about their preparations for combat, frequently prefacing comments about their officers with "bloody-fucking." But after taking seemingly endless time for morning and afternoon teas, they fought like wild animals, without any evidence of fear. For them, frontal attacks were commonplace, and losses commensurably high. Hulks of burnt-out British tanks lined up one behind the other were typical relics of their dogged assaults.

On 11 November 1944, while still bivouacked in Geleen, E Company, Second Battalion was ordered into the line to support a cavalry unit in action along the Dutch-German border. This operation was the first combat operation for the division. Four men were wounded, and six were reported missing in action in the "skirmish"—a premonition of things to come.

After their organized retreat across France and defeat at Aachen, the "exhausted" German Army took refuge behind its West Wall, the Siegfried Line, to regroup and prepare for the defense of the "Fatherland." Behind Aachen, north and south, was the German "inner-fortress", an elaborate chain of fortifications of pillboxes, tank traps, and mine fields, covered by withering enemy fire.

This border defense was placed between the Wurm and Roer Rivers, obstacles in themselves.

Within five miles of the Dutch-German border stood the German town of Geilenkirchen—a major focal point of the German defense. Geilenkirchen set astride the Wurm River. The Roer River, three times the size of the Wurm, was seven miles to the east and provided the German force an excellent fallback position, if needed. For the 84th Division, the decisive battle for Germany would be fought between the Wurm and Roer Rivers.

Ashley moved with the Second Battalion from Geleen, Holland to the front on 17 November. The First and Third Battalions of the regiment made the attack on Geilenkirchen on the 18th. The fact that the Second Battalion had a new commander and executive officer was obviously a factor in Colonel Meddler's decision to initially hold the Second Battalion in reserve. From the initiation of the regimental attack on the 18th, attacks by enemy air, artillery, mortars, and small arms were intense and continuous.

It wasn't until the 22d of November that the Second Battalion was committed to seize and hold the high ground between the towns of Wurm and Beck. F Company captured seven pillboxes in route to its objective before being stopped. G Company advanced only a couple of hundred yards, before being pindowned by artillery from high ground to the northeast of their position. The attack failed, despite the personal effort of Major Thompson, the new battalion commander, to rally the troops and keep the attack moving.

From the 18th of November, the day of the regimental attack on to German soil, until the Second Battalion was relieved on the 25th, enemy fire was so intense that any movement was near impossible. One regiment, whose M1 rifles were inoperable due to mud, charged wildly toward the entrenched enemy with fixed bayonets. As a result of this action, the shocked defenders called the division with the shoulder patch, a white ax in a red field—*"President Rosenfelt's Bloody Butchers."*

Ashley and the Second Battalion staff spent most of the time in a cellar, well to the rear of the rifle companies. He soon realized the obvious—the longer the time spent in the cellars, the more difficult it was to come out. For several days one staff member sat in the corner of the cellar in a state of shock—wide-eyed and staring straight ahead.

Finally, Ashley and his sergeant crawled out of the basement to find artillery and bombs had pulverized the town of Prummern. With anxious fascination, they watched a dogfight between an American P-38 Lightning and a German Messerschmitt 109. It seemed unreal, until one of them was hit, caught fire, and crashed in the distance. It happened so quickly, that they were never able to determine who won the battle. He prayed that it was not Cal Sinclair, his best friend and former college roommate,

Except for the battalion commander and the battalion S-3, few knew what was going on. The best sources of intelligence were the rifle company troops in route to and from the front. It was from a platoon leader from the Third Battalion moving back from the pillboxes that he learned of Jeb Carrington's fate.

"Hey Bud, what do you hear from my friend, Jeb Carrington?" Ashley asked.

"Not much anymore, since he was evacuated. Didn't you hear what happened to him?" Bud, the platoon leader said.

"No, what happened?"

"While leading an attack on a pillbox yesterday, he was 'raked' across the legs by a Kraut machine gun. For a while they thought he might lose his legs, but a later report said that except for a stiff leg he would be all right. He is on the way to a hospital in England and then home," the lieutenant said.

"My God," Ashley yelled back loudly so as to be heard over incoming mortar fire. "So, Susan Wiley's curse is finally broken. Her fifth lover will live!"

"What did you say?" the platoon leader asked, moving nearly out of voice contact.

"Oh nothing," Ashley said. "It was something that Jeb and I got involved in while in England. Take care of your self. By the way, I think I'm going to change jobs soon. I don't know what the hell I'm doing here. They keep shelling the hell of the command post, and I can't fight back. It's a helpless feeling. I'll see you."

Ashley had a lot of respect for his young battalion commander. Major Thompson was a good looking, clean-cut regular army officer and a distinguished ROTC graduate from a mid-western university. Ashley rightly surmised, however, that the major was too busy learning his own job to make a battalion S-4 out of a second lieutenant. Ashley knew he had to find a job that he had been trained to do. He made up his mind to ask his boss for a transfer that night while they were together in the cellar command post.

"Major Thompson, I have a request, Sir," Ashley spoke in an unsure tone.

"What is it, Ashley?" the battalion commander asked.

"Sir, I'm obviously not making much of contribution as your battalion S-4. I think you would be better served to get someone who is a supply specialist. At Fort Benning, they trained us to be platoon leaders—nothing more. I think I can do a better job with a line company," Ashley explained.

"Lieutenant, why in the hell are you asking this? I know. You heard that the battalion S-4 of the First Battalion and his driver were ambushed last night. They were captured too. Is that what's on your mind now?" the major asked.

"No sir," Ashley said." I've had this on my mind for a long time."

"OK, in the morning I'll send you to E Company with Captain Grant. He has more combat experience than the other rifle company commanders," Major Thompson said finally.

"Thank you, Major."

Grant was not exactly overjoyed at having a new second lieutenant to worry about, particularly a former battalion staff officer. Having seen combat at Guadalcanal, he had learned never to become too attached to those with a limited life expectancy. It was also become apparent to Ashley that he had contempt for anyone who served behind the front lines—rifle company front lines. The captain was a man of little warmth. He spoke as little as necessary, and then only about the business at hand. Ashley would come to have more respect than love for this physically and mentally tough combat officer.

When he entered the company command post, Grant was involved with the upcoming attack. He showed no recognition of Ashley's presence, and continued to direct his orders to the platoon sergeant, the acting platoon leader.

"Sergeant, we will attack with two platoons. Your platoon will be on the right, First Platoon on the left, Third Platoon will follow. F Company will be on our right and for this one, G Company will be in reserve. The objective is the high ground northeast of the town of Lindern. It is from this area that Kraut artillery has stalled our advance and kept us bogged down in these God dammed, muddy beet fields. Any questions? Lieutenant, go with the Second Platoon. OK, move out!" So with this welcome, Ashley began his war at the front with a rifle company that he had volunteered for. He began to wonder if he had made the biggest mistake of his life.

The platoon sergeant led the platoon in a north-easterly direction as vaguely described by Captain Grant. To the left of the platoon column there was an orchard of stunted trees and beyond a beet field, now a sea of mud brought on by daily downpours of freezing rain. Ashley assumed his assignment was that of an observer. He brought up the rear of the column of squads. He could see beyond the orchard and the gradually sloping terrain leading to the high ground beyond. Nothing could move below without being observed. The platoon sergeant guided the platoon into the orchard. Then as if the orchard were sacred ground, artillery fire from the high ground began to pound the area.

Ashley leaped into the nearest foxhole, the excellent work of a German craftsman. His entry was especially timely, as he saw his last position had become a shell hole. The previous occupant of the foxhole was either a large or a cautious soldier or both. The earthly dwelling was over six feet deep. From the bottom of the hole, Ashley contemplated his position. He was *persona non grata* in a strange world of friendless fools, he thought. He could hear the voice of his former OCS tactical officer: "Well, candidate you got yourself in a hell of a mess, what the hell are you are you going to do now, give up?" Yeah, why not, he thought. The Captain never put me in charge of anything. This platoon is going to get its ass shot off, and mine too if I get out of this safe haven.

The shelling intensified. Ashley looked upward,

and there was the extended hand of soldier he had never met.

"Can I give you a hand, Lieutenant?" he said.

"Who in the hell are you?" Ashley responded.

"Squad leader of the Third Squad, Sir."

"Good, get me out of here now, or I'll never come out. My coming out seems to make a difference to you. You are only one who seems to give a shit whether I live or die. Your help is appreciated," Ashley said, with a feeling of disgust with himself.

Luckily, there was now a lull in the shelling.

"Sergeant, where is the platoon sergeant?" Ashley asked.

"Over there, by there by the edge of the beet field, Sir," the squad leader said.

"Good, thanks." Ashley said, now moving towards the platoon sergeant with more determination.

"Platoon Sergeant, we gotta get the hell out of here. If the Krauts decide to `fire for effect' on us, nothing will be left alive in this fucking orchard. The only direction to go is toward the big guns, before they get their desired target bracket," Ashley advised.

"I think you are right, Lieutenant," his platoon sergeant agreed.

"Good, let's move all three squads in a skirmish line," Ashley suggested.

"Platoon—skirmish line! Move it on the double!" the sergeant yelled. The men responded instantly. Ashley, for the first time since he had been in the division, found a sergeant who knew what he was doing.

The platoon moved scarcely a hundred yards, when the orchard behind then turned into a furnace.

"Good call, Lieutenant!"

"No," Ashley said. "It was either good luck or someone is watching over us—my guardian angel. We have got to keep moving."

They moved quietly for 200 more yards, when suddenly they came to the edge of a tank trap—an enormous ditch, built deep and wide enough if not to stop tanks—to slow them down. In the mud of the beet fields it was a significant barrier.

"Get in! Quick, get in!" Ashley yelled.

The timing was perfect. As soon as the last man hit the trench, the German machine gunners sprayed the top of the tank trap. Fortunately, their gunners must have been temporarily hypnotized by the sight of bunch of crazy GIs heading into no-man's land. They had delayed firing for a few seconds too long.

The platoon riflemen secured their position, and waited for further orders from the company commander. They didn't have to wait long. It was near dark, when they heard a thrashing noise to their rear. It was the company runner.

"Platoon Sergeant, the captain has lost touch with F Company. They were supposed to be on your right flank. He wants you to send out a patrol to find them," the runner said excitedly.

"OK," the Sergeant said. "Tell the captain we can use a little more water, K rations, and ammunition."

"All right, take it easy. I'll see you about this time tomorrow," the runner said, happy to return to the cellar in the rear.

The platoon sergeant wisely sent out only one man to attempt contact with F Company—He never came back. Poor communication in F Company between the platoons and the company commander continued to plague the command. One of Ashley's OCS classmates led an attack just two miles west of his present location a week earlier. Lacking specific objectives, he moved too far into a town called Mullendorf. The town was filled to capacity with more than a thousand German infantry and supporting armor. Under the circumstances, F Company rifleman were easily overwhelmed and taken prisoner. Their war ended with their first attack on 22 November 1944.

A week later *a deja vu*, but this time the losses were higher. It now became clear why Ashley's platoon could not make contact with F Company, which should have been within close proximity. A runner, as was the custom, delivered the attack order on behalf of the F Company commander: "Attack, attack now. Take the high ground northeast of Lindern and dig in." There was a misunderstanding as to where the exact location of the high ground was. Since they did not initially receive fire, they advanced four to five hundred yards more—too far! A much larger German tank-infantry unit killed four members of two lost platoons, and captured all the others except four who managed to escape and tell of the tragedy.

As it turned out, Ashley's E Company platoon had also advanced too far. Unknown to them and the enemy, they were but a small finger protruding into strong, German defenses. The shelling continued day in and day out. The cries of new, teenage replacements in holes by themselves could be heard above the earth-shaking explosions. Ashley and his platoon sergeant shared a foxhole. At night each took turns at two-hour watches. They had seen training movies of soldiers decapitating their "enemies" or being decapitated by them with piano wire. That thought kept them awake, until completely overcome with fatigue. The sergeant and the lieutenant stored their grenades around the lip of their foxhole to prevent them from accidentally going off in their hole. That changed after a couple of days when a sniper's bullet cracked the casing of a white phosphorus grenade. The leaking, liquid phosphorus nearly burned through the sergeant's overcoat before it could be extinguished.

There were days that were more exciting than others. A few haystacks, or German camouflaged positions, were scattered around the battlefield. The platoon soon found out that they could set them on fire with tracer bullets, and enjoy seeing the rush of the enemy devils to avoid or put out the fire. They had a sobering experience, however, when they realized how close the German lines were to their own.

One typically cold and hazy morning, they spotted German stretcher-bearers within 50 yards of their line carrying what appeared to be their wounded to the rear. Red crosses clearly marked their helmets. Time and again they went back and forth, each time removing a body or two. At first, Ashley gave the word to hold fire.

"Hey look, Lieutenant. In the distance one of those Krauts just jumped off a stretcher and walked away as good as you and I could," the platoon sergeant said excitedly.

"I'll be damned, you're right. Let's test 'em. On their next pick up we will fire over their heads and see what happens. Get the word out to the squads about what we plan to do. If they are faking it, we will shoot them all," Ashley said.

The plan worked. Two stretcher-bearer teams appeared, loaded their "wounded," and began their movement to the rear. The platoon sergeant fired an overhead burst above the heads of the aid men. At that moment, healthy German soldiers jumped off the stretchers and dashed to the rear.

"Fire, fire, open up. Let 'em have it. Kill 'em!" Ashley yelled.

"Lieutenant, those bastards had crawled up so close they could have spent the night with us, after killing us of course," the sergeant said.

"Yeah," said Ashley. "I wonder how much longer the captain is gonna keep us up here."

"Last night the runner told me that the `Old Man' was going to rotate platoons soon."

"Good, we are overdue for some good news, Sergeant. This place is beginning to get to me. Do you remember that lieutenant in F Company that was with the first lost platoon?" Ashley asked.

"Yeah, I remember," the sergeant answered. "I heard his old man owned a big liquor business in Kentucky."

"That's him," Ashley said. Well, he used to hang out at the club a lot. I was the club officer at one time. The lieutenant was a hell of a party guy. He played the piano well, and had a great voice. Well, I could have sworn I heard him last night singing the song—`*Spring Will Be A Little Late This Year*,' a favorite of ours."

"Couldn't have been him, Lieutenant. He is probably in a German stalag some place in the rear, eating stale bread and cold potato soup every day."

Ashley and his platoon were finally replaced by the Third Platoon that had enjoyed relative quiet in company reserve. The reserve billet consisted of the remnants of a farmer's house, but more important a thick-walled basement. They were able to get their first hot meal in a week, and shave and bathe out of their steel helmets with moderately warm water, courtesy of the company cook and helpers. E Company received some replacements but F Company received most of them, since they had lost most of their riflemen in only nine days of combat. Of a full complement of 200 officers and men, they now had only four officers and 32 men left. The sight of clean-shaven, well fed replacements whining about their sleeping conditions on one occasion caused Ashley to completely lose it.

"Lieutenant, I don't have any place to sleep," the pathetic replacement said.

"Soldier," Ashley growled with his hand tight around the collar of his man's fatigues, "I want to tell you something—we have all been sleeping standing up in muddy foxholes, and have been shelled every day and night for a week. We are lucky as hell just to be breathing. Now go find your squad leader. I'm sure he will find you a place to lie down. If not come back and see me."

Ashley was no longer a platoon observer, he was the platoon leader. It was an improvement, albeit slow in coming. His platoon sergeant welcomed the change. He wasn't being paid to do a lieutenant's job. For the first time since leaving Holland, Ashley had a clean shave, warm food in his belly, and less self doubt. The time had come for him to meet his company commander on more equal terms.

Ashley found Captain Grant in his comfortable, cellar command post. He was surrounded by his first sergeant, clerks and other command post "strap hangers," enjoying a cup of coffee.

"Sir, may I have word with you in private?" Ashley asked.

"Yes, Lieutenant, what can I do for you? Have a seat. First Sergeant, excuse us a moment."

"Sir, I want to give you a quick run down on some of the things we saw up in the trenches last week."

Ashley gave the Captain a capsule review of the major events and then the major reason for the interview.

"Captain, there is one thing that troubles me. Your dealing directly with my platoon sergeant puts me in the position of observer. I think the sergeant by now knows who's in charge, so I would appreciate your passing orders to me, and I in turn will pass them on to my platoon."

"Sorry about that, Lieutenant," Captain Grant said. "My platoon officers don't seem to last more than a couple of days, so I've gotten in the bad habit of dealing with the sergeants. It's amazing how many out-live lieutenants. If you live long enough, we will see if we can't straighten things out."

"Thanks Captain," Ashley said while excusing himself. He was relieved at having had what seemed to him to be a positive discussion. Yet he knew that the captain, by reputation, didn't suffer fools lightly—particularly lieutenants who told him how to run his business. Ashley had become smart enough to know that the boss had a number of options at his disposal to make life miserable for him if he wanted to. He wouldn't have long to wait for his commander's next move.

13

Major Okie was the Executive Officer (XO) of the Second Battalion. The XO was not exactly the plain fellow who lived next door. Among other things, he was half-Cherokee and descendant of Chief Dragging Canoe. The chief is remembered for his failed attacks in 1776 against the US Army at Fort Watauga and Eaton's Station in North Carolina.

The Cherokee were among the most literate and courageous of the American Indian tribes. One of their own developed an alphabet for their language, which accounted for their remarkable assimilation of white culture. They were also survivors of the forced march from Georgia to Oklahoma during the bitter winter of 1838-39. Of 18,000 who made the westward trek, called the Trail of Tears, 4000 died from disease and exposure.

Unfortunately, Major Okie did not exhibit very many of the commendable traits of his noble ancestors. Ashley's recollections of this aging National Guard officer were less than favorable. He had spent a night or two in the command-post bunker with Okie before moving to E Company. The old major talked incessantly about the battle of the hedgerows across France, which had little or no relevance to the battle of the pillboxes in the mud fields of Germany. No one seemed to know what division he came from or what his job had been. The battalion commander had not exactly figured out how to use his peripatetic XO, and as the result he became a freelance operator—an unguided missile. Like his Indian antecedents, he had a genetic weakness for "firewater." He became an alcoholic.

Ashley's second meeting with Major Okie was sooner than he would have liked. Less than two weeks after his assignment to E Company, Captain Grant "volunteered" him to lead a battalion night patrol of a half dozen men. At the battalion command cellar he discovered Major Okie, Major Thompson, the battalion commander, and Lieutenant Saklos discussing an enemy sighting of the previous day. Lieutenant Saklos was the regimental intelligence and reconnaissance platoon leader. Ashley had met him at Camp Claiborne during division maneuvers. He did not envy him of his requirement to work closely with Colonel Meddler, his old stateside nemesis. He remembered Meddler's unconscionable humiliation of Saklos in front of his men, and several regimental staff officers. Saklos had made the cardinal sin of the maneuver. He was captured with a map showing the regimental defensive positions. Since then he had done everything possible to redeem himself in the eyes of his commander. Unfortunately, his actions at times were foolhardy, exposing himself and his men unnecessarily

"Lieutenant Saklos, tell Lieutenant Ashley what you saw yesterday," Major Okie said.

"Yes, Sir, I was making a reconnaissance of the regimental front for Colonel Meddler, when I saw a couple of Krauts going in and out of a building a few hundred yards in front of our lines. I figured we ought to capture them, and find out what's going on out there," Saklos said with an air of self-confidence.

"OK, Sergeant," Major Okie said turning to his assistant. "Issue the lieutenants and the men a double K ration, an extra canteen of water, extra clips of ammunition, and a rope to tie-up the prisoners and bring them back to the command post for questioning."

Ashley listened in shock and disbelief. The mission as he saw it was to pass through American lines into known mine fields, penetrate the main German defensive line, find a house, capture its occupants, tie their hands with a rope, and bring them back alive—all of this in the black of night. He was speechless. Ashley was particularly concerned about mines in the area. The battalion commander, having listening in silence, now added his guidance.

"Major Okie, I don't see any need for two officers to go on this patrol. Since Lieutenant Saklos has been out there in daylight and apparently knows the route well. I suggest he take the patrol. Do you have any problem with that, Saklos?"

"No Sir, Major Thompson. This fits the mission of my platoon," Saklos said, gladly accepting another opportunity to settle the score with his unpredictable colonel.

The patrol was a short one. Once they entered the German main line of resistance, Lieutenant Saklos stepped on a mine that blew both his legs off and killed one soldier instantly. Trip wires set off flares, lighting the battlefield, enabling German gunners to accurately spray the area with deadly machine gun fire. The remaining members of the patrol never had a chance to fire a shot. They wisely and hastily retreated to the rear. They recalled the brave Saklos' last words: "Oh Jesus, help me. Oh Jesus help me, help me!" Then the hated darkness returned. For a moment, there was an eerie silence in the beet fields, as though God himself had ordered time-out for a prayer.

PART FOUR

THE BATTLE OF THE BULGE

1944-1945

14

Colonel Meddler's regiment was not a major participant in the battle for the Siegfried Line. The other two regiments were chosen by the division commander to lead the effort. Casualties were, however, nearly equally spread among the three regiments—the heavy, enemy artillery fire was more random than selective. Meddler and his "boys" would get their chance in the battles to come.

By the 18th of December 1944, the 84th Division, with the help of the 102nd Infantry Division and the 2nd Armored Division, drilled a sizable hole in the formidable Siegfried Line. By the end of its one-month campaign, the 84th had captured eight strong points, 28 German officers, 1521 enlisted men, and 112 pillboxes. It was now the mission of the 102nd Division to relieve the 84th of its mission, to mop-up the remaining strong holds, and to move on east to the Roer River. The 84th turned its attention to increased enemy activity in the Ardennes forest of Belgium, which would become the most famous battle of the war—The Battle of the Bulge.

With the fall of the Siegfried, Adolf Hitler—the little Austrian corporal, the Fuhrer of the Third Reich—found himself in a desperate situation. It became obvious even to the fanatical Hitler that he could not win an extended war of attrition from a defensive position along the Roer and Rhine rivers. He needed a quick counter punch, one that, with the element of surprise, might succeed. He began preparation for the operation in September 1944. He ordered his generals to prepare for a lightning strike through the Ardennes, one that would cross the Meuse River, seize Antwerp with its supplies, and split the American and British forces. Using the mass principle of war, Hitler ordered all of the men and materiel that could be spared from the Eastern and Northern fronts be moved to the Ardennes. He counted on battle proven veterans and children raised as fanatics by the Nazis for a final solution to the war. They were his *Hitler Jugend*, ages 16 to 19. In this campaign they would be thrown against some of America's best and brightest, ages 19 to 22, led by platoon leaders ages 20 and 21 from college classes of '44.

At exactly the planned moment—0525 hours on 16 December—the massive German force made its move. Conditions were perfect, frozen, snow-covered ground, and poor visibility. They achieved total surprise. Field Marshal Von Rundstedt, the German commander in chief of the Western front, committed the major elements of three armies (his precious strategic reserve) into the Belgium Ardennes area of operations. The mainly armored force quickly overran the thinly held Allied defenses. By late December the German forces reached the vicinity of the Meuse River, a distance of nearly 50 miles. But this was the high water mark of the German counteroffensive. For on Christmas Day 1944, the skies over the Ardennes cleared, enabling Allied Air to pound the enemy's overextended logistical tail. This was the big picture, but it was of little concern to front line infantry. They were worried about what the next hour or the next day would bring.

On 20 December at 2100, within seconds of the prescribed hour, a quartermaster truck company with 48 two and a half ton trucks arrived in the Second Battalion area to move the battalion units to the south.

Except for the change in direction of the convoy on several occasions to avoid the advancing Wehrmacht, the trip to Belgium was surprisingly uneventful. It was a welcome change in scenery from muddy beet fields, battered towns, and gaunt hardwood trees to quaint, clean villages surrounded by beautiful, blue-green spruce. The air now was cold and crisp, and the first snow of winter had begun to cover the ground. At night on the 21st of December the unit arrived at the vicinity of Marche, Belgium at the designated assembly area. Things were looking up. A few days earlier, the troops had bathed at Dutch miners' showers. They had received clean clothes, additional combat rations, ammunition, and a few wide-eyed replacements. If that were not enough pleasure, the battalion was designated division reserve.

15

Ashley was standing in line with his E Company platoon having a reasonably warm meal when he noticed Captain Grant approaching. Despite freezing conditions and a foot of snow, the cooks did well with the turkey, cranberry sauce, hot rolls, and mincemeat pie.

"Merry Christmas, Lieutenant Ashley," Captain Grant said in a cheerful, unaccustomed mood.

"Merry Christmas, Captain. So it's Christmas. I wondered why we were having a hot meal for a change."

"Ashley," Grant continued, "I've got some news for you. You are being transferred to F Company. As you may know, they were nearly finished-off in the battle for control of the Siegfried. They need rifle platoon leaders badly. You have been selected to give them a hand."

The thought of transfer to another unit with new faces was a shocker at first for Ashley. He had hardly gotten to know the members of his E Company platoon. But he had met Captain Tipper once at the Camp Claiborne officer's club. He liked him and looked forward to a more compatible relationship than he had had with Captain Grant.

Captain Tipper was commander of F Company, the Second Battalion of Colonel Meddler's regiment. He was one of nicest, most caring officers in the battalion. He was nondescript in appearance, average build, thinning brown hair, and a freckled nose too large for his face. A Norman Rockwell cover for the

Saturday Evening Post would have shown him in a white lab-coat standing in front of his own drug store in some far away mid-western town. Tipper must have wondered how and why he had become an infantry commander. His company had faired poorly in the Siegfried line—nearly all of his riflemen and platoon leaders in his three rifle platoons were either killed or captured. The captain himself was plagued with chronic back problems and other ailments. Lieutenant Fortner, his executive officer, took over command from time to time to give the "old man" of 30 years a respite from the stress of command. There was some question as to whether or not the captain had the physical stamina and mental toughness for command of a rifle company that became known as the—"Company Of The Lost Platoons."

"Welcome aboard, Lieutenant Ashley," Captain Tipper said with his hand extended and a warm smile on his face despite his many problems. "It has been a long time since Camp Claiborne. I wish the hell we were all back there right now in one piece. But for now, I've got a real choice assignment for you. Take your pick—First, Second, or Third rifle platoon. They are all without a platoon officer. I lost them all."

"I'll take the Second Platoon, Captain Tipper, if it's all right with you. I had the Second Platoon in E Company. Two must be my lucky number, I'm still here!"

"OK, Ashley, you got a new command. By the way, did you hear about your good friend, Lieutenant Coke?" the Captain asked. "I remember seeing you two together back at Claiborne."

"No, Sir, how's he getting along? I haven't seen him since we left the Camp."

"Not well I'm afraid. His unit was one of the first in action down here. They took a small Belgium village without too much resistance. Coke had his platoon dig in on the higher ground beyond the town. Then, at daybreak the next morning a sniper from the second floor of a building shot him, while still asleep in his foxhole. They say he got it right between the eyes," the captain said, breaking the bad news.

"My God, Captain, that's awful. Coke and I were on the same floor at OCS. We raised many a glass together. He knew more about soldiering than the instructors. Before OCS, he had been a Regular Army sergeant and had seen action in 1942 against the Japs at Attu, one of the Aleutian Islands off Alaska. If Coke couldn't make it, Captain, there's not much hope for any of us," Ashley warned.

"Sorry, I had to bring it up, Ashley, but I thought you ought to know."

"It comes as a shock, Captain, but thanks for letting me know. I appreciate it."

"Good luck, Lieutenant."

"Thanks, Captain, I think it has been more than luck so far. Somebody has been watching over me. I've tried not to do anything stupid either. It seems like the brave and fools die young, Sir. That in itself means I should make it. I'm neither."

Ashley joined his platoon in a deserted Belgium farmhouse. The platoon was at about 60 percent of authorized strength. Under normal conditions units less than two thirds strength are pulled out of the line for replacements, supplies, and retraining. But these were not normal circumstances. Three German armies were chewing-up American divisions piece by piece. In the beginning, American units were outnumbered by a ratio of three to one. Ashley's rifle platoon, like others, was made up of young replacements and a few combat-seasoned veterans.

Sergeant Fisk, a wiry Texan stooped from a month's shelling in the Siegfried line, greeted his new lieutenant. But it was only a matter of minutes into the sergeant's orientation that a tremendous explosion shook the aging farmhouse. Fortunately, Fisk and Ashley dove in among the sleeping men lying on the floor. A missile the size of a cannon ball passed through the walls of the building.

"What the hell was that?" Fisk asked, justifiably unnerved. "Anyone standing could have been decapitated."

"Don't know. It was a hell of a noise. Let's find out," Ashley answered.

The two of them instantly spotted a rising cloud of smoke within 50 yards of their building. Beyond the smoke, several parachutes floated gracefully towards a snow covered clearing surrounded by tall pine and fir.

"It was a B-17! I saw it! It took a direct hit right above us," said an excited soldier from an adjacent platoon.

From out of nowhere a jeep appeared, followed by an ambulance. Their direction was unmistakably toward the falling chutes. On second look, Ashley saw a familiar figure, none other than his old nemesis, Major Okie, the battalion executive officer. Ashley began to laugh without restraint.

"What's so funny, Lieutenant?" Sergeant Fisk asked.

"Well, I was laughing at the major in the jeep. He's Major Okie the battalion executive officer. Do you know him?"

"No, Sir," the sergeant replied.

"Well, you don't want to. Whenever he's around look for things to be fucked up. So he has finally gotten a chance to lead a patrol to capture someone—

an American. I'll bet the battalion clerk will write him up for a Bronze Star for gallantry in action as soon as he gets back to his basement at battalion headquarters."

The major and his crew located the downed flight officers and crew. They were in a state of shock. They thought at first they were being attacked by a German patrol. Upon discovering that their "attackers" were Americans, they gladly offered their all, leather flight jackets, nylon scarves with escape routes printed on them, fur-lined boots, and other gear in exchange for foxhole blankets, a ride in a warm ambulance, and a cup of coffee. The airmen were a sorry sight when they walked out of the ambulance into the aid station, stripped naked except for their long underwear.

"Fisk, it looks like that monster hole we saw in our hooch could have been a dud from our friendly B-17," Ashley surmised.

"Could have been, Lieutenant. The bombardier was probably dumping his extra bombs before crossing the channel."

"Well anyway, Fisk," Ashley said. "You were telling me what gives around here. Looks like I'm the new guy on the block. The way things are starting out, I may not be the last. I heard you were with F Company—the least loved in the regiment—from the beginning."

"I know we don't look too good so far, since we have had a bunch of guys killed and captured under strange circumstances. The captain is doing the best he can, considering he's been sick a lot. Lieutenant Fortner, the executive officer, had a bad run in with the brass back at Camp Claiborne, and it's left him with a sour taste in his mouth. We never see much of the first sergeant. He hangs out around the command post. I guess it takes a lot of people to help the headquarter's company clerk make out the morning report. More than anything else, we have had a lot of bad luck. That's about it, Lieutenant, as I see it. Except for one thing. Since you are new they will be giving you, and us, a lot of the dirty work in the beginning," Fisk explained.

"Thanks, Fisk. I think you might be right; they gave me the same treatment in E Company. Between the two of us, we gotta figure how to do what they tell us to do—no more, no less—and stay alive at the same time," Ashley said relaying his survival philosophy to his new platoon sergeant.

In military jargon, the initial situation in the Ardennes forest was very fluid. That is, no one seemed to know where the Germans were and vice versa. There were unplanned encounters, skirmishes, withdrawals, and counter attacks. Men, we will "find them, fix them, and destroy them," the commanders said from their comfortable positions in the rear. It was easy enough to say, but difficult to do.

"Ashley, your platoon will lead the column into the enemy's suspected area of operations," Captain Tipper said. "Turn right at the road junction about mile away, cross a bridge, and continue to march until told otherwise."

It seemed simple enough even if open ended. Ashley was beginning to find out that nothing is simple in war; confusion is the norm. The road junction consisted of a turn to the left and two right turns. An MP corporal stood on an improvised platform at the crossing. He motioned to Ashley and his Second Platoon to take the left of the two right forks. Bad guidance! After ten minutes in never-never land no one showed. In the far distances an enemy column was on the move.

"Lieutenant, I think we took the wrong turn," Fisk said, reminding his platoon leader of the obvious.

"Yep, you got it right, Fisk. Did you see all of those God damned Krauts out there just waitin' to make us prisoners? Must be at least an armored company. I can see a lot of tanks and personnel carriers. It could be the advanced reconnaissance force of an even larger unit. They are pouring into that wooded area over there. It could be their forward assembly area," Ashley said.

"Yeah," Fisk said, "I see 'em."

"Fisk, I don't think they have seen us yet. We've got to get our asses back to the road junction and have a word with that fucking MP. And then try to find the company. They sure didn't send anybody out looking for us. Hope that's not standard operating procedure."

"It is! I forgot to tell you about that, Lieutenant."

"Corporal," Ashley yelled. "Why in hell did you send us down the wrong road? Nobody's out there but a woods full of Krauts."

"Trying to thin out the traffic, I reckon. Don't seem like a big deal to me," the corporal replied in a tone arrogant enough for Ashley to make the MP remember the encounter for the rest of his life.

"Corporal, two things: First you almost got us killed before our time, which will come soon enough; second your mother did a poor job of teaching you the fundamentals of common courtesy. Now I want you to salute, and say that you are sorry, Sir. If you don't within 30 seconds, I'm going to have my biggest squad leader, who played football at Michigan, pull you off that fucking pedestal you are standing on and kick your fat ass. Any questions?" Ashley snarled.

"No questions, Sir. I'm sorry. It was bad mistake," the corporal said, visibly shaken.

"All right, that's better. Now, which direction did you send the rest of our company?"

"The other right fork, Lieutenant, sorry," the corporal said, apologizing again.

"Corporal," Ashley advised. "You better get word to your company commander right away that the woods are full of Krauts about a quarter of mile down the wrong road that you sent us on. They may be heading this way at any moment. You will be needing a lot of help if they do."

"Fisk, we had better have the platoon move out on the double, before the company leaves us for good."

"OK, Lieutenant, we are moving out. I think you scared the shit out of that poor corporal," Fisk said laughing.

"I hope so."

Captain Tipper wasn't too displeased with the mishap. As Ashley soon learned, the captain had the unique ability to camouflage pain and discomfort with an innocent smile. What Ashley could not understand was why a company runner was not dispatched to retrieve them and turn them around. Maybe the captain figured that Ashley's platoon was way out front, and the main body of the company would eventually catch them. Wrong assumption!

After a long day's march, the company reached its designated assembly area on time, despite the early miscue. The snow continued to fall. Ice replaced the mud of the beet fields as the temperature dipped well below freezing. It was late December, or was it early January? Ashley had lost all account of time. Blue-black darkness came early. At times there was an eerie stillness among the tall, blue-green fir. Morning would come too soon and another day of hunting would begin.

The day didn't begin too badly. The cooks served a breakfast of cold eggs and pancakes, but hot coffee. Then Capt. Tipper called Ashley and his platoon sergeant over with the orders for the day.

"Lieutenant," Tipper said, pointing to his map. "See these three towns?"

"Yes, Sir."

"I'm going to send your platoon on a probing mission, to see how far we can get without too much resistance. The division tank company has let us have a platoon of three light tanks. They'll transport you and your people. They'll also help out if you get into trouble. OK?"

"OK, Captain. Where are the tanks?" Ashley asked.

"They are the ones lined-up on the street out-side. The tank platoon lieutenant has been briefed by his commander, and he knows the general mis-sion and direction. Good luck."

Ashley introduced himself to the tank platoon leader, and went over the captain's instructions with his squad leaders. It was a new experience for them to ride tanks the way the German Army did during their blitzkrieg through France and the Low Coun-tries. They mounted the tanks rather awkwardly, but with one man giving a hand to the other they man-aged. The tank commander gave a hand signal indi-cating a forward movement. The scenery now had become commonplace—trees, more trees, snow cov-ered blacktop roads, and an occasional farmer's barn and field. In this virgin territory every house and barn could have an enemy soldier lying in wait to kill them. Ashley knew that there was no time for day-dreaming. He had the natural infantryman's dislike for being too close to noisy tanks, the armored soldier's iron coffin, infantrymen called them. Around armored units stealth was impossible. Tanks and tankers drew fire, but they had some protection inside their metal box. The foot soldier had only the irregularity of God's good earth.

The tank officer with his head now out of his turret made a quick move of his lead tank to avoid a body lying in the road. He looked at Ashley and shook his head in disgust, as vultures flew away to avoid contact. It was the decayed, flattened body of a German soldier. He had been run over and over by his own tanks and trucks. It was a ghastly sight. His bones were pulverized, and little was left of him but muscular tissue turned to threads.

"Ashley," the tank officer said. "Looks like those bastards were in a hurry. No time to bury their dead. Just maybe they are pulling out and going home."

"Now that would be nice, wouldn't it?" Ashley responded nervously, making conversation only because it was expected.

"Sergeant Fisk, I'd guess that we have come about five miles so far, and we haven't seen a soul. I have an uneasy feeling that this lull is too good to be true," Ashley said.

The tank officer apparently saw something suspicious or had the same uneasy feeling. He raised his hand halting the column as they approached the outskirts of the first village that Captain Tipper mentioned in his briefing.

"Hey, Ashley, I think you had better have your people clear those two buildings up front before we move on," the tanker said.

"Yeah, I think you are right, Lieutenant," Ashley said in agreement.

"Fisk, let's dismount and check out those buildings ahead."

"Roger!"

The men cautiously inspected each building, outhouse, and the surrounding area. While waiting for further instructions, the squad leaders had their men disperse in a half moon-shaped defensive position facing in the direction of march. There were only about 25 men left of the some 40 authorized. Ashley was impressed with their discipline and precautionary measures. The squad leaders seemed to know what to do, and did it without being told. He commended Fisk who had taught them a few things about the art of survival.

The small tank-infantry unit did not have long to wait. There was an open field between the buildings and surroundings that they occupied and a road to their front that ran perpendicular to the road they were on. Their visibility was good, too good. The impotent little platoon of tanks stood out like a sore thumb. The first indication that they were in trouble was the roar of the German tank engines and the squeaking, clanking sound of tank tracks. Then they appeared moving at high speed from right to left. They were some of the latest and best tanks in the Wehrmacht inventory—the 43-ton Panther and the invincible 56-ton Tiger. They were armed with the 88mm that could easily penetrate the armor of America's best, the 36-ton Sherman whose 75mm cannon usually bounced off the heavier armor of the German tanks.

Ashley and his group watched in awe as the first echelon of about 50 enemy tanks passed to their front as if on parade, daring their light tanks with their popguns to give it their best shot. At least it seemed that way, but they were unobserved by the first tank armada. The second group of about the same strength that appeared, however, stopped for a break. A few of their tankers opened their hatches, crawled out to urinate, stretch, and take a drink of water or schnapps or whatever suited their fancy. One of their light tanks took a position as flank guard facing the American intruders. The surprised German tank commander suddenly spotted the small American force.

Ashley found himself in a highly vulnerable position, lying on the ground in front of his lead tank. The features of the sunburned face of the fair-skinned German crew chief, appearing out of the open tank hatch were clearly visible. Looking through his field glasses at the American tanks facing him, he calmly called out his fire order: *"Ein hundert meter, schiessen nur wann Ich sprache."* My God, Ashley thought, translating the German's warning order. He's just over a hundred yards away. That's a little more than the length of a football field away. He can't miss. Oh shit!

The American tanker lieutenant stood his ground, but took no action. He rightly concluded that it would be stupid to start a problem with a bully who has ten times more firepower than you do. Then the inexplicable happened, the German crew chief closed his hatch, as did the others and calmly continued in the direction they had started, as though it was all in a day's work. The radio from the American lead tank emitted an unpleasant crackling sound. An emergency message was on its way.

"Ashley," the tank leader said. "I have a report that division headquarters is being threatened by a bunch of big tigers. Probably the same ones we saw pass us by for a juicer target. I've been told to get out of here to support division headquarters. Sorry, I can leave you a daisy chain of a couple of antitank mines (mines connected by a rope) that you can use to cover the road into your position."

"Great, we got two mines, one bazooka and two antitank rounds for it. What other action do you suggest for us sacrificial lambs?" Ashley said disgustedly.

"Don't know. You'll be duck soup if another bunch comes in this direction," the tank leader warned.

"With our worthless walkie-talkie, we are out of everyone's radio range from here. See if you can get a hold of Captain Tipper for me and tell him of our bad situation. We will dig in here, and be prepared to pull our mines across the road if required to slow them down. But if I don't hear from you or the captain in couple of hours, we are out of here," Ashley said.

"OK, sounds good to me. Good luck," the tank officer said, while hurriedly moving his tanks to the rear.

At about the agreed upon withdrawal time, a smiling truck driver showed up to take the platoon back to the company assembly area.

"You are as pretty as Betty Grable," Fisk told the Black driver of the two and half ton truck, as the platoon loaded up for the return trip.

"The cap'n was some kinda worried 'bout you folks. But I told him, 'don't worry Cap'n, I'll bring 'em back,' " the driver said, showing a perfect set of white teeth.

"You done good. We're glad to get outta here," Ashley said, joining Fisk in the happiness of the moment.

Captain Tipper seemed relatively unconcerned about Ashley's cat and mouse game with the German armored units, but the battalion commander was.

"Ashley," Tipper said, "Battalion wants a report

of the incident. After you get yourself a cup of coffee, take my jeep and go up to battalion and brief the old man."

"OK, Captain."

Technical Sergeant Sovernalli was a principal battalion clerk and jack-of-all-trades. At times when Ashley was assigned to the headquarters as the Battalion S-4, he got the feeling that Sovernalli often was running the Battalion Headquarters Company. He was among the minority who had earned Ashley's respect.

"Lieutenant Ashley, good to see you again. Understand you have seen a lot of action lately," Sovernalli said, in his usual up-beat manner.

"Well enough, I suppose. Is the battalion commander around? I've been told to report to him," Ashley answered.

"No, Sir, he had to leave in hurry to go to regiment to report to Colonel Meddler. Lieutenant, I think there is a big push coming up soon. Major Thompson looked real nervous when he left to go to see the colonel. But Major Okie says he wants to see you to find out what the hell is going on down in F Company," Corporal Sovernalli said.

"Oh, shit!"

"What did you say, Lieutenant?" Sovernalli asked, with a smile on his face.

"Nothing," Ashley said as he moved toward Major Okie's desk, located in a dark damp and dreary corner of an ancient Belgian house near the village of Marche.

Major Okie was pacing back and forth, muttering—"Attack, attack! We have to be aggressive at all cost."

"Lieutenant, the tank officer that went with you on that little charade you were on told me that you two let a whole column of tanks pass your way without firing a shot. Is that correct?"

"Yes, Sir."

"Will you pray tell me, why?" Okie ordered.

The major looked tired and drawn. Ashley surmised that the alcoholic battalion executive officer had missed his liquor ration since the liquor warehouse in Liege had been recently destroyed by a German buzz bomb.

"Well, Major Okie, it was a stand off. We were both prepared to fire, the Kraut tankers and ours, but neither did. If they had elected to fire, it would have been curtains for us. They had 50 or more tanks, none as small as our three. We had an under strength platoon. I'd say they had a battalion. We were over five miles in front of our company area with no means of communication except for the tank radios. The tank platoon leader was told to deploy his tanks to protect division headquarters, leaving us stranded. We held on for two hours after they left, before finally being picked up. Looks to me like we were considered a fair exchange for a couple division staff officers," Ashley said, trying to explain.

"Should have attacked, Ashley, should have attacked," the major mumbled.

"Had we done so, Major, we would have been the fourth platoon of F Company to have been killed or captured in less than two months of combat. I chose not to."

"OK, dismissed. I will give your report to Major Thompson."

Ashley never heard any more about the situation but he would hear a lot more from Major Okie, the ubiquitous and unpredictable Cherokee.

16

On 28 December, E and F Companies of Colonel Meddler's regiment established a defensive position along the Marche-Hotton road at the northwestern tip of the salient. Ashley's new Second Platoon had what seemed to be a rare assignment—company reserve. Finally, they thought they would have the chance to get a few hours sleep before more trouble began. The new residence was the cow barn attached to a small Belgian farmhouse. They were too tired to bathe. Their last real bath had been in a Dutch miner's shower a few miles to the rear of the Siegfried Line. The faces of the riflemen had the gray-black color of chimney sweeps, reflecting a lamp-lit existence in the pillboxes near the Roer River. They had no problem huddling on the ground in the straw and cow manure. Their accommodations were an improvement.

In a few minutes of stillness, they were all out like a light. For a brief moment Ashley's thoughts turned from the horrors of war to a world of dreams. Then came an aggravating noise, too close for comfort:

"Lieutenant, Lieutenant, wake up. The company commander wants to see you now," Corporal Hartman, the company runner, said, excitedly shaking Ashley's shoulder.

"God damn it, Hartman," Ashley growled, "I was in the middle of hell of a nice, sweet dream and you screwed it up."

"I'll bet it was about that Belgian beauty you

were talking to in the last village. I could tell she had her eye on you."

"It was only a dream, Hartman. But you were right, she was good looking. And I have to confess; she did invite me into her cozy little cottage. There the lovely creature made me something to eat. She called it a European favorite—steak and eggs, potatoes smothered in steak gravy and even a green salad. It may have been horsemeat, but I didn't care. I was starving to death. We polished off one bottle of great French Burgundy. She said it was from some place called Beaune, the wine center of the world. We had just moved close to her glittering, coal fireplace to do justice to another bottle, a soft Beaujolais, when she then began undressing me, insisting that I join her in a tub of steaming hot water. It was at this point," Ashley reminded him, "when things were looking good, that you, the commander's right arm, broke in with some God damned nonsense about this frigging war. Gimme a break, Hartman!

"OK, what's up?" Ashley sighed, wishing he hadn't heard a thing Hartman had said.

"Don't know, Sir, but the Old Man doesn't look too happy," he whispered in a confidential tone. "I think he may have another big job for you. The word's out that you guys fucked up that last tank-infantry patrol, so I'd guess you could be getting another chance to excel."

"You could be right. You know, Hartman, you damned, high IQ, ASTP soldiers are smart enough to be generals. The trouble is you got no ambition and don't want to risk getting your ass shot off, like us second lieutenants."

Senior First Lieutenant Fortner occupied the main house, with his platoons dispersed in holes or outbuildings. He looked up from his rumpled, dog-eared German map and motioned Ashley over to take a look. Acting Commander Fortner was the company executive officer. He was a small-framed fellow of medium height, black hair and eyes to match. The war had aged him but he was only about 26, which fit the optimum ages of 21 to 28 for his current employment. His pinched face gave him a look of perpetual displeasure. Perhaps, rightly so. In the scheme of things, he had become a part time player, a relief commander, when the going got rough. He must have felt like a bridesmaid who never became the bride.

This was Ashley's first encounter with the new commander. He had no idea where the captain was at the time, and he was not about to get into a lot of small talk about where he was either. While in E Company, he had learned the hard way from Captain Grant that second lieutenants don't ask a lot of foolish questions. So he listened. But as time went on, he realized command arrangements in his new company were like a game of musical chairs. (In a couple of weeks Fortner would be moved to G Company, when that commander went down with frozen feet.)

The runner had guessed right—another damned platoon patrol.

"OK, Lieutenant Ashley, your sorry platoon will find out what's holding up a unit from another regiment. Take a look here on the map. Follow this tree-lined road for about half a mile and you should come to a farmhouse at a road junction. There you will find a unit from the division's 335th Regiment. Whoever is charge there will give you further instructions. Any questions?" Fortner asked, closing the short conversation.

"No, Sir."

"OK, then get your ass moving."

Ashley figured they would be given a find and

destroy mission and/or be asked to bring back a prisoner. You would have to be crazy to like doing something like this, he thought, but occasionally he had found a few nuts and drunks that did. They were not smart enough or sober enough to realize that death is a permanent condition. Ashley had learned the hard way that in comparison to taking a patrol, being in a company attack was a piece of cake, particularly, in this snake-bit outfit—the "Company of the Lost Platoons." He knew that if you are hit while the company is in the attack, there is usually someone around to get you back to the medics, but on a platoon patrol you are all alone and there is no help. You crawl back with whatever you have left or you don't get back at all.

Following their leader's orders, the platoon moved out (albeit cautiously) in a column of squads on each side of the road. The platoon was the only movement. No one, not even a nice Belgian, was out there to give them a send-off with a *"vive la Amerique, vive la Belgique"* salute. The temperature was freezing, but not bitterly cold as it would be in a few days. There was a light cover of snow, but the ground was not yet frozen so they could dig in if the situation required. The gray overcast seemed appropriate for the occasion. It was about noon when they reached the outpost unit. Ashley and his platoon sergeant were given more definitive information on the enemy terrain and their mission—"find out what's holding us up." They were loaned the big SCR 300 radio, which would permit them to call in artillery or 4.2-inch mortar fire, if needed. The big pack radio was a welcome replacement for the near worthless platoon "walkie talkie", the SCR 536. The platoon runner, however, was not overwhelmed with the idea of carrying the much heavier piece of equipment, which also made him a sitting duck for enemy snipers.

Ashley was told that he would pass through a rifle platoon of E Company, 335th Regiment that was pinned down by small arms fire. Of course, the thought occurred to him, if they are pinned down, what the hell are we doing here? Who in the hell are we, supermen? "No, but maybe we could fake it," he mused. They found the platoon where they said it would be: at the end of a draw near the edge of a thickly wooded area that sloped gently downward from right to left. The surprise came when Ashley discovered that he knew the platoon leader, a classmate and ex-"star" football lineman—Lieutenant Dick Derek. If he remembered right, Derek had been a "walk on", but he was good enough to play in the big game at West Point in 1941, when the little military college almost beat the big one. The game was nip and tuck for two quarters, but the bigger and better Army team triumphed in the end.

"Dick, is that you in the hole over there?" Ashley yelled.

"Yeah," he said, rather sheepishly, "you duck butt, what the hell are you doing here?"

Ashley was not about to tell him he was scared (expletive) so he figured he would play the macho role. What did he have to lose?

"I'm here to pass through your outfit and win the war, so we can both go home. What are you doing here? You are the only jock I've seen at the front. I figured most of you football heroes would be back at division rear issuing bats and balls to the troops, and banging the doughnut dollies," Ashley said, making a bad joke.

Lieutenant Derek was about six foot two, and still weighed over 220 pounds even after a two months' diet of K-rations. His head was big enough to fit nicely in the one-size-for-all helmet, and his broad, square shoulders made his GI-issue fatigues look like they were tailored by Brooks Brothers.

"What are you, a smart ass?" his face changing from a scowl to smile as he crawled out of his foxhole and came over to greet Ashley. "Did you see Charlie when you came through the CP?" Derek asked.

"No, I missed him," Ashley said.

"Charlie and I rotate between this platoon and the weapons platoon."

"Wish I'd seen him," Ashley said. "Charlie and I were cadet sergeants in the same company."

Having played out the small talk, Ashley knew unfortunately that the time had come to get on with the business at hand.

"Dick, I've got a problem. My platoon has been given the job to get out there and find out who's shooting at you and take 'em out. Do you know how many there are?" Ashley asked.

"Nope."

"Do you think they have got the area mined and booby trapped?" Ashley asked.

"Yep," Derek said, a little embarrassed that he had not cleared out the pocket himself.

The outward display of bravado gave Ashley a little confidence and even a temporary swagger.

"OK, Dick, I'll be seeing you, based on what you've told me we will start out in a column of squads.

"Fisk, scout out, column of squads."

"OK, Lieutenant."

They left Derek with an astonished look of disbelief. The acting was over!

Private Murph, the scout, was a fearless little street fighter from Brooklyn who loved trouble about as much as his "Dego red" wine. When he could find a bottle of the terrible stuff, he even filled his canteen with it. Fighting armies are full of Murphs. They are good to have around when the going gets rough. But when the fighting stops they are—miserable and usually in trouble—the personification of Kipling's Tommy Atkins:

> *"O it's Tommy this, an' Tommy that,*
> *An' Tommy, go away;*
> *But it's thank you Mister Atkins,*
> *When the bands begin to play."*

Following a few yards behind their scout, the platoon moved as quietly as Indian braves from tree to tree, the bigger the better for protection. Ashley had also formed another good, stay-alive habit in suspected mine fields by stepping in the safe haven of the scout's footprints in the snow.

The German unit had picked the higher ground with fields of fire directed temporarily away from the platoon toward the cleared area to their right front, leaving their rear exposed—good break! Murph raised his hand, signaling halt and pointing like a bird dog in the direction of his prey. Ashley and his squad leader crawled over to see what his problem was. Derek was right, they were certainly here. But, how many? Ashley couldn't tell. But he could see three of them, well scrubbed, big guys with shiny black helmets facing away from the platoon toward the open field near the top of ridge. They were obviously expecting an attack from the opposite direction.

Ashley moved one squad up to his position to form a base of fire and kept the other two squads in column behind them in reserve for the moment. The Krauts had the better position; they could easily toss their "potato-smasher" grenades down the hill on top of the platoon. "What are you going to do now, candidate?" the OCS tact-officer would have said had he been here, looking over the lieutenant's shoulder. In sizing up the situation, Ashley assumed they had a bunch of bad guys behind the ones they could see. So why not keep the ones in the rear pinned down with the big guns, while taking care of their forward outpost. So, he called in on the SCR 300 for a marker round. In no time flat, they responded—"OK, on the way." Bad choice of options, the round landed in the trees above them, saturating the area with limbs and shrapnel in one deafening explosion. The forward observer for the 4.2's was only about 100 yards behind, so he didn't have to be told something went wrong, he could hear it. Next call—"up 500".

"That should get the stuff off our backs, and allow us to creep the barrage back toward us at 100 yard intervals at a time. Screw the standard bracketing procedures," Ashley yelled over to Sergeant Fisk, who was clearing the debris off of himself.

"Good solution, Lieutenant. Our friendly fire was getting too close for comfort," Fisk said calmly.

The second round landed so far out, it could hardly be heard. Good, enough of that. At this point their "friends" to the front turned their attention toward them and sprayed their position with machine gun fire, neatly manicuring the limbs and leaves a few inches above their heads. For a fleeting moment, very fleeting, Ashley considered sticking his helmet up on the end of his carbine to get a hole through it for a souvenir, but decided against it. He thought it would be nice to live at least until his 21st birthday and even a little longer, if possible. Instead his squad on line returned fire.

"I don't know how I missed them. I had a perfect sight picture and missed with a couple of rounds," Ashley said to the squad leader lying beside him in the heavy undergrowth.

While the firing continued sporadically from the

first squad, Ashley had the squad leader of squad number two move his squad to a flanking position on the left. In this situation the platoon could deliver flanking and frontal fire. They now had the attackers in an L-shaped box.

Since they were like pawns in a chess game, it seemed like the right time to try a sensible approach to ending this nonsense. Ashley tried his best college German, to urge them to come out: *"Deutcher Soldaten, kommen sie aus, schiessen sie nicht, handen hoch."* That really pissed them off. Did he miss pronounce *schiessen* and say *scheissen*—to evacuate the large intestine? He would never know, five big monsters in a wedge formation with submachine guns (burp guns) blazing away, charged directly toward the sound of his voice. The flank squad opened up now with their Browning automatic rifle, pinning them down once again. Before closing on them, which can get you hurt, Ashley decided to first try a fragmentation grenade. It would have to be tossed so as to miss the trees, and be an air burst to keep it from rolling back down the hill on top of them. This meant holding the grenade for four seconds, and pray the fuse length was eight seconds as advertised. John Wayne, where the hell are you, when we need you?

Ashley pulled the pin, let the handle fall free, counted four, and threw a perfect, high arched strike, up hill between the trees. The Krauts, unfortunately, stood up to make a final charge.

A moment of silence followed, then Murph began yelling loudly, "Lieutenant, Lieutenant, you got 'em. A direct hit: You blew five of 'em away. My God, Lieutenant, the young kid's face is gone, poof! The old sergeant's got a big hole in his stomach. I can see another guy—some kind of Kraut officer lying beside two others. They aren't moving. They look deader than hell to me."

The firing stopped. Then the crackling sound of a welcome transmission from the SCR 300 split the smoke-filled air.

"Lieutenant, we have been hearing a lot of noise, are you guys all right?" the outpost officer in charge asked.

"Yep, so far," Ashley replied.

"It's getting dark," the officer in charge said over the radio, "you ought to get out of there."

"Will do, gladly. We are out of here now!" Ashley quickly obeyed.

They turned and faced in the opposite direction, with the last squad now becoming the first in the column.

Derek had not been in on the conversation. Because of all the firing, he wasn't sure who was advancing in the near dark toward his position, and he came close to ordering his platoon to begin firing.

"Get ready to fire you guys—on the count of three: one, two—hold it, hold it," Derek yelled, "they are GIs!"

Ashley debriefed the outpost group. They were amazed that no one in the platoon had been killed, based on the noise they had heard. He said good-by to Dick Derek and headed his platoon back towards the barn. (Ashley never saw Derek after that. He lived through the war only to die in Korea, as a captain.)

Totally drained, they moved in silence through the welcome darkness like shadows of the walking dead.

"Lieutenant," Fisk broke the silence in a near whisper. "A penny for your thoughts?"

"I was thinking about what Murph said he saw. We left some dead people back there, that young kid with his face blown off and the old sergeant with the big hole in his gut. My God that's pretty bad. I never examine the dead. If I did, I would be nuts by now. Maybe we only stunned the others and they were playing dead. In a way, I hope they make it back, and after the war they get together at the *Hofbrauhaus* in *Munchen* and have a tall one," Ashley answered.

Lieutenant Fortner seemed to be preoccupied. He showed little interest in Ashley's and Sergeant's Fisk's report of a successful mission, a number of enemy kills and no losses of their own.

"Lieutenant Ashley, you are the newest cannon fodder around here now, is that right?" Fortner asked.

"Yes, Sir. I'm the newly assigned officer from E Company. I was a rifle platoon leader there for over a month."

"Yeah, I know. They tell me you got a hell of a temper. I thought I'd gotten rid of you and your bunch of misfits, what the hell are you doing back?" Fortner asked.

"Sir, I'm here to tell you that we cleaned out a hot-bed of Krauts in front of E Company, 335th as we were told to do and—we didn't lose a man," Ashley said, raising his voice.

"OK, so you are all a bunch of heroes," Fortner said. "Right now I've got more important things to do than listen to your miraculous escapades. So haul ass—both of you. I'm needed on the phone."

The briefing, and Ashley's first meeting with the executive officer, left something to be desired. Fortner returned to his comfortable command post for presumably more pressing matters.

"Lieutenant, you think the acting commander is a caustic son of bitch?" Fisk asked.

"I will withhold comment on that one for awhile,

Sergeant. For now, I think I would have to say that, like all of us, he probably wishes he was running a PX in Paris where he could screw every cocotte in *Pigalle*. Besides, the Army needs a few sons of a bitches, like Patton for example, who prides himself in being one—hated by his men, feared by the Germans, and loved by the media, if you can believe the Stars and Stripes."

17

Specialist Sovernalli, the likeable battalion headquarters' clerk, had guessed right—the division was getting ready for a big push. The initial objective of the divisions of General Hodges First Army north of the bulge and General Patton's Third Army south of the bulge was containment of the enemy. This allowed the build-up of reinforcements and materiel in the area and the use of Allied Air, now blessed with improving weather, to pound the over-extended German lines of communication. By the end of December 1944, the objective of the mostly American force to contain the enemy within the deep salient in their lines was accomplished. Now it was time for the more difficult and costly job—to reduce the bulge, and to drive the enemy back to the original defensive position along the Belgian-German border.

During the first week in January 1945, there was a turn for the worse for the ground forces. Temperature fell into the low teens for the first time. With the wind chill considered, it was well below zero. Blizzard conditions prevailed—blinding snow and snow-drifts of two to three feet. Tanks and vehicles had difficulty moving on the icy secondary roads. Automatic weapons now fired sluggishly—single rounds at a time if at all. Frozen feet and hands and hypothermia were commonplace. Commanders were no longer able to find comfortable basements and bunkers for their command posts. They were forced to share the inhospitable, frozen forest of the Ardennes with their men. They were at near equal risk for the first time in the war, and their shocking losses would reflect it.

For a change, Colonel Meddler's regiment would now take the lead for the division. The British relieved Major Thompson's Second Battalion from their defensive duties in the Hotton-Marche sector. The Second Battalion would now lead the march to contact. With or without contact the objective was to secure the critical Laroch-Houffalize road net and deny its use to the enemy in their attack or retreat.

The attack convoy, a single motorized column, was a well-organized balance of rifle and heavy weapons companies. Captain Tipper had been discharged from the hospital and was now in command of F Company. Lieutenant Fortner was moved to G Company to replace the commander there who had to be evacuated with frozen feet. F Company led the column. Ashley and his Second Platoon, with an attached section of heavy machine guns, found themselves at the head of the long column. They were perched on tank destroyers that noisily crunched their way through the ice and snow into "virgin territory", a beautiful, unmolested place, but one where only fools would tread.

"Lieutenant, look at that long column following us. This is big. This is the real thing, and we are right at the front of it all," Sergeant Fisk yelled out over the deadening noise of the smoke-belching, tank destroyers.

"Yeah, it is absolutely amazing. If we live through this we will never forget it. Nothin' in life will ever compare with what's in store for us in the next few days. But right now, I have a strange feeling we are being watched. Look down the road about a hundred yards. What do you see, Fisk?" Ashley asked.

"Looks like three or four soldiers milling around

a jeep. Should I shoot over their heads to get their attention, just in case they are GIs? We've been warned about Germans dressed in American uniforms roaming around in the rear area, cutting throats, and bayoneting GIs in their fartsacks."

"Let's wait until we get a little closer," Ashley responded.

"Fisk, tell me I'm wrong. I think I see Major Okie, waving his arms around like a mad man."

"I'm afraid you are right, Lieutenant. I think that's him all right. I bet you wish you had said fire and ask questions later," Fisk said, with a frozen grin on his face.

"Yeah, we are in real trouble now," Ashley replied.

"Lieutenant Ashley, dismount!" the major yelled in a grating, whiskey-tenor of a voice that Ashley knew so well.

"Lieutenant, in the edge of those woods up there you will find a couple my guides who will lead you to the assembly area," the major said.

Okie had hardly finished his instructions, when the sound of incoming artillery roared through the air. The major and his driver, without further to-do, jumped into their jeep and headed for the rear. Chief Dragging Canoe, his Cherokee ancestor, would have been shamed by his cowardly conduct. Ashley and his group knew exactly what they had to do to reduce the risk—head for the cover of the woods toward the sound of the big guns.

When they reached the edge of the woods, Ashley discovered that only his platoon and a lieutenant with a section of machine guns from the heavy weapons company had made it. The Artillery had separated them from the rest of column.

Heavy snow continued to fall at a rate they had

not seen before. With the descent of darkness, bone-chilling winds tore at their exposed flesh. There was a general consensus among the two lieutenants and the senior sergeants that the only solution was to locate the guides and follow them into the assembly area as Major Okie had ordered. After wandering around in the blackness through the thick under growth, they discovered two huddled, pitiful creatures.

"Who in the hell are you two miserable souls? Where in the hell are we? Do you know where you are? Where is the assembly area?" Ashley demanded in disgust, realizing that the major had sucked him in again.

"I don't know, Sir," the guide-sergeant said in a quivering voice, as his corporal-helper looked on in shock.

"Fisk," Ashley ordered, "You take over and find out what you can, before I lose my head and shoot 'em both."

Fisk was equally disgusted with the incompetence of the two guides and particularly their leader. Fisk treated them as spies, who had been planted by the Gestapo with an English speaking German officer, disguised as an American Army major (Major Okie). He was so convincing, the guides seemed to believe the story. Finally, they broke into sobbing masses of humanity. They knew nothing, because they had been told nothing by Major Okie that made sense.

"Lieutenant, I think we are wasting our time. These poor bastards weren't given very good instructions or directions. This is the first time they have been out of the cellars, where they have been shoveling papers or manning radios for the whole war. To tell you the truth, I feel sorry for them," Fisk said.

"Yeah, I had a couple of days in the cellars.

The longer you stay there, the more frightening the world outside becomes. We've got to figure a way out of this," Ashley said, as if talking out loud.

They huddled in a circle by design, with the machine gunners and riflemen alternately dispersed. It seemed like a reasonable formation. From it they could spot a friend or shoot a foe. But neither came. Ashley nibbled on salted, roasted pecans—the remnants of a care package from Kit Montague, surely the best, most caring girl in the world. But would he ever see her again? She said he would. She had been right so far. After all, she was a physic. He had no alternative but to believe her, he thought.

Ashley and his group leaders, after many hours of waiting, decided on a course of action. It was obvious that no one would be making contact with them. If they continued to remain still or lie in the snow, they could freeze to death.

"Let's move in the general direction we were going in when we were cut off. Maintain a column of squads, and stay close together. We don't want to get lost in this blizzard," Ashley said in a quiet voice expecting a Nazi would be found behind every tree. It was nearly an hour of trudging along in knee-deep snow before they discovered signs of life.

"Halt, who goes there? Give the pass word or be shot!"

"Hartman, cut out the bull shit. I recognize your sorry ass, how could I forget that sickening Jersey accent. You know who we are. You bastards left us stranded again. This is getting to be a bad habit in this God damned company," Fisk growled back at the freezing Hartman.

"Sergeant Fisk, is that you?"

"You bet your sweet ass it is. Now don't point that fucking rifle at me."

"Lieutenant Ashley, the captain is looking for you. He has already briefed the rest of the unit on the attack plans for the morning," a nervous Hartman said.

"OK, what time is it now?" Ashley asked. "I'm too tired to look at my watch."

"Three AM—0300 Sir," Hartman answered.

"Three AM. My God, will this hell never end."

"Ashley, sorry we lost you in the move up," the captain said greeting his lost lieutenant as though he were being invited to a cocktail party at the Camp Claiborne Officer's Club.

"OK, here is the deal for tomorrow. There is an opening over there in the line we saved for you. We knew you'd find us. You always do. We will attack at first light in a skirmish line—three platoons abreast: first, second, and third from left to right. Our job is to take and hold the Laroche road, which runs perpendicular to our line of attack. Keep your heads down. We have a line of tanks massed behind us who will fire a preparatory barrage right over our heads. I'll give the signal to move out as soon as the tankers finish their job. Any questions?" Captain Tipper asked.

"Yeah, we need coffee, we are all about to freeze to death," Ashley responded, without the usual military courtesy.

"No problem, see the mess sergeant. He told me he had saved enough coffee and chow for your group. Good luck."

Ashley lined his platoon along the line of departure, as Captain Tipper had ordered. The ground was frozen solid—a foot deep. Only a stick of dynamite could have broken through. Digging-in for the remainder of the short night was out of the question. Sergeant Fisk found them two adjacent slit trenches, courtesy of the dreaded enemy, that served their purpose. What did it matter anyway; even if the ground was soft as the beet fields of the Siegfried, they were too exhausted to dig a foxhole.

The mess sergeant was as good as his word. Although not hot, the coffee was still as warm and as soothing as a mother's milk. With the momentary comfort given them by the warm coffee, their exhausted bodies begged for sleep. Yet, fear and the cold kept them awake. An occasional break in the overcast allowed a sliver of moonlight to give them a view of the ground to their front over which the assault would be made. It was a setting made for a Hollywood movie. Between their woods and the woods defended by the German Infantry, there was a clearing several hundred feet deep and wide enough to easily accommodate two rifle companies abreast. There was the sound of enemy mechanized vehicles moving either in or out of the objective area. The battalion commander had chosen to do nothing but wait until morning. Then turn his rifle companies loose, and hopefully still achieve some element of surprise. There was nothing left to do but wait, hope, and pray for victory and another day of life.

Even though Ashley knew it wasn't fair to pray only when in trouble and forget God when things were going well, he prayed anyway. And he was sure he was not alone. The Lord's Prayer did not seem totally appropriate for the occasion, but the 23rd Psalm did. He was thankful now, that as a boy, his mother had dragged him and his sisters to church every Sunday. Finally, he could now say to God with conviction: "Yea, though I walk through the valley of the shadow of death I will fear no evil for Thou art with me." To make sure he was closer to being on the same frequency with God; however, he reminded the Almighty that if he were taken in tomorrow's battle, he would be the last of his line.

"Fisk, are you able to get any sleep?"

"Afraid not, Lieutenant. I've been listening to them moving around over there. It's pretty scary. That snow in that field in front of us could be covered with blood in the morning—ours!"

"You could be correct. You are a Texas Baptist, if I remember right," Ashley said.

"That's right, have been all of my adult life."

"Well, there is something about religion that maybe you can help me resolve. And I realize in this situation I shouldn't have any doubts about eternity, because in a couple of hours it may be too late. That fellow over there that we are going to kill in the morning has a logo on his belt buckle that says, as you know—-'*Gott mit uns!*' We also believe that God is with us. How can God be with both of us? Is there an explanation that God is not the G-3 of the world, that is, not the chief of day to day operations but rather He is the G-5 of the world, and as such is only in charge of plans and policies," Ashley asked his old friend of many battles.

"I don't know, Lieutenant, but if Jesus Christ is not with us on the battlefield tomorrow, we could be in big trouble."

Daylight came at about 0700, and with it the voice of the commander of the attached tank company broke the stillness of the seemingly innocent morning light.

"Tankers, get ready, load your guns. All clear?"

"All clear, Sir." The pause allowed the Infantrymen on the line time to bury their faces in the snow and cover their ears with frozen mittens.

"Fire prepared mission when ready!" the tank commander yelled. And within seconds, the scream of the first volley passed over the heads of the infantry on line. They repeated volley after volley, until the steam from the barrels of the guns reminded the tank crewmen that the fire-mission was complete.

Then Captain Tipper's voice was heard—"F Company, get ready to move."

"Fisk, let's fix bayonets, win or lose we will scare the shit out of them. Second Platoon, fix bayonets!" Ashley yelled.

"F Company, move now. Move out!" Captain Tipper yelled again.

And with that, the Second Battalion began its fight for the critical Laroche-Houffalize road net. And in other sectors of the front—companies, battalions, and regiments were on the move. The battle for control of the Ardennes forest had begun.

Four platoons abreast, two each from F and E Companies got up from the frozen ground and moved cautiously forward. They were nearly shoulder-to-shoulder. Too close for comfort, their dark uniforms against the snow made them easy targets for enemy lying in uniforms the color of the snow. Ashley's squad leaders led the way, running and stumbling but getting up and running again. He fell back a few feet in knee-high snow. He wondered where his men found the final burst of energy. As they reached the forward edge of the objective area, a piercing rebel yell filled the morning air. "My God, they are great," Ashley thought.

The exchange of fire was surprisingly light. The tank barrage had either driven them deep into their bunkers, or the noise they that they had heard the night before was a retrograde movement of the main force to a safer and more defensible area. But each bunker, deep holes with over-head protection of timber and dirt, had to be cleared. Ashley carried a "grease gun", a semi-automatic, 45-caliber submachine gun, so nicknamed because they looked like a mechanic's grease gun. He moved with the others from bunker to bunker firing into them and yelling at the occupants—-*"kommen sie aus—schnell!"*

His frozen gun now fired sluggishly. The thickened oil had turned it into a single-shot weapon. He decided on a different approach. He pulled the pin on a white phosphorus grenade and tossed it into what appeared to be a larger, command bunker. To his surprise a poor devil, the single occupant flew out of the bunker with his overcoat on fire, yelling for mercy.

Near by was the corpse of another German, face down in the snow.

"Fisk, come here and look at this," Ashley called-out. What do you think happened to this guy? I see no visible evidence on his body of penetration by bullets or shell fragments."

"I don't see any outward damage either. He coulda had a heart attack or froze to death last night," Fisk said, rolling the body over.

A ray of sun briefly penetrated the branches of the tall trees, sending a reflected beam of light off the dead man's buckle, inscribed with—-*"Gott mit uns."* Ashley and Fisk looked at each other, shook their heads, and without saying a word read the other's mind.

The first objective—the Laroche road—was now in sight. Control of it was, however, temporarily delayed by a light German tank, stuck in a ditch alongside the road itself. Try as hard as he could, the driver could not dislodge it due to the slippery ice. It was a beautiful trophy, and Ashley and his platoon wanted it badly, but so did E Company on their right. Both companies fired at it with rifles, pistols, and rifle-launched fragmentation grenades, all of which ricocheted off the armor plate of the tank. Ashley yelled for his bazooka man to get the tank. He was the smallest soldier in the platoon, which always seemed to be the case. He ran forward stumbling through the snow to get into a position to fire. He tried again and again to get off a round without success. Ashley ran over to help the gunner get it to work. Nothing! Must have been the sub-freezing temperature. But the German tanker only a few feet away took notice. He slowly rotated his turret until his cannon was directly in line with Ashley and his bazooka operator. Then he slowly lowered the muzzle of the gun until it was pointing directly at them. When will he fire? What is he going to do? they thought, scared witless.

He didn't fire. He began to move. Maybe the angle of his gun gave him better balance or traction. He now turned on to the road. He seemed assured of getting away. For a while, the platoon hoped he would make it. But E Company riflemen, having witnessed the F Company problem, had their bazooka ready when the tank rolled into their area. They got a direct hit and killed or captured the crew. However, a German halftrack made it through a hail of F and E Company rifle and grenade fire to warn their unit of the location of the Americans.

The sun had set, and darkness was would soon arrive. Laroche road, the connecting link to Houffalize, and one of the key objectives in the bulge had been taken, and it now had to be secured for the night.

Ashley and Fisk set up their platoon defensive positions along the road for the night. An American tank now found it safe enough to join them on the road. The crew chief, popped open his tank hatch and looked at the strange world around him. From his relatively warm interior, he enjoyed a steaming cup of coffee.

"Lieutenant, would you and the sergeant like a cup?" the tanker said thoughtfully and meaning it.

"We wouldn't mind, if you could spare a cup," Ashley said.

"Where are y'all going to stay the night?" he asked in all innocence.

"Right here on God's white earth in a sleeping bag with our clothes on, boots and all," Ashley answered.

"What do you do in the middle of the night, if you have to take a piss?" he grinned.

"Well, we do it in a k-ration box and throw it out. So don't get too close," Fisk joined in on the conversation.

"I'll be damned. Last night I met an infantry lieutenant who walked up and down all night. He said he was afraid to lie down for fear of freezing to death," the tanker said.

"It's cold enough all right, but those GI candy bars help. The `D bar' is about the size of big Babe Ruth and has 2000 calories in it. It will give you a lot of energy-heat. I gotta go report to my company commander before we turn in. See you in the morning if you are still alive," Ashley said in closing out the conversation.

With that the tanker said good night, and closed his hatch much the same way a turtle would pull his head under his shell when danger was near.

Ashley located Captain Tipper in the bunker he had taken earlier in the day. Except for the smell of burnt human flesh and white phosphorous, it seemed cozy enough.

"Captain we are deployed along the road in shallow slit trenches that the Krauts left. A platoon of E Company is off to our right."

"That sounds good. Any casualties today?"

"No, so far so good. But there is something that is bothering me," Ashley said.

"What's that?" his company commander asked.

"Captain, I don't think we should stop here very long. The Krauts know exactly where we are. I'll bet right now their artillerymen have us plotted on their maps for a shelling tonight or tomorrow. If we move just a couple of hundred yards beyond this road, I think we will be safer," Ashley warned.

"I think we will be all right for tonight. The cooks are going to get us some hot food up here tomorrow. After that, we will be able to think better. Try to get as much rest as you can tonight. See you in the morning," the captain replied.

"OK, see you in the morning, Sir. Good night."

"Good night Ashley."

Ashley pulled his sleeping bag over himself, chewed the remnants of his chocolate bar, and closed out his world of horror to a slumber-land of peace and quiet.

The sun did come up in the Ardennes forest the next morning. The warmth of sunrays through the tall trees dispelled, if only for a moment, the feeling of hopelessness. The smiling mess sergeant and dirty, bearded cook's helpers delivered their pancakes, heavy cane syrup, and hot coffee at sun up just as Captain Tipper had prescribed. After breakfast and a drag on a Raleigh cigarette left over from an old k-ration package, Ashley's small world seemed a little better. He forgot all about advising Tipper on the need to move out of the area. After all, the captain was in his late twenties or early thirties and Ashley had only reached his 21st birthday few days earlier. "What tactical wisdom could a "shave tail" offer a seasoned company commander anyway?" he asked himself.

The day also began with a pleasant surprise. Major Thompson, the battalion commander, came to the front. This was the first time since the war began that Ashley had seen anyone above the rank of captain up on the line. The only one the Major recognized initially was his former battalion S-4. Even though Ashley had a communication problem with his battalion commander, he still held him in high esteem.

"Ashley, good to see you," Major Thompson said, shaking his hand. "Glad you are well. I knew you would do a good job."

"Thank you, Sir, good to see you again," Ashley answered.

With that, the major located Captain Tipper. They talked for awhile, walking along the Laroche road, and he was gone.

On the 11th of January, the day after the Laroche road had been secured, the company had an opportunity to rest and reconnoiter their immediate surroundings for a few hours. The area was quiet. No sight of the enemy. Maybe the fanatic devils had pulled back a few hundred yards to regroup and prepare to fight another day in defense of the critical crossroad at Houffalize. By nightfall, however, they would make their presence known. Fisk and Ashley had just settled into their shallow slit trenches, when the first heavy barrage fell into the F Company area. Ashley's prophecy had come to pass.

Fisk cried out. "I'm hit, I'm hit. The bastards finally got me."

Ashley could see that his old friend was seriously wounded. His face was shattered and bleeding, and his right arm looked as though it was nearly severed. Ashley called the medic for help but without response. He crawled back to the company bunker. He realized that he had lost use of his left arm and had trouble breathing. He found the medic attending other wounded, but got help for Fisk as quickly as possible. While waiting for an examination himself, Ashley lost consciousness. When he woke from the dream world of morphine, he found that he and Sergeant Fisk were in an ambulance with other wounded—destination unknown.

Ashley and Fisk later discovered that they were transferred first to the 2nd Armored Division medical detachment, and next to the 102nd Division Evacuation Hospital. At this point, the two men lost track of each other. It was a significant separation for both. Not only were they close and trusted friends, they depended on each other for survival.

Ashley was convinced now more than ever that some guardian angel continued to watch over him. The next four days following his hospitalization would be the bloodiest fighting of the war.

Major Thompson was shot in the abdomen by a "burp gun" (a machine pistol). He survived, but his injuries were so severe that he would never return to the division. Captain Grant, the E Company commander, was killed while leading a patrol. Two days later, Grant's executive officer, a close personal friend of Ashley's, was killed leading the company. The next day, a second lieutenant and another friend took over the command and was also killed. It was difficult for those unaccustomed to the war outside the basements and bunkers to survive at the front.

On the single day, the 12th of January 1945, F Company losses alone were eight men killed, and 31 were wounded. When the battalion was finally relieved on the 15th, it was at 50 percent of authorized strength. The three rifle companies had only 25 riflemen per company left of the 118 authorized.

When the units of the First and Third Armies met at Houffalize, Belgium on 16 January, the Ardennes campaign for all practical purposes was over. By the end of January, the lines were restored to their original position along the German-Belgian border. Hitler's 40-day folly was a costly one—19,000 Americans were killed, 23,000 captured, and 81,000 wounded. It was the largest land battle that the United States Army had ever fought.

PART FIVE

DESTINATION BERLIN

1945

18

When Ashley arrived at the F Company head-quarters pillbox, he found that Lieutenant Fortner had again assumed command from Captain Tipper. The captain was hospitalized for hypothermia at the end of fighting in Belgium. Division units were rested and refitted in Holland and returned to their original pillbox defenses along the west bank of the Roer River. Here they relieved elements of the 102nd Division who had relieved them for battle in the Bulge. The 102nd had a relatively easy time of it after taking over from the 84th Division. The sizable German force that controlled the area pulled back to more easily defensible positions east of the Roer.

The F Company command group was having a wild party when Ashley reported in. But the mood was more one of relief than of celebration. Fortner had come very close to being court-martialed. The division commander was determined to make a secretive return to the Roer from the Belgian Ardennes. Division patches were removed from all uniforms, markings were removed from vehicles, communication silence was declared, and movement made at night.

Fortner was charged with blowing the cover. As soon as he arrived in his company's defensive sector, he sent out a squad patrol to find out the threat if any to his front. The patrol was captured immediately—without firing a shot in self-defense. Unfortunately, some members of the patrol provided the enemy with more than their required name, rank, and serial number. The incident proved to be a personal embarrassment to the entire command. Ironically, the unit that relieved F Company, when it left to cross the Roer, discovered a sizable enemy force in front of the company's defensive position.

"Ashley, have a drink," Fortner said, greeting the new arrival in a rare civil manner. "You're in luck. The scotch ration is in. The Brits don't do much fightin', but they sure make good booze."

"Thanks, I think I will have one, Sir."

"What the hell are you doing back? You could have gotten lost back there in the stock piles of supplies in Liege, and nobody would have ever known the difference."

"Maybe not, Lieutenant," Ashley said. "But I would have. Besides, I wrote Captain Tipper from the hospital that I would like to come back to his company. He paid me a compliment once—one of the few I ever got from anyone in this battalion. He said, `Ashley, you somehow manage to get back from tough situations no matter what happens.' There also may still be a few people left in the company that I recognize. If I had opted for the replacement system, I could have ended up in a new division and not have known a single, swinging dick."

"Amazing logic, mister, have another drink. So you decided to come back to the least loved regiment, the unluckiest battalion, and the most fucked-up company in the division. You may have heard that the regimental and division commanders were just about ready to court martial my ass for doing my job. The company's loss of three rifle platoons in taking these pillboxes we are in was considered business as usual a few months ago. But now, the loss of this one dumb squad brought more heat on me and this "snake-bit" rifle company than you can imagine. The

Division Review Board, however, ultimately ruled in my favor. They arrived at the obvious. All commanders since the beginning of warfare have been held responsible for the security of their own units. I was exonerated," Fortner exclaimed.

"Lieutenant Fortner, I understand what you are saying about coming back to F Company. But I chose the lesser of the evil."

"Forget it! You play cribbage, Ashley?"

"A little."

"Tell you what—you beat me in a game, and I'll give you the weapons platoon. There is probably no one in your old Second Platoon that you know anyway. Most of them got killed or froze to death in the Bulge after you left. Your chances of surviving in a weapons platoon versus a rifle platoon are about four to one. But I don't have to tell you. I'm sure you know that, don't you?" Fortner said.

"Yes, I do, Lieutenant."

"Good, this should be exciting. In effect, you are playing for your life. Cut for the deal!"

Ashley won the cut, which gave him the initial advantage. But Fortner was no slouch. He soon won a crib or two that put him well in the lead. Fortner paused for a drink, swigging a hefty slug from his private bottle of Johnny Walker.

"Drink?"

"No thanks, think I'll pass on this one," Ashley answered.

Then the game turned. The alcohol began to take its toll on the company commander. Fortner's normally astute pegging failed him, as did his pairing and selection of cards. He lost, and lost heavily.

"OK, the fun and games are over. Go out there in the dark in that filthy mud with all those stinking Krauts on the loose, and find your Second Platoon,"

Fortner ordered.

"Thanks a lot, Lieutenant!"

Ashley turned and disappeared into the night, realizing that the duplicitous side of Fortner was now in command. The company runner, seeing what had happened, sneaked out of the headquarters pillbox long enough to point out the pillbox to Ashley that would be his temporary home.

Once inside the concrete bunker, it took Ashley a moment to get his bearing. He looked about at the two or three faces either sleeping or on guard. None looked familiar, except one. Huddled in a corner asleep was a man with a lean, pinched face, lined and burned by the hot Texas sun, which he would never forget.

"Fisk, Fisk. My God, is that you?" Ashley asked.

"Sure is, Lieutenant. I been waitin' for you," Fisk responded, with a welcome smile on his face.

"Damn, Fisk, I thought you were in a hospital in England waiting for transport to Walter Reed for serious fixing-up. What happened?"

"At first, the doctors thought I had a skull fracture. But the X-rays didn't show nothin', so they concluded that I had a concussion, and a bad cut in my scalp. Once they stitched that up, I was out of there in a couple of weeks. How about you?"

"Not much with me either. Torn muscles, but no broken bones. My nose was blown out of shape. That was the reason I had trouble breathing. They ran a wire up my nose a few days—no anesthesia. They finally got it straightened so they could drain some badly infected sinuses. They gave me some antibiotic, and held me around for a couple weeks. I was in some hospital ward in Liege, I think, where a buzz bomb landed so close; it almost blew me out of bed. I figured it was time to leave." Ashley explained.

"I'm as beat as you probably are, Lieutenant. Let's get some rest."

"Good idea. Maybe you can show me around in the morning, the way you did the first time I saw you in the Bulge. Thank God you made it back, Fisk. Good night," Ashley said, crawling into his sleeping bag.

Sergeant Fisk's defensive plan was as simple as it was sound. He had two squads deployed along the river's edge where they enjoyed good fields of fire. The Third Squad occupied trenches surrounding the platoon command post pillbox. The squads were connected to the platoon command post, using a part of the existing German telephone system.

Occasionally, they were able to hear Hans talking to Fritz on the line, but no one seemed to care. Thanks to Fortner's loose-lipped patrol, the Germans now knew who was where and in what strength. Anyway, there were enough Mexicans and American Indians available for handling secure traffic. The Germans must have been totally disgusted to hear messages in Spanish and native Indian dialects.

While the weather in early February 1945 was no comparison to the blizzards of Belgium in January, it was still below freezing at night. During the day, the sun turned the frozen ground to mud—much the same as it was when the division left in December for Belgium.

Ashley was awakened by the smell of coffee in another world of misery with his third rifle platoon.

"Coffee, Lieutenant?" Fisk asked.

"You bet. Where did you get that portable gas burner?"

"Our good Sergeant Joe Muller here liberated it from the 2nd Armored Division. They are always loaded with rations and other goodies. I think they expect us to help ourselves. Seeing us grubbing around in the mud and ice like this all the time, I think they actually feel sorry for us," Fisk said.

"Muller, you remember Lieutenant Ashley," Fisk said turning towards Muller.

"Yeah. Hi, Lieutenant, glad you are back with us. We seem to be lucky when you are around," Muller said and meant it. He was known to "speak his mind."

"Howdy, can't exactly say I'm happy to be here, but I'm glad to see you are still alive," Ashley said greeting his old friend.

Muller was not exactly a runner-up for an Army recruiting poster. He was a scrawny little guy, with sharp features, a stooped posture and deep-set, expressionless, faded blue eyes. His steel helmet dwarfed his small head and narrow shoulders. He had been a corporal in the Bulge, and had just been promoted to sergeant. Ashley was well aware of his one distinguishing asset—he had more guts than any one in the company, and probably the whole battalion.

"Lieutenant," Fisk said, "let's go up on the river and check on the Second and Third Squads. Keep your head down. This has been interesting up here. We've been getting continuing small arms, mortar, and artillery fire and we have also been strafed by their fighter-bombers. And those damn buzz bombs— they fly over our pillboxes all the time. The Krauts are not about to quit."

"OK, Fisk, lead the way."

"You saw Joe Muller," Fisk went on, "His First Squad dug in around our platoon headquarters bunker. The Second Squad is up here on the left along the river. Bill Murtha is the squad leader. About half of his squad are Mexicans, Tex-Mexicans from the San Antonio area. They speak very little English.

Murtha has had to learn some Spanish to talk to them. You would have to be crazy to come up here at night. They have nervous fingers. They shoot first and ask questions later. Battalion is always complaining about them shooting up the landscape at night. But they swear the Krauts are coming. So what the hell are you going to do?—nothing!

"Murtha was a mid-western university football player. He is probably the only one in the platoon who can out walk you and me. He is aggressive and happy only when he is in the attack—shootin' and killin'. But in defense, he gets restless. When there's booze around, he turns into a nasty drunk. One of these days when the shooting stops, he'll probably get busted back to private. Too bad. He is one hell of a combat soldier when he is sober.

"The Third Squad is over here. Sergeant Jerry O'Rourke has this one. O'Rourke is interesting. He is a true replacement. This is his first combat. He is getting kinda old for this business. About 28, I'd say. He is the only one of us who has a college degree. He is a big, awkward guy. He moves by the numbers— just the way they taught him in basic training. But he is loyal and dependable. We can count on him.

"All O'Rourke talks about is getting back to Kentucky so he can open a bar-restaurant and make enough money to raise race horses. You will find out he is a good cook, too. He can take a can of this or that and make it really taste like something. Amazing!

"Sergeant O'Rourke, this is your new Lieutenant."

"Hello, Lieutenant, nice to meet you. Understand you have been around since the shooting started," O'Rourke said, making small talk.

"Yeah, too long. It seems like eternity. I heard

you graduated from a good university in Kentucky. What did you major in?" Ashley asked.

"English Lit," O'Rourke answered.

"Great, that ought to help up here. Maybe you can write us all up for Congressional Medals, so we can go back home and sell war bonds. Nice seeing you, O'Rourke. I'm sure we will be seeing a lot of each other. Don't let the Krauts come across the river and get to us back in the rear," Ashley joked.

"Sleep well tonight, Lieutenant. The Third Squad is in control up here," O'Rourke said.

"OK, I'll remember that," Ashley said, terminating the conversation.

With the tour of their sector complete, Ashley and Fisk returned to their pillbox.

"Fisk, I think we've got a good group."

"We have a few eight balls but, all and all they are about as good as you can get," Fisk said, agreeing with Ashley's assessment of the platoon.

The phone rang from the old leather EE8 telephone holder. Fisk answered.

"Good," Fisk said. "We will send a couple of runners back to pick 'em up. "Muller, that was the supply sergeant. He says they got a couple of Jerry cans full of beer for the platoon. Send whoever you need to pick them up."

"OK, will do."

"That sounds like a good deal, Fisk," Ashley said.

"Yeah, some things are pretty nice in this static situation. The squads all have their beer and water containers. They bring their empties to us here at the pillbox; we fill them, and send them away happy, usually. We return our empties to the company supply clerks who repeat the cycle when they can."

Shortly after dark, a call came in from the Second Squad. "Sergeant Fisk, this is Murph. I gotta bitch."

"Wait one, Murph," Fisk said.

"Hey Lieutenant, listen in on this one. It's Murph. You remember him from the Bulge."

"Yeah, sure do. Glad he is still around," Ashley said smiling.

"Sergeant, I'm drinking this God damned beer you sent us," Murph complained.

"Yeah, so!" Fisk growled.

"Well, I'm an old beer drinker, as you know. But this is the damnedest tasting stuff I have ever had. It tastes like gasoline. I think those supply fucks forgot to clean out the gas from the Kraut jerry-can before they put the beer in."

"OK, Murph, I'll raise hell with them. Maybe they will be more careful next time. You want to send it back?" Fisk asked.

"Hell no, I'll drink the shit anyway. It is better than nothin'."

"Fisk, he is a riot. He'll never change, and I hope he doesn't," Ashley said, laughing.

The company mail came with a resupply of C-rations. Ashley hadn't heard from anyone in over a month. But it would have been better if the news he was about to receive had not been received at all.

There were the usual letters from family and friends, reporting how tough things were getting with a shortage of sugar, gasoline, nylons, and other of life's necessities. There was a temptation at times for Ashley to ask them to write on toilet paper due to the critical shortage. But he managed to restrain himself.

Then there were two important letters—one pink and perfumed from Kit Montague. The other was an official looking envelope with a return address from Calvin Sinclair, Sr., Newport Beach, California. He naturally opened Kit's letter first. Maybe she would give him a clue as to what to expect in the elder Sinclair's letter.

My dear Brett,

I had a telephone call from Cal's dad, asking for your address. He will be getting in touch with you soon. He has some unpleasant news about Cal. Better that he tell you. I know you are going to make it. I am already planning for the day when you come home. The war can't last forever. Survive for me. I love you.

Kit

Ashley opened the second envelope.

Dear Brett,

There are two letters in this envelope. I wrote one and have seen the one Cal wrote to you some time ago for me to hold for you in case of a disaster. To better understand the situation, read his letter first.

Cal Sinclair, Sr.

Dear Brett,

I flew my first bombing missions for the Canadian-British units from England, and then from their forward airfields in Holland. The Canadians are courageous airmen who earned my respect on every mission. And they really cared about my welfare. I spent all my free time in England visiting London, and the beautiful English countryside. I also learned to love and admire the British people.

My last flight with the Brits and Canadians was on Christmas day over the Belgian Bulge. We met the biggest German aerial resistance we had faced in any of our previous bombing runs. It was sort of their last hurrah. I completed my required 25 to 35 missions and was offered an opportu-

nity to go either to Canada or the States to spend my remaining time at a training base. Instead I asked for, and was granted, permission to fly with the American Eighth Air Force. After all, I am an American.

On February 14th, I flew a B-17 with the Eighth Air Force. It was against a defenseless city, a city without a single military or industrial target. The city was Dresden. Firestorms burned for days. Thousands of men, women, and children suffocated in air raid shelters or were baked alive—all done in the hope that it would destroy the will of the German people to continue the war. The bombing failed in its purpose—but it destroyed one of the most beautiful cities in Europe. I was not a proud participant in that mission, but it in no way diminished my pride in being an American.

Now Brett, I wanted you to get this letter in case anything happens to me. If you do, you know it is all over for me. It was not God's will that my life end this way. I was just on the wrong mission at the wrong time. At 22, I was no longer a kid. But I had a kid's great dreams of tomorrow. I had so much I wanted to do. But it wasn't to be. Robert Burns had it right when he said: "The best laid schemes o` mice and men Gang aft a-gley."

Long ago, I had a premonition that something tragic like this could happen, so I did make some arrangements. I had planned to give you my convertible as a graduation present. Just in case I didn't show, I left the car with Kit Montague. You will find that the title in the glove compartment transfers the car to you.

Brett, forget this catastrophe. Get through this war in one piece and get on with your life. When you and Kit think of me, let it be about the good *times we had together. Please live a little for me.*

Goodbye dear friend. May God bless and keep you safe always.

Cal

Dear Brett,

Cal's letter pretty much tells the story. It is an awful loss for us. He was our only son—our only child. We can never get over it. He was scheduled to come home in the spring but his aircraft was destroyed over Germany soon after the Dresden raid in February. I know you are almost as proud of him as we are. He flew nearly a hundred combat missions, even though he could have come home after 25. He was awarded both the Canadian and American Distinguished Flying Crosses. But they are an empty substitute for him.

There are some important things you can do for Cal's mother and me when the war ends. First, please find out where Cal is buried, and send us a photograph of his grave and the surroundings. Second, we want you and Kit Montague to visit us here in California. Call me as soon as you can when you get home, and I will arrange the transportation for the two of you.

I have an important job for you that I will talk to you about when I see you.

Please keep us posted on your plans and whereabouts from time to time. May God watch over you.

Cal Sinclair, Sr.

Tears came easily now for Ashley. When Captain Tipper told him Lieutenant Coke, his closest friend in OCS had been killed, he was ashamed to show any sense of feeling in front of his company commander. He made believe it never happened. But now Cal Sinclair, his inseparable college roommate for three years, was dead. He couldn't deny it; he had letters to prove it.

"What's the matter, Lieutenant?" Fisk asked. He had never seen his platoon leader lose his cool before.

Showing the Fisk the letter, Ashley said, "He didn't have to stay. He did his time. He could have gone home. He didn't have to prove anything to General Pealot or Colonel McNutt, or anybody at the college or anywhere else," Ashley answered, badly shaken by the news of the death of his college roommate and best friend.

Ashley walked alone out of the pillbox, through the trenches toward the Roer. The partial moonlight gave the battlefield an eerie yellow-gray color. Bright flashes of cannon fire could be seen beyond the shining black river. Fisk, seriously concerned about his distraught platoon officer, followed quietly to allow him a moment to himself.

Suddenly Ashley paused, took the German luger that Fisk had given him in the Bulge from its holster. Put it to his mouth and kissed the end of the barrel.

"No! Don't do it, Lieutenant!" Fisk pleaded.

Then before he could reach him, Ashley slid a round into the chamber, turned toward the river, lifted the pistol to the sky, and fired until the magazine was empty.

"Fisk, any more of that gasoline tainted beer left?"

"I think so."

"Good, let's go back into that cement monster and get drunk. That stunt I just pulled was the only way I knew to salute the best friend I ever had. If battalion calls about our making too much noise, tell them to 'go fuck themselves'," Ashley said lifting a canteen cup full of the warm beer. "Murph is right. This stuff is poison!"

19

After an hour of drinking the gas-spiked beer, Ashley easily fell asleep.

"Muller, let's go outside a minute," Fisk said in a confidential tone. "I don't want the Lieutenant to hear me. You may have heard some of the conversation I had with him. He just got the word that his college roommate, a B-17 pilot, was killed over Germany. As you can imagine, he is pretty upset. We need to boost his spirit. The only one who can do that is that clown Murph. Get him up here at 1000 hours tomorrow."

"Right, will do. Murph has got to tell the lieutenant about his R&R trip to Paris. I'll tell him the name of the game. If he will follow the script, which is difficult for him to do, that ought to get the Lieutenant laughing again," Sergeant Muller said.

Muller arrived with a muddy, unshaven Murph at the scheduled time.

"Lieutenant, we are honored with the presence of your Platoon Scout," said a smiling Muller.

"Murph, how you doing?" Ashley asked.

"Doing great, Lieutenant. We been sitting up here overlooking a pretty river for about a month, resting our asses and having a ball. It's fun and games. Every morning, the Krauts come out of their holes to, let's say—relieve themselves. And as soon as they drop their pants, we go for white bulls' eyes. You ought to see them run with their pants down," Murph said laughing at his own story.

"That must be nice way to start your day,

Murph. Hey, I see you made corporal. Corporal Jim Murph, USA has a nice ring to it. I knew Captain Tipper would recognize leadership sooner or later."

"That wasn't the Captain. Lieutenant Fortner promoted me for being the only one that escaped from his ambushed patrol. They were a blabbermouth bunch, you know. They got him in real trouble with the commanding general. In a few days after the patrol was lost, Kraut air and artillery delivered propaganda leaflets fell all along the front lines. There were no longer any secrets. The Krauts now know everything about the division's past and recent history, the hometowns of members of the patrol, even the lousy shape they were in. They said: `Poor Sergeant Bruner, he is in such bad health he should never have been drafted,' " Murph said.

"Yeah I heard. They will be eatin' potato and cabbage soup for the rest of the war, if they are lucky," Ashley said, wanting to hear more.

"Murph, tell the Lieutenant about getting laid in Paris," Muller said, trying to keep Murph on track.

"Well, Lieutenant, since I was the only one that survived that fucked-up patrol—not only did Lieutenant Fortner promote me—he gave me a pass to Paris. I think I might change my mind about him being a horse's ass, and get to really like him. The platoon even took up a collection for me. They told me that when I got to Paris to find a good looking 'Lady of the Night`—screw my head off, and come back and tell them about it. I had a little money of my own I had won in poker since leaving the States. With the money the platoon gave me and my winnings, hell, I left here with over a hundred bucks. Didn't have a nickel, though, when I got back.

"As soon as I got to `Gay Paree', I headed straight to Pigalle and some place called Cafe Le

Amour. It was Amour all right, Amour for my money. I had two big glasses of red wine, and then began to look around a bit. I didn't have to look very far. This good-looking, sweet thing was sitting right beside me, ready to make a move on me. As soon as I caught her eye, she said—`mon ami,` would you like to buy me a drink?' Like a big shot, I said `of course, *Mademoiselle.*` Well, after a couple of drinks, she suggested we go to her apartment. By that time she had her hand in my trousers, and I was in no position to refuse.

"Her place wasn't an apartment at all, just a room with a toilet, douche bowl, and a wash basin. We got better in Brooklyn. By the time I cleaned some of the German mud off myself, she was already in bed—naked as a jaybird. She was a beauty all right: pale white skin, dark brown hair, green eyes, and built like a brick shit house. Boy, it was love at first sight. But then reality began to set it in. She said: `20 dollars American—up front'! I had to go along, of course. The platoon had given me a pussy allowance, and it would have been embarrassing to have to return it. They said I'd earned it the hard way. You might say things were hard right then, so to speak. So I quickly jumped into bed, and started screwing like a mink. During the entire exercise, she was either reading a frog love story or eating an apple. If that wasn't enough of an insult to my American manhood, she told me she didn't care whether the French, Germans or Americans controlled Paris—so long as they had *beaucoup* francs."

Murph's stories worked, Ashley joined the group in his pillbox in tear-jerking laughter.

"Corporal Murph, based on your shortage of funds, here is five bucks on one condition," Ashley said.

"What's that, Lieutenant?" Murph asked.

"You won't ask me again to examine the bodies of the Krauts that you and I kill—the way you did in the Battle of the Bulge."

"It's a deal, Lieutenant!" Murph agreed.

With that, the telephone rang. Fisk answered.

"Lieutenant, Fortner wants to see you at his command post right away."

"OK, tell 'im I am on the way."

Lieutenant Fortner began his surprise briefing to the platoon leaders of the remnants of his three rifle platoons and a near full-strength weapons platoon in his usual devil-may-care manner.

"Gentlemen, fiddle-farting around in this defensive position is about over. Everybody wants a piece of Berlin, the British, the Americans, and the Russians, particularly the Russians. Imagine the prestige, and the glory for one of our generals who leads his soldiers down the *Unter Den Linden Strasse* through the *Brandenburg Tor*—Eisenhower, Bradley, Simpson, Patton, yes particularly Patton. Can you imagine the show he would put on? Who will become the American Caesar? Remember how we let Charles De Gaulle go into Paris first, so that he could lead his armored division through the *Arc de Triomphe* down the magnificent *Champs-Elysees*. Some day he will likely be the President of a new—`La Grande France.'

"OK, enough of the glory crap. In the Siegfried and the Bulge we plodded along. This will be different. We will be driven hard day and night by our division and regimental commanders to our objectives with fire and movement and plenty of both. But it still ain't gonna be easy. It is still more than 300 miles to Berlin. There are major river obstacles that must be crossed—the Roer, the Rhine, the Weser, and finally the Elbe. And there are also still many battles to be fought against an enemy who doesn't know the meaning of the word surrender, particularly under unconditional terms.

"In summary, D-Day for the final campaign is 23 February 1945. It begins with the crossing of the Roer. Initially, our regiment will be in corps reserve. As such, we will follow the other two regiments across the river. We will by-pass them or attack through them, if they are delayed for the slightest reason. The operation could well be called "rat race." On D-minus-1 and D-minus-2, we will participate in feints that will include firing all of our weapons on call. The magnitude of the artillery and air strikes will be unlike anything we have ever seen before. Our objectives should be nothing but rubble by the time we reach them. We will pass through a dozen towns and villages before we even reach the Rhine. It will be no picnic. Be prepared to move out on short notice. If there are no questions, that's it for now."

Ashley had seen the dark side of Fortner many times, but this speech showed yet another side. The text seemed above and beyond the reach of a lieutenant company commander. The content was more in keeping with the briefing of regimental commanders by a division operations officer—a lieutenant colonel. Was Fortner parroting something he had been told earlier by higher command or had he now become an excellent actor?

Initially, the attacking regiments were highly successful, leaving behind a trail of bodies and blood. On the first night or two out, Ashley and his platoon shared foxholes with the enemy dead. One German soldier had been killed and propped-up against a tree with a hairbrush in his hand touching a hairless, shining head. They passed enemy, teen-aged soldiers lying on the floor of a farm house covered in their blood crying out for help that the platoon could not stop the attack long enough to provide. Ashley hoped follow-on medics would heed their pitiful cries. An American soldier from one of the leading regiments was left for dead. A bullet had passed through his neck but missed his vertebrate and major blood vessels. He was either in a state of shock or too scared to move for fear he would be hit again. He reportedly survived.

On 1 March, stiffening resistance slowed the attacking units. The Second Battalion took over the lead, with a new battalion commander at the helm. At first, the battalion advanced by truck for nearly ten miles. Then suddenly determined German infantry and artillery near the town of Dulken stopped the rapid motorized advance.

On reaching the outskirts of Dulken at mid morning, Lieutenant Colonel Norwell, the new battalion commander, decided against charging headlong into a force of unknown strength and capabilities. He chose instead a more cautious approach. Perhaps it was because of his experience as the G-3 (Operations Officer) with a division that had been mauled in the Battle of the Bulge. He tried a form of Psychological Warfare. He used public address systems, a jeep mounted with loud speakers, in an attempt to persuade the German defensive unit of the advantages of being American rather than Russian prisoners. They were given an hour to surrender. Hordes of civilians heeded the call, but not a single German soldier did. Norwell's conservative approach, that could have saved lives on both sides, failed. However, his tentativeness didn't go well with his regimental and division commanders. He lost a valuable hour in the race for Berlin, the prize of the war. This single mistake may have been the beginning of the end of his promising career in the Regular Army.

The time spent waiting for the anticipated enemy surrender was enjoyed by riflemen dispersed in houses along the line. Ashley's platoon took full advantage of the respite.

"Fisk," Ashley asked. "Where is O'Rourke?"

"He is in the kitchen, Sir."

"Perfect, let's get him to fix us some good Kraut food to eat."

"That's what I'm doing, Lieutenant," O'Rourke answered, already in the middle of making piles of French fries. "How do you like your fries, Lieutenant?"

"Doesn't sound like a Teutonic specialty, O'Rourke, but I'll take them any way you make them," Ashley said.

"The first course will be soup, the farmer's pumpernickel bread, and his homemade brew. I found some of his jars of tomatoes, and a bag of his onions. I had enough of my own powdered milk to make a perfect cream of tomato soup. There will be enough here for all of us when I get through," a happy O'Rourke reported.

"Don't think he put poison in this homebrew, do you?" Fisk asked.

"No, the stove was still hot," O'Rourke answered. "That fat Kraut probably high-tailed it out the back door as we came in the front.

Luckily, the platoon finished its exceptionally good feast before Colonel Norwell's pre-attack, artillery barrage began. There were no orders from Lieutenant Fortner. He could not be located. Ashley lined up his platoon along the edge of a large clearing, separating the platoon from the town of Dulken. About a half mile from their position, there were a number of two and three story stucco buildings to the left and to the front in an L-shaped configuration. To his right Ashley could see a tree-lined blacktop road leading into the town.

"Fisk, look out there. Things have gone to hell in a hand basket. There is one platoon, at least, pinned down in the middle of that open field about half way to Dulken. It is probably the First Platoon. If we hadn't pulled in late, Fortner would have had us out there. They are being ripped apart from fire from the top floors of the buildings to their left and front. They are digging in like mad, men about to die. Their wounded are yelling for medics. Looks like three of our assigned light tanks have been stopped at the entrance to the town. They are scared shitless without infantry around them. Don't blame 'em! I wonder where the hell Fortner is? I wonder where the Third Platoon is?" Ashley asked as if talking to himself.

Ashley didn't get an answer. But a German antitank, antipersonnel 88 mm answered for the Germans. A single round passed just over their heads, destroying most of the farmer's barn a few yards behind them, and setting it on fire.

Then a clean-shaven first lieutenant, in a freshly pressed uniform, appeared on the scene. Neither Ashley nor Fisk recognized him. He was blond guy, a "neat freak", with a good military bearing. But at the moment, he was also stumbling drunk. Was he the new company executive officer? Was he a German plant? They would never know the answer. The deteriorating situation was moving at triple time.

"Attack, attack," the drunken officer screamed as another 88 mm round passed closer over head, barely missing him. At first, Ashley and Fisk tried to ignore him, thinking he would pass-out or give up playing soldier and go away. But he didn't. Ashley considered the possibility that the stranger could be a somebody, or was a somebody's messenger or liaison officer. That could be a problem.

"Attack where, attack where?" Ashley screamed over the sound of incoming and outgoing Artillery.

"Through that platoon, pinned down in front of you," the stranger said.

"That would be suicide," Ashley responded. "We would be pinned down and slaughtered just as they are!"

"That's an order, attack now or—I'll take over your stupid platoon and lead the attack myself," the sloshed lieutenant muttered.

"Fisk, that son of bitch is crazy!" Ashley said "We got to make a move now. We will move toward the platoon out front, and then after about 25 yards out turn quickly to the right and run like hell—straight for that road leading into the town. Before that weird lieutenant and the Krauts figure out what we are up to, we should be in the outskirts of Dulken.

"Ok, let's go. Platoon, follow me on the double," Ashley yelled.

Before the drunk and the Germans could react, the Second Platoon was on the road. Using the protection provided by the trees and drainage ditches, they advanced rapidly toward the stalled tanks at the edge of the town. After convincing the tankers they were Americans, they began moving with the platoon into Dulken. From their right, the Third Platoon came out of nowhere, cut in front of them. The three rifle platoons had now been accounted for. Once in the town, firing ceased, except for an occasional fanatic sniper. The organized German force had withdrawn.

Within a few minutes, they reached the northern edge of Dulken. It was the highest ground in the area, and provided an excellent, panoramic view of the surrounding terrain and the adjoining village of Bistard. Here in this nothing of a farming community, the elite defenders of Dulken who had refused to accept an offer to surrender now decided to make a stand. But Fortner hadn't figured it out. He was enjoying the show.

Ashley saw Fortner for the first time since before the Dulken attack. He had not seen him at all during the operation. For whatever reason, he seemed sober, rested, and prepared to continue the battle.

"Ashley, we have orders to press on. You take the lead. Move down the slope of this rise and then pick up the road at the end of that row of houses in the connecting town of Bistard down there. If you don 't meet any resistance keep moving on the only road out of the town. The rest of us will follow," Fortner ordered.

Ashley had an uncomfortable feeling about the situation. He hated to move over open areas. He had learned the hard way that when the shooting begins in open field, there is no place to hide. But he moved his platoon as ordered. He chose a line of skirmishers to maximize fire to the front. Looking back, he saw a large company group watching. It was a circus atmosphere. It was as though the curtains of a theatrical performance were about to open, and he was the star of a show he had grown to despise. He luckily caught the eye of Lieutenant Louis, one of his college classmates, who had recently taken over the Weapons Platoon that he had been denied. Lou nodded in recognition, but otherwise he typically made no comment or gesture. But Ashley was relieved to see someone he could trust who could tell what happened, if the operation went sour as he sensed it would.

It was strangely quiet for the first hundred

yards. Then some 25 German civilians with white flags and hands raised jumped up in front of them. Ashley motioned for them to pass through. They hesitatingly obliged. The civilians had barely cleared the platoon lines when the German infantry opened-up with a heavy salvo of rifle and machine gun fire. Muller and his squad were in a line to his left. Fisk was on right with the two other rifle squads. Before they could find shelter in mounds of earth, Muller caught a round between his web belt and his canteen. The force spun him in a 360-degree circle. He continued moving for a few seconds in the original direction before diving for the ground. For the first time, Ashley saw a look of fear roll over Muller's usually stolid face.

O'Rourke broke his dive to the ground in perfect form. His right hand griped his M1 rifle at the small of the stock and his left held the stock near the forward edge of the sling swivel. Without being able to determine the origin of the firing, Ashley directed firing toward the vent holes in a brick barn immediately to their front. But without the desired result. Firing continued.

"Fisk, take the two squads and clear those houses on the right," Ashley yelled. "That may be where the bastards are firing from."

Ashley and Muller were left in the middle of field, firing randomly with no safe place to go. Their hearts pounded so rapidly that their hearing seemed impaired. Their nervous spit had the look of liquid cotton. They craved water, but were too preoccupied to steal a drink from their canteens. The browning automatic rifleman lying between Muller and Ashley was hit, and died instantly from a round that passed through his shoulder into his heart. A supporting machine gunner from the Weapons Platoon was killed as soon as he began to fire. His assistant gunner took over, but he too was hit and cried-out for help.

Ashley imagined for a moment that they were surrounded by a large, tank supported force. In desperation, he pulled the pin on one of his fragmentation grenades, determined that if surrounded he would take some company with him to hell. The enemy assault didn't come. But his hand had now become frozen around the grenade.

"Muller, my hand is glued to this damn thing. I can hardly pry my fingers off of it. Have you got a suggested target?" Ashley asked now concerned about the possibility of losing his hand.

"Yeah, toss it across the street behind that building over there," Muller said.

Within seconds there was an explosion, and accompanying screams of pain.

"Sounds like there is a bunch of them behind that building," Muller said, now recovered from his initial shock from being hit and spun in a circle.

"OK, Bazooka-Man, fire a round into that building where the noise came from," Ashley ordered.

More screams of frightened men. It was now time for the other side to be introduced to helplessness and fear.

"Max, let me borrow your M1, I am out of ammunition for my carbine," Ashley said to his platoon runner, radio operator, and protector.

"OK, Lieutenant, I haven't fired too much so far," Max said.

"Muller, take out that Kraut 76 mm anti-tank gun beside the building where the screams came from, I'm going to try for the building."

"Got it, I'll be right behind you." Muller said.

Ashley made a dash across the road, and found temporary cover in the door inset. An adrenaline-assisted boot easily broke the door in. The entrance was dark and musty. The farmer's jars of preserved fruit and vegetables were neatly arranged on shelves at the end of the dark entrance hall. For lack of something else to do, Ashley fired a single around from Max's M1 into a jar of berries. The result was an explosive sound that echoed throughout the small house.

"Camarade, camarade," they yelled as they poured out of the darkness with hands on the back of their of heads. There were seven in all—over six feet, cleanly shaven and dressed in recently pressed uniforms. They were likely some general's honor guard, Ashley surmised. Max moved in and took over. With Ashley's empty carbine, he marched them to the rear. Ashley now turned his attention to other matters. Muller's squad made quick work of the anti-tank gun crew and blew-up the gun using a hand grenade in its breech. A lone soldier crawled around the side of the building, catching Ashley by surprise. He turned quickly to his right and fired a second round—this one catching the poor devil between the eyes.

Fisk and the remainder of the platoon met at the end of the town of Bistard. The battle was over. A beer cellar was discovered, and its contents were quickly consumed. Forty of the enemy had been killed or captured by an under strength rifle platoon.

Ashley reported his platoon's situation to Lieutenant Fortner at his company's headquarters. Fortner had surrounded his headquarters with the attached platoon of light tanks. They were never committed to the battle. Ashley filled his pockets with ammunition for his carbine and the Max's MI. He then reluctantly asked Fortner for further orders. He assumed his platoon would now be given some slack, since they had spearheaded the attack. He should have known better.

"Lieutenant Fortner, my platoon is pretty-much bushed. Request our order of march be behind the First and/or Third Platoons," Ashley said.

"Lieutenant, your request is denied. Be prepared to move out in 20 minutes."

By the time Ashley reached his platoon, a second cache of the farmer's beer had been located and was being consumed in large quantities. Ashley passed on the next company operational order and joined his group in the temporary beer bust.

"Lieutenant," Murph said, "Did you take a look at that Kraut you killed? The back of his head was nearly blown off. That M1 you borrowed from Max sure packs a wallop."

"God damn it, Murph, when I contributed five dollars toward your pussy fund awhile back, I thought we had a deal—that I wouldn't be your undertaker! I don't like the looks or smell of the dead. You gotta kill your own Krauts. Let mine rest in peace." Ashley said, reprimanding Murph.

"Sorry, Lieutenant, I forgot," Murph said, hurt by the strange attitude of his platoon leader. He cornered Sergeant O'Rourke for an explanation.

"Sergeant O'Rourke, you heard the Lieutenant chewing my ass out about talking to him about dead bodies. Is he cracking up or going crazy? I seen him kill a lot, but that's no reason to flip-out, is it? You been to college and are the oldest guy in the platoon. Maybe you can help me figure what's with the Lieutenant," a concerned Murph said.

"Murph, I don't have all the answers but maybe I can offer something. We are like being in a jungle in front line combat. It's nasty business. It affects different people in different ways. It doesn't seem to bother you, I noticed. On the other hand, take some of the others.

Sergeant Murtha gives the impression that he enjoys killing, but I don't think so. I think he drinks himself into a stupor when it's over to cleanse his soul. You see he is still not yet a complete animal. He has a soul!

"You ever heard of that guy they call 'Tex the Gun Slinger', from the Heavy Weapons Company?" O'Rourke asked.

"Yeah, I heard of him. He is really a weird son of bitch. He wears that low-slung 45 pistol, tied around his leg just above his knee. Likes to make believe he is a gunner fighter. After the rifle platoons have cleared an area, he comes out of his hole and mops-up, he calls it. I saw him out draw a Kraut in the Bulge. After he shot him dead, he jumped on him like a wild animal and pulled all of his gold teeth with a pair of pliers that he carries on his cartridge belt all the time. They say he's got a pound of gold teeth in his back pack," Murph explained in wide-eyed excitement.

"Yeah, Murph, that's the guy I was talking about. He is an example of a guy who has gone over to the animal kingdom. He is a soulless geek. His next step could be cannibalism," O'Rourke said, explaining his theory.

"The Lieutenant's situation, on the other hand, is a little different, a little more complex. He has been in the line longer than most of us and has done and seen an awful lot of killing. Over half of his classmates out of 60 from his OCS class who came to the division with him are either dead or missing. His problem is, he is two people—one a civilized person, and the other a vengeful killer. He is like a man with a double. He's smart enough to know that to survive he has to be the killer double. His torment is which double to shoot—the good guy or the bad guy. You see, when you ask him to examine the bodies he has broken, it is difficult for him," O'Rourke said summing up his theory.

"Thanks, Sergeant, you have given me something to think about," a relieved Murph said.

The company marched most of the night, following a road that led them in a northeasterly direction. Ashley's platoon continued in the lead all night without relief. Some of the men were so exhausted they fell asleep and out of ranks and had to be retrieved. They arrived at a town called Suchteln before daybreak. Suchteln was not unlike the dozens of other towns they had overrun in the "break-out", except for the fact that this one had a large hospital with warm rooms, hot and cold running water, and electricity. The men piled into soft, clean hospital beds and slept for twelve, undisturbed hours.

On 4 March 1945, the Second Battalion and assigned units entered the city of Krefeld on the Rhine. Before the war, Krefeld had been a major German chemical and dye-manufacturing city. Because of its importance to the German war effort, the city had been reduced to a rock-pile by British and American bombers. Even so there were still enough beautiful houses left to easily accommodate F Company and the rest of the battalion.

A week's stay was enough time for the company to continue its inescapable trail of trouble. At the end of the respite in Krefeld, Captain Tipper returned and took over his old command from Lieutenant Fortner. His return to the company that he had commanded off and on from the landing at Omaha Beach to the present was full of surprises. Tipper found out that his first sergeant had been sentenced to life imprisonment for shooting an unarmed German soldier. Colonel Meddler, the regimental commander, had been relieved of command, and replaced by a young, gung-ho, lieutenant colonel. Meddler's time had come. He had lost too many of his men in the battle for the Siegfried line and the Battle of the Bulge. His failure to press the attack at Dulken gave the division commander the excuse he needed to send the tired old man to the rear to a less demanding job.

20

As a result of the shooting of the unarmed German, those found not guilty of a crime but indirectly involved were transferred to another company. Additionally, F Company was moved out of Krefeld to Rumeln, a smaller town near the Rhine. While division units were preparing for the crossing of the Rhine, part-time training schedules were followed. Instruction in demolitions and explosives were included in the makeshift training program. At one of the classes, a lieutenant from the company Weapons Platoon gave a lecture and demonstration on the German anti-tank weapon—the *panzerfaust.* It looked a lot like a bulbous warhead at the end of a three-foot pipe.

"Hey, Lieutenant, that thing looks like a plumber's friend," a platoon joker called out to get attention.

"That may be, but it's a deadly weapon," the lieutenant responded to his detractor.

Everything seemed to be going well during the lecture, until the detonating charge in a dud went off unexpectedly, leaving 30 bleeding men lying on the ground. F Company had rightfully earned its title—the "Snake-Bit Company" of the division.

With all of its romantic legends and impact on men and nations for centuries, the Rhine to Ashley and his platoon was just another narrow, slow-moving body of dark, dirty water. Near midnight on the 1st of April the battalion was loaded on trucks driven by black soldiers, and moved across the river on pontoon bridges at Wesel. The sky was illuminated with more searchlights than an opening night on Broadway. The troops and their commanders would have been happier without the exposure of the lights, but they were a valuable aid to the engineers who had already begun to build a more permanent span of the river. Thanks to a British unit and an American Airborne Division who made the initial crossing, the battalion crossing was unopposed.

In this, the beginning of the final dash to Berlin, the battalion was organized into three task forces. Each task force consisted of a motorized rifle company with attached heavy machine gun and mortar units from the battalion Heavy Weapons Company. A platoon of tanks or tank destroyers on loan from the 5th Armored Division accompanied the lead task force.

Ashley was told that the battle from the Rhine to the Weser River would cover a hundred miles, and not be an easy trip. It was a good assessment. It took six gut wrenching days. The Wehrmacht resistance that was left was touch and go—a costly delaying action that took a heavy toll on both sides of the line. The German commanders knew it was all over. But their small disciplined units, made up of kids and old men, fought bravely for every mile.

On 6 April, the division and its regiments crossed the Weser at Porta Westfalica on pontoon bridges laid across the river by the supporting 5th Armored Division. For inexplicable reasons, the enemy resistance stiffened between the Weser and the Elbe Rivers.

Shortly after crossing the Weser, the Second Battalion would spearhead the attack. At times the battalion dashed across the countryside at heretofore unheard of speeds of 10 to 15 miles per hour. But frequently units would be stopped at wooded road junctions and small villages, where the enemy could safely hide, spill the blood of the invaders, and run.

It was the first week of April. Spring was not to be denied to the sweeping German plains. For the first time, Ashley and his troop realized how truly beautiful the country really was. Gone were the dark, gray days of winter spent in the Siegfried line. "Why had the German people allowed a madman to bring their nation to near extinction?" Ashley said to himself.

Sergeant Brown was a tall, strikingly handsome black. His assistant, a short, untidy corporal, was the opposite. The sergeant did the driving and the corporal did the talking.

"Lieutenant, I wanna get myself a Kraut on this trip," the corporal said. "I been up front many times, and I ain't fired no shots yet."

"That's interesting, Corporal, what's your name?" Ashley rejoined. "We try to avoid 'em. And you want to find 'em. Maybe we have been here too long."

"Washington, Sir, but they call me 'De Cap' cause I love to wear this knit cap that goes under the helmet. The "wool knitty", I calls it, is sure nice when it's cold."

"Cap, you ever heard of General Patton?"

"Yes Sir. That's that red-faced white man wit dem pearl handle pistols, who rides up and down the road with sirens going full blast, stopping every now and then to chew GI asses. Yes Sir, I heard of him," the smiling corporal answered.

"You got it. That's the man. He's real bad. If we run into him, he will really chew your ass out, and mine too, if you don't keep your helmet on. He even makes his truck-mechanics wear ties. Now, do you know how to operate that ring-mounted 50 caliber machine gun on your duce and a half?"

"You bet, Lieutenant."

"Good, that's gonna be your job. I'll tell Platoon Sergeant Fisk to give you first shot at any Krauts that we see on the ground or in the air," Ashley promised.

Washington joined the platoon in the back of the truck, and with a big smile of white teeth took his place behind the 50 caliber. Ashley took his seat beside Sergeant Brown in the cab of the truck as they moved toward the next roadblock, then the next and the next. "Someday soon," he thought, "maybe with God willing—Berlin, and then it would all be over."

"He's a talkin' little Nigger, Lieutenant, but he will do all right," the likeable black sergeant said in a friendly tone.

"I think you're right, Sergeant Brown. I like his spirit."

Within a few miles inland from the Weser, artillery fire from the surrounding hills brought the long column of GI-filled trucks led by a platoon of tanks to a halt. The tanks stopped first, then the lead riflemen jumped from their trucks and sought shelter along the roadside.

Captain Tipper ordered F Company into the wooded hillside to put the German resistance out of commission. He moved his company along the road with the First Platoon on the left of the road and Ashley's Second Platoon on the right. Captain Tipper initially positioned himself between the two platoons. On reaching the first road junction, both platoons came under fire. The First Platoon to Ashley's left received both machine gun and 20 mm cannon fire from a German flak wagon. A number of men in the platoon took hits including the platoon sergeant, whose arm was shattered by 20 mm cannon fire. The sergeant had received a battlefield commission, and needed only to pass a physical to receive his well-deserved gold bars, but that now seemed unlikely.

Captain Tipper yelled to Ashley over the sound of rifle and cannon fire to keep moving forward. He then faded back into a building between the two platoons, presumably to radio for help. Ashley moved his platoon forward to the edge of the crossing, with an unimproved gravel road to his front. There, with his platoon dispersed in a line along the edge of the road, he was pinned down again. The machine gun fire from the flak wagon was now firing from the left directly down the road in front of them. He decided to hold his position for a while until he could figure out what to do next, when one of his corporals with blood streaming down his face crawled over to his position.

"Lieutenant, Lieutenant, when are we going to cross the road?" The corporal screamed.

"Now Corporal, now! But the medic will take care of you first. Fisk, pass the word along the line. We will make a go for it between machine gun bursts. Tell 'em to watch for my hand signal. Ready, one, two, three, go!" Ashley yelled over the machine gun chatter.

One near-straight line swept across the road as one, except for two men at the end of the line who never got the word. (The next day the two were picked up in the rear in a state of shock and held by military police as deserters. They were eventually returned to the platoon, since Ashley refused to prefer charges against them.)

The platoon made it across the road on to the heavily wooded high ground.

"Fisk," Ashley said, "I've got to get back to the captain and tell him what's happened and give him our position. Otherwise, the company could leave us here with the Krauts all around us. As you recall, they have a bad habit of doing that. Wish me luck in rerunning the `steel gauntlet'."

"You got it. Be sure you count the time between machine gun-bursts carefully," Fisk warned his platoon leader.

Ashley followed that good advice and, to the disgust of the German gunner, he made a successful dash between the bursts. He reported the situation to Captain Tipper, who was preoccupied with the losses in his First Platoon. He seemed satisfied with Ashley's report and told him to hold the ground where they were, and that the battalion column would come their way as soon as possible. It did. After seeing Ashley's unit cross the road, the commander of the German delaying force withdrew.

Once the enemy withdrew, the battalion made its fastest advance of any operation to date—nearly 40 miles in two hours through seven villages of shocked civilians waving white flags. It was dark by the time they reached the town of Weetzen, a clean, pretty town not yet damaged by the invaders from the west. Deciding to keep it that way, 100 German soldiers (without a fight) surrendered to E Company as they entered the town.

The battalion task forces had been on the move for two days and nights. It was assumed that this would be the place for a few hours of rest. The companies poured into any house or shed they could find for at least a temporary break. The angry German force, now in the hills surrounding the village, had other ideas. Exactly at midnight, artillery began to fall into the American billets and vehicle parking areas with deadly accuracy. It was a clear message from the enemy that *"Der Krieg ist nicht zu Ende,"*—

the war is not over. The bombardment would last continuously for two hours.

After much confusion Ashley located Captain Tipper in his basement command post. Within a few seconds, a shell landed at the entrance, knocking him down into the basement in the midst of the captain's surprised headquarters group.

"Captain, are we going to stay here until daylight?" Ashley asked, hoping for an affirmative reply.

"I'm trying to find out now, but I doubt it. Better have your outfit ready to move out at any time," Tipper answered.

When Ashley returned to his platoon, he discovered that the platoon had taken a direct hit. Squad leader O'Rourke had a minor shrapnel wound in his knee. But one member of his squad had a serious intestinal wound. The attending medic had little success in stopping the bleeding.

"Fisk, we have got get this guy in the truck and get him to an aid station, any aid station." Ashley said.

"Roger, but we gotta be careful moving him. Sergeant Brown, give me a hand in ripping this door off its hinges. We can use it as a stretcher."

"No problem, Sergeant Fisk. I think I can handle this one by myself," Brown said, jerking the door off its hinges with relative ease.

Both Quartermaster truck drivers, Sergeant Brown and Corporal Washington, were amazingly calm as they drove the critically wounded soldier under a hail of Artillery fire to the close-in battalion aid station. They could now tell their peers around campfires in the rear that they had had their baptism of fire.

The battalion was unable to get artillery counter-battery fire to silence the incoming artillery from the hills to the front and flanks. The regimental commander finally ordered the battalion to pull back out of the town until they could get the situation under control. After much difficulty and confusion, the convoy was re-formed and moved out in total darkness in the midst of continued shelling. That within itself was a remarkable accomplishment. Nearly every company had vehicles damaged or destroyed. An attached platoon of 4.2 mortars was put out of action. Of more importance, within two hours in the death trap, the battalion suffered 48 killed or wounded. So much for going so far so fast within the past 48 hours.

Hannover, the largest city along the route of march, was now within a day's fighting. Before the attack commenced it was necessary to secure the near bank of the Mittleland Canal and to reconnoiter and secure the bridges that crossed the canal. F Company was assigned the unpleasant task. Captain Tipper advanced in his preferred formation—two rifle platoons abreast and the third in reserve. It was a "no brainer" for a commander to say —First Platoon on the left, Second Platoon on the right, Third in reserve. Ashley now, as in many previous attacks, found himself on the right. So far it had been the position of good luck and light resistance. Ashley often wondered whether it was his good luck or the psychic power of his girl, Kit Montague, which seemed to be controlling the course of events.

As the company approached the first series of bridges, it was slowed by moderate small arms fire from the vicinity of the major canal crossing. Again the Second Platoon had the best of it. The First Platoon was in direct line of the heaviest fire. At times, the battalion surgeon personally attended the wounded at the front. A steady stream of battalion stretcher-bearers carrying the wounded from the First Platoon could be seen moving back and forth to the aid station.

Once atop the bridge, Ashley's platoon came under sniper fire for the first time. Sergeant Muller and his squad were the target of the heaviest fire. One round ricocheted off of Muller's German retina camera, hitting Ashley under his right ear, knocking him down the bridge embankment. Although not seriously injured, it didn't improve his disposition. He climbed back to the top of the bridge and yelled for the defenders to surrender. One did. The others apparently withdrew into the city.

As the prisoner approached, Ashley yelled for him to go back and bring the rest of them out. Either he didn't understand or he was too frightened to do so for fear his sergeant would shoot him on the spot. Ashley fired close to the prisoner's head. But to no avail.

"Lieutenant, you almost shot the guy's ear off," Muller reminded him.

"I think you are right. He really pissed me off. Thank God I missed. I was just trying to get the son of bitch's attention."

They discovered six 500-pound bombs under the bridge. With the help of a squad of the battalion's Ammunition and Demolition Platoon, the bombs were defused and removed. Darkness settled on the now secured objective. Firing ceased, except for the sound and light of artillery explosions in the distance.

"Max, get the captain on the phone," Ashley said.

"OK, Lieutenant."

"Captain, Ashley here. The platoon has secured the objective—one prisoner, no serious injuries, Sir."

"Good show! You are sitting on the line of departure for tomorrow's attack. Your platoon and the Third Platoon will lead. The First Platoon took some bad hits. They will start out in reserve. I'll give you the word later on the time for the jump-off in the morning. Be careful," the captain cautioned.

"That you can be assured of, Captain. Thanks!"

21

   The attack on Hannover, Germany's 12th largest city, began at 0500 hours, 10 April 1945. The American plan of attack was a surprise and a disappointment for the German general who was responsible for the defense of the city. On the night of 8 April, the Second Battalion took a prisoner who was carrying a map of Hannover's defenses. The map and corroborating intelligence showed the German defense was concentrated in the south and southwest of the city. Based on this information, the 84th Division commander chose to attack with three regiments abreast from the north and northwest.

   F Company had seized the major Weser-Elbe bridge in their sector, Ashley and his platoon would be the first to cross it, followed by the remainder of the regiment's Second and the First Battalions. The bridge that the First Battalion was to have crossed was destroyed by German engineers before the battalion was able to cross it. Thus, the Second Battalion would again spearhead the attack.

   A thick, soupy fog covered the entire battlefield. It was impossible for the enemy to detect the movement of the American infantry. Hannover was now ripe for seizure. Within an hour after crossing the canal, Ashley and his platoon surprised a group of Wehrmacht stragglers and warehouse security guards in the outskirts of Hannover, and relieved them of their weapons. The platoon had become skillful scroungers. Nearly every soldier had a German weapon or bayonet. Ashley jumped a security guard and added a second 38-caliber pistol to his collection. The other company platoons accused Ashley's platoon of having one guy shooting and 39 looting.

At a break in the action, such as it was, a head count was taken. Sergeant Muller reported one malcontent, who spoke fluent German, missing from his squad. There was no reason even in the fog to be lost. Frightened soldiers stay close together. Speculation was that he was a German spy who found this his last opportunity to return to the Fatherland before the war ended or risk being shot.

The other surprise was the sight of Lt. Colonel Norwell, the new battalion commander. This was only the second time Ashley had seen anyone above the rank of captain at the front. The other officer was Major Thompson, the former commander, who was shot while visiting forward positions in the Battle of the Bulge.

Ashley was determined to be remembered by this commanding officer, a tall, impressive looking man with thick, graying black hair and a strong profile.

"Sir, Lieutenant Ashley, Platoon Leader, Second Platoon, Company F reporting, Sir."

"Good morning Lieutenant. Looks like things are going well with you and the platoon this morning," the new battalion commander responded.

"Yes, Sir, we are mopping-up here, and will be moving on into the city in a few minutes. Colonel, here is a souvenir pistol for you from the platoon. One of the Krauts graciously parted with it just a few minutes ago."

"Thank you very much, Lieutenant. I'll treasure it. Maybe we will both remember this occasion for many years to come."

Colonel Norwell shook hands with Ashley, said

good-bye, and was on his way. Within an hour, he was relieved of command of the battalion. The regimental commander thought that he spent so much time looking for German souvenirs that he failed to press the attack. One staff officer thought that he lost control of the attack, resulting in E and G Company firing on each other. Another Lieutenant Colonel assumed command—the third battalion commander since the landing at Omaha Beach. Ashley never saw the new leader until the war was over.

Ashley's platoon continued deeper into Hannover's sprawling industrial area. The city was nearly 70 per cent destroyed as the result of saturated Allied bombing. The heart of the city was nearly flat. Only the outlying area seemed to have been spared.

The platoon began a building-by-building search as they moved toward the southeast section of the city. It was a clear and/or destroy operation—an assumed mission since no one was around to give the orders.

The first warehouse/office complex provided an interesting and revealing situation. Ashley kicked in the first office door, expecting to see either shooting or surrendering troops. He saw neither. Instead he met a smiling, round-faced civilian who appeared to be in complete control of himself and his surroundings. The rotund figure looked like a butcher or shopkeeper from Chicago.

"*Machen sie nichts. Hande hoch! Wo sind die Deutschen Soldaten?*" Ashley yelled, as his finger tightened on the trigger of his carbine.

"Don't get excited, Lieutenant. I have just been on the telephone with the commander of German troops. They are now leaving the city to you with all of its many problems," he said in perfect mid-western English. At that moment, for all practical purposes, the battle for Hannover was over.

The division had been given a city that had more than its share of problems. Allied bombing left it without a single functioning water supply system. The populace suffered from malnutrition, diphtheria, scarlet fever, tuberculosis, and typhus.

By the afternoon of 10 April 1945, the capture of Hannover, the capital of the state of Saxony, was universal newspaper copy:

"American troops captured Hannover today in an armored sweep that caved in Germany's northern and central defenses, and rolled forward at a mile-an-hour clip to within 115 miles of Berlin. From a population of more than 475,000, Hannover was now down to 250,000 Germans and 60,000 displaced persons, including 15,000 allied prisoners of war... It had been an important German metropolis—the meeting place of five railroads and seven major highways."

"Platoon Sergeant Fisk, do you know what we will be able to tell our grandchildren, if we make it back?" Ashley asked.

"Don't know, Lieutenant," Fisk replied, "I have been afraid to think that far ahead. What will we tell 'em?"

"Well, I think we ought to tell them that you and I and the members of Second Platoon, Company F, Second Battalion, 333rd Regiment were with the first wave to seize the largest objective in the history of the 84th Infantry Division. And ours was the first foreign division to invade Germany since Napoleon Bonaparte came this way in the 19th century."

"Do you think it will mean anything to them, Lieutenant?"

"My God, I hope so, Fisk, after all we went through to get here."

The advancing troops found some joy in the drive from Hannover to the Elbe River in seeing the happiness in the faces of liberated American and Allied prisoners of war. But these brief moments of elation were short lived, as prisoners of concentration camps were freed. Even battle-hardened soldiers were sickened at the sights. Some of the prisoners had been in the extermination camp at Auschwitz, where they had been forced to live horrible and unnatural lives. The division commander did his best to provide a caring atmosphere, with the hope that it would help lead them back to a decent and normal existence. But most were left with visible and invisible scars that could not be healed in a week or a month or ever.

One woman, completely detached from reality, moaned:

"I am supposed to go back to Paris. I was supposed to go yesterday, but the train did not come. Then it was supposed to be today, but I don't think it will be today. It may be tomorrow or next week. At first, I was crazy to go home but now I am not so crazy. I do not know whether my husband is dead or alive and I do not know where my friends are. They say it is very expensive to live in France now and I have no money. I think I am afraid to go back because of what I may find. No, I do not know whether I want to go back or not. But, of course, I will go. I am French!"

Division units met only light resistance in the long awaited drive from Hannover to the Elbe. Thousands of displaced persons lined the roads to cheer the long columns of grinning American troops as they continued their march to their final objectives. Thousands of German soldiers, broken in spirit and exhausted by years of war, headed west to a destroyed nation and starving families. But some organized units and vengeful rogue groups continued to counterattack. The regiment's logistical and administrative column was ambushed in the last few days of the conflict. The personnel officer was killed and the regiment was cut-off from its supply source. For an extensive period, forward units suffered from an acute food shortage. Living off the land became the norm.

On 16 April, F and G Companies reached the Elbe River and were ordered into a defensive position along the river near the small town of Beuster. The remainder of the battalion occupied the town. On the 24th of April, E Company was committed to clear a pocket of resistance near the town of Wittenberge. (not to be confused with the historic town of Wittenberg to the south, the home of Martin Luther— leader of the Protestant Reformation). Two men from the company were killed and three wounded in the questionable action.

Ashley and his platoon found themselves again at the head of F Company's column in the movement toward their assigned defensive positions along the Elbe. To reach the objective it was necessary to cross a flood-control dike, more than 20 feet high with a narrow unimproved road on top. They made it over the dike about the same time that the Germans across the river decided to have target practice. They fired several 88 mm rounds across the top of the dike. The rest of the company chose not to cross. They found more comfortable quarters near or in the town of Buester with the remainder of the battalion. Ashley vividly recalled the time that he and his platoon had been separated from the company in the Battle of the Bulge. At that time, the platoon marched through the night in a blizzard to find the company. He decided this time to let the company find them. They never did. They were too busy enjoying the fruits of "their victory." This time the separation would last nearly a week.

"Lieutenant," Fisk said, "Do you see what I see up ahead? Look at that neat farmhouse near the river. There is a nice looking main house, a big barn, and other smaller buildings."

"Sure do. Think we ought to hold up there until we figure out what to do next?" Ashley asked, after having already made up his mind.

"Yep," Fisk responded, "I see only one problem. See that church steeple in the little town across the river. From there they can see every move we make."

"That's true, but in this flat river bed they could see us for a mile anyway with a pair of good field glasses. Let's risk it, Fisk, and hope they are as tired of the killing as we are."

The farmer's spread suited their needs perfectly—a hen house complete with fat chickens and large, brown eggs, an ample supply of pigs, and a lone milk-cow in need of milking. If that weren't enough there was a smoke house of several cured hams. Near by, the prosperous farmer had a well-stocked trout pond. He must have been caught by surprise or he would have taken some or all of his cured hams and eggs with him.

"Fisk, as Brigham Young would have said—'this is the place for our people.' Let's use the same type defensive set-up as you had back on the Roer, two squads in outposts near the river and one in reserve in the barn. Since O'Rourke is the good cook, let him have the barn. How does that sound?" Ashley asked.

"Outstanding, Lieutenant, I think we still have enough telephone wire to hook them up to our command post here in the main house. If not, we can 'borrow' some of the farmer's wire. Maybe the company will forget us for a while and we can take a break from the God damned war," Fisk said.

For a day or two, all was quiet on the platoon's river front property with the nice view. Spring was in full bloom as were the beautiful flowers in the *Frau's* flower garden. Then a major, Corps of Engineers, and his driver arrived in their jeep.

"Fisk, look out. I smell trouble," Ashley said.

"Yeah, we have learned that nice things don't last forever."

"Good morning, Major," Ashley said, saluting the field grade officer.

"Good morning, Lieutenant, how are things going up here?" The major inquired.

"Going good, Major," Ashley continued. "Hope you've got more good news for us. We don't know where our company is, and tell you the truth—we haven't missed them. How did you get over the dike without being shot at? They had a couple of 88 rounds with our names on them but missed when we scampered over it."

The major smiled. That was a good start, Ashley thought. "Major, would you and your driver like a glass of our host's beer?"

"Thanks, Lieutenant. That would be nice, and then I'll tell you why I'm here. Your platoon is located near Buester, which is just about in the middle of the division defensive zone. You have Wittenberge to your north and Seehausen to your south," the major explained, pointing to the area on his map.

"We don't have any idea where we are. I think the company outran the maps quite a way back," Ashley said keeping the conversation going.

"Well, anyway I'm going back, and recommend to the Big Brass that we cross the river right here in your area. It is the best spot I've seen so far. As I said, it is centrally located. Good soil, and the slopes up to the river and on the other side are perfect. The roads will support the traffic, too. The 5th Armored Division can put a pontoon bridge here in no time flat."

"Oh, shit!"

"What did you say, Lieutenant?"

"I was getting ready to say, too bad. You are going to open up a big range-war in our peaceful little valley, as they would say in Hollywood."

"Sorry, I gotta go. Thanks for the beer," the major said, as he and his driver drove southwest in a trail of dust at high noon.

"Fisk, we gotta prepare for a big artillery duel, right in the middle of our world. We have to dig in deeper. This time behind the buildings, away from the river, and out of sight of that church steeple in the town over there—where they are sure to have their artillery observers. The buildings will stop or slow down some of the shrapnel. Call the squad leaders in for a briefing."

It had been nearly a week since the platoon crossed the dike and set up camp in the German farmer's spread. All hands were beginning to enjoy a quiet break in the war. Being separated from the company had its advantages, not the least of which was no patrolling across the river and becoming the last KIA of the war. But all of this was about to change. The phone rang. Sergeant Fisk answered.

"Hey, Lieutenant. It's Muller on the line. He sounds nervous. He wants to talk to you."

"It must be bad news. It's three in the morning. Muller, what's up?" Ashley asked.

"Lieutenant, there's somebody coming from the direction of the river right toward us. I can hear them

thrashing around in the brush 25 yards from us."
Muller's heavy breathing and pounding of his rapid
pulse could be heard over the phone. His normally
clear, confident voice turned into a whisper.

"Halt! Who goes there?" one of his men yelled.

"Muller, I can hear some of the things that are
going on. Tell your men not to shoot until we can
figure out their intentions." Ashley ordered.

"Hold your fire," Muller screamed.

The "invaders" must have heard and understood enough of the command to hold their fire. There
was then a few minutes of silence. Then Muller came
back on line.

"Lieutenant, there are a couple of Kraut lieutenants down here and about 24 men with them. They
want to speak to you. One other thing, Lieutenant,"
Muller said.

"What's that?"

"You won't believe it, but one of the lieutenants
looks enough like you to be your brother. It's unbelievable."

"Now aren't you glad you didn't shoot them?
Don't answer that. Max and I are on the way. Stay
cool!" Ashley advised.

"Max, grab your M1 and let's go. Fisk, hold
down the fort. Maybe Max and I will bring you back
some company in a few minutes."

Max was a good, God fearing farm-boy from
the foothills of North Carolina. He had been Ashley's
platoon runner since the campaign began. He was a
natural combat soldier—strong, loyal, and innovative.
If anything broke, Max could fix it. He could even
butcher a pig and have it on the grill in less than two
hours.

When Ashley arrived on the scene, the German
lieutenants called their individual squads loudly to

attention, did a very military about-face, and rendered perfect Nazi salutes. It appeared to Ashley that they were beginning to stage a Lee-Grant type surrender ceremony. Fearing the noise could bring artillery from both sides, Ashley immediately put a halt to the formality.

"*Stille, Ruhe*—silence, quiet, *bitte*!" He yelled in his best command voice.

"*Warum sind sie hier? Was wollen sie?* Why are you here? What do you want?" Ashley asked in rapid-fire questions.

"Muller, have your men collect their weapons."

Ashley looked at both of the young officers. Neither was more than 19 years old. The soldiers under their command could have been their fathers. One of the lieutenants was a tall gangly looking kid with thin blond hair, parted in the middle and cut to hang loosely to the top of his ears. He wore wire oval-shaped, granny glasses. Ashley sized him up as a former Hitler *Jugend*—fanatical and dangerous. Then he turned to the other smaller, dark-haired German lieutenant. "My God," Ashley thought. Muller was right. Looking at this one was like looking into a mirror. It gave him a strange feeling. "What if in some way there was a family connection," he thought.

"*Setzen sie sich, bitte*, sit down, please," Ashley commanded.

"*Herr Leutnant*, I speak some English. I think I can answer the questions you've asked to your satisfaction." His look-alike's English was better than Ashley's German.

"OK, my first question is. We have the weapons of the other officer and the men. Where is yours?" Ashley asked.

"I threw it into the bush over there, when I heard your sergeant say, `Hold your fire.' " the German lieutenant replied.

"Get it for me, please."

"*Jawohl, Herr Leutnant!*" the young officer said, disappearing into the dark night for a few minutes, long enough for Ashley to realize that he had become careless. The German could have easily slipped back behind him in the dark and blown his brains out. After all, they outnumbered his men two to one, and they knew it. But as promised, the German lieutenant returned with a beautiful luger pistol. Rear echelon GIs would pay a fortune for it.

"*Bitte, Herr Leutnant,*" he said, handing Ashley his pistol.

"*Vielen dank,* thank you very much," Ashley responded, admiring his new treasure.

"*Herr Leutnant,* our situation is this. The other *Leutnant* and I graduated from Officer Candidate School in Prague this past December, and were immediately assigned to an Infantry division on the Russian front. We were winning the war. The Russians are nothing. They have nothing. But we ran out of supplies, no *benzin* (gasoline) for our trucks, for our tanks, or for our Luftwaffe. A few days ago as we were leaving Berlin to the west, the Russians were coming in from the east. They acted like wild animals, stealing or destroying everything in sight, and raping all the women who were crazy enough to have remained in the city. Most of them have never seen a flush toilet or ever owned a watch. So those were the reasons we came to the American lines. M*ein hauptmann,* my captain, sent us over here to arrange for the surrender of his command of about 200 men. He has only one request—that your men let us keep our watches. It is about the only personal thing that we have left. You are probably much more aware of that than we are, since you have probably seen more of our destroyed homes than we have so far. We have enough boats to bring them all over at once." the German said.

"*Ein moment, bitte*! I have no problem with you keeping your watches. But having all of your men come at once is too much. How many men can you put in a boat?"

"Seven."

"OK, tell your *hauptmann* to send only a boat of seven men every 30 minutes. That way, it will allow us time to make arrangements to receive you. It will be safer for both sides." Ashley suggested.

"*Herr Leutnant*, you look familiar to me. Have we met before?" the young German officer asked.

"I think not, but the same thing did occur to me," Ashley said, wishing he had more time to discuss the obvious, but he knew that this was neither the time or place for fraternization.

The *hauptmann* came with the next boat. By then it was daylight, as Ashley had planned and hoped it would be. The German commander was a pathetic, rumpled little old man of about 40 years. The poor fellow had been a professor at Heidelberg University. Military Science was not exactly his chosen profession.

Fisk had Max take the first group over the dike. Fisk told Max to turn them over to F Company. If he couldn't locate the company, he then told Max. "Say goodbye to the Krauts and tell them to go home." By mid-day, the entire company of 200 Germans was within or had passed through Second Platoon area. The company-rear personnel, having now discovered a new source of souvenirs, descended on the helpless Germans like vultures. Ashley was embarrassed that his agreement to let them keep their watches was ignored. He genuinely felt sorry for them. They had nothing left and nothing left to go home to.

On the afternoon of the 2nd of May, a patrol from G Company reported contact with the Russians at the Elbe. Berlin was no longer the objective. The Russians now owned the pile of rubble and the starving population.

The 8th of May 1945 was declared the official Victory-Europe (VE) Day. But there would be two V-E Days for most men: the official date and then the most important date—the date thcy returned home. For Ashley and his few classmates that were still on the battlefield, the most important date—going home would still be a long time coming.

PART SIX

THE SPOILS OF WAR

1945-1946

22

"Lieutenant Ashley, you got a visitor from company rear. It's that damned Hartman, the company runner," Fisk said, in a happier mood now that the war for Europe was over.

"Sir, Captain Tipper wants to see you right away. Somebody at division headquarters has been trying to get a hold of you," Hartman reported.

"God damn it, Hartman, the last time I saw you in the Bulge you were a corporal. Now you are a sergeant and I am still a second lieutenant," Ashley said, giving Hartman a welcome handshake.

"Well, Lieutenant, you told me when I last saw you in the Bulge that us ASTP soldiers were smart asses, maybe that's the reason," Hartman said with a smirk on his unshaven face.

"OK, you win. What the hell does division want with a worn-out, has been like me?"

"Don't know, Lieutenant," Hartman continued. "Maybe Captain Tipper has an answer for you."

"OK, let's go see him."

Captain Tipper was one of the first officers in the battalion to be sent home. He was selected for early redeployment based on earned rotation points. Points were awarded for such things as age, marital status, time in service, battle stars, decorations, etc. As a general rule enlisted men were rotated before their officers. It was a fair system.

When Ashley and Hartman arrived at F Company headquarters, they found the Captain packing his gear with the help of his company clerk. Captain

Tipper had to be at the port of embarkation at Le Havre, France within two days or miss the boat. At this point he had little time for small talk. It was obvious that he had done his share of celebrating his early selection for return home to his wife and a son he had never seen. His eyes were blood-shot and swollen and his face a purplish red.

"Hi, Ashley, good to see you," Tipper said hurriedly. "I'm on the way home. It's time to say goodbye and good luck. Major Buckley, your old stateside boss, is now the acting division G-5, whatever that is. He wants to see you ASAP."

"Good luck to you, Captain. Hope you find your family well. Being in F Company has been an experience I will never forget."

Despite his shortcomings, Ashley still liked the "Old Man." He knew he would miss him.

A company jeep and driver were standing by to take Ashley to division headquarters.

"Where to, Lieutenant?" the driver asked.

"Division G-5. Do you know where that is?" Ashley asked.

"Yes, Sir."

"Good. Then *macht schnell.* I am late already."

Ashley hadn't seen Major Buckley since landing at Greenock, Scotland on 2 October 1944. At that time, the major was the regimental S-4. It was now 1 July 1945. Ashley was curious as to what had happened in the meantime. How did the major suddenly become a G-5? That's big league stuff! He had worked directly for the major for a few weeks while at Camp Claiborne, Louisiana. They had gotten along well together. But no one told him that once in the field, his real boss would be the battalion commander. Serving two masters was more than a twenty-year old could handle. The ultimate result was that he served neither very well. After only a couple of days in the Siegfried Line, Ashley had asked the new battalion commander to send him to the front. This way he figured he would avoid the disgrace of being fired. In retrospect, he realized it was not the smartest thing to have done. He spent the whole war as a rifle platoon leader, first with E Company and finally with F Company. Major Buckley must have thought he was some kind of nut, which led him to wonder why the major would wanted to see him now. At this point Ashley knew he was lucky to be alive, and he really didn't give a Goddamn.

"Hello, Ashley, haven't seen you in a long time. Glad to see that you are still in one piece. Have a seat," Major Buckley said, motioning to a dirty, over-stuffed German chair.

"Nice quarters, Sir," Ashley acknowledged.

"They will do. I have a job for you that will allow you to find nice quarters for yourself and a select group from your platoon. They tell me you turned out to be one hell of a combat platoon leader. If you recall, Captain Gunner was the investigating officer in your straggler problem. He reported to me that you handled yourself very well under heavy enemy fire the day he went to the front to see you. He was particularly impressed with your refusal to press desertion charges against your two men involved. As a result, he recommends that the general court martial be dropped, thanks to you. Those two GIs of yours owe you a life-long debt of gratitude. They could have been shot for desertion."

"Well, Sir, I do recall Captain Gunner. He was the company commander of the regimental service company that I was assigned to while we were in garrison at Camp Claiborne. He was a stickler for rules as I remember. He reminded me once that I should

never turn in my carbine to the company armorer
with dust in the chamber. I was naive enough in
those days to believe that the company armorer was
paid to take care the weapons of the company officers, who were supposed to have bigger problems to
worry about.

"Now to tell you the truth about the straggler
situation, I didn't want someone at a trial to stand up
and say that I couldn't control `forty men and a medic.'
I wasn't being noble; I was just covering my ass. The
only thing that I feel good about is that more men in
my platoon survived the war than in any of the other
rifle platoons in a very strange company."

Ashley responded in a more self-confident manner than he had in previous encounters with his old
boss. He had made a commitment to himself that he
would do his best at whatever job he was given, but
there would be no more unquestioned—yes sir, no
sir obedience. His role as Pavlov's dog was over. After all, no one could now send him on any more suicide patrols. The war was over! His future plans
when discharged form the Army were simple—go back
to Charleston and finish his final year of college, and
make mad passionate love to Kit Montague.

"Good, now let's get down to business. I have
been told to set up some form of temporary civil government in our huge division rear area. Eventually,
specially trained personnel will arrive from the States
to relieve us of the responsibility. But in the meantime, we have the job. The division rear area will be
divided into four sectors, with a control team in each
sector. You will be in charge of team one. You will
function like an area commander, except you have
no command, other than your small team of four men.
You will be allowed to pick any three men from your
platoon. Your company commander has also been

told to let you have a jeep and trailer for the project. I will see to it that you get an interpreter. I know a GI at regiment named Weinstein who speaks Yiddish. I've heard you speak some German, so you should be all right. Now here is a map. I will let you take it with you. Your area is shown here. I suggest you find a nice house for your headquarters somewhere near the center of your area. But your location should take into account the location of American troop units, because you will have to make your own arrangements with them for logistical and operational support. You will have a written statement of your mission and support requirements signed by the division chief of staff, just in case unit commanders in your sector challenge your authority. I will also give you an approval stamp with an American eagle on it. You can use it to approve any reasonable, official civilian request for assistance. That is a lot of authority; be careful how you use it. With the judicious use of this seal of authority, German bureaucrats will do anything you tell them to do. I know, I've tried it. It works like a charm. They are trained to jump through their asses for anyone who acts like he's in charge. You now fit that mold, at least a lot more than you did as a nineteen-year old, when you came to work for me. You will report directly to me. How does that sound?" Major Buckley said, with smile on his large round face.

"Never better, Sir. It will give me a chance to live again. For all practical purposes, I have been a dead man for seven and a half months. One thing, Sir, I was twenty years old when I reported to you at Camp Claiborne, Louisiana."

"OK, nineteen, twenty—you still look like a kid. Now git going," Major Buckley said, waving Ashley toward the door.

Following Buckley's orders and armed with a letter of authority to do about anything, Ashley returned to F Company headquarters. He picked up his authorized company jeep and trailer and moved on to his platoon. He briefed Sergeant Fisk and the three men he decided to take with him on his first of many post-war adventures. He would like to have had Fisk with him, but someone had to be in charge for the indefinite period of time that they would be absent. He choose squad leaders Muller and O'Rourke—Muller, the fighter in case they ran into trouble; O'Rourke, the wise, educated elder statesman and good cook; and Max, the platoon runner, his trusted jack of all trades.

The now mobile entourage stopped at regimental headquarters to pick up Weinstein, the designated interpreter. Since all seats were now taken in the Jeep, Weinstein had to take a seat in the trailer with the luggage. He didn't seem to care. He said that he was looking forward to a respite from his typewriter.

"O'Rourke, take a look at the map and pick a town in the center of our area of responsibility," Ashley said, happily looking forward to what could be a most enjoyable change of pace.

"Roger."

"OK, Max, you are the driver. O'Rourke is the navigator, Muller, Weinstein, and I are observers," Ashley said giving instructions to his new team.

O'Rourke's selection of a team headquarters-house was excellent. It was generally in the center of the area of responsibility and reasonably close to the division logistical and administrative units. The town had been off the main route of advance and had escaped the ravages of war. The team "command post" was one of the best houses in the area, one of the few that were not already occupied by senior officers and their staffs. Now it was time to tell the owner that it was time for him to leave.

"*Mien Herr, sprechen sie Englisch?*" Ashley asked.

"*Jawhol Herr Leutnant, ein bisschen,*" the homeowner said.

"Good, then you will be able to understand some of what I have to say. We are taking over your home for a while. I have to ask you to leave in a couple of hours. You will be allowed to take your personal things with you. Any questions?" Ashley asked.

"*Leutnant*, why my house? I am no Nazi. I am a Catholic! My neighbor over there (he points) is a gross Nazi. He lives in a finer house. You would like it much better than mine," the disturbed German pleaded.

It would be an understatement to say the response was not well received by the team commander.

"Weinstein, I want you to tell this son of bitch in your Long Island German that I don't care if he is a first cousin of the Pope. Also tell him I am sorry that his Propaganda Minister Goebbels and Gestapo Chief Himmler have made him and the German people a nation of informers. I want his sorry ass out of here in one hour."

"I got it, Lieutenant. I'll take over gladly," Weinstein said. And he did, with appropriate hand and arm signals.

The situation improved considerably after moving into the nice house. The jeep trailer load of combat K and C rations made excellent trading material for local fresh bread, vegetables, ham, and eggs. O'Rourke's cooking continued to improve. A middle-aged German woman, fluent in English and the proud owner of a typewriter, volunteered to serve as secretary for the operation. Hilda, as she was called, typed the daily activities report for submission to Major Buckley. She was willing to work for O'Rourke's leftovers, and even cooked a few potato-heavy meals for the team.

The next addition to the enterprising group was a French soldier and temporary owner of an American two and a half ton truck painted in French colors and unit markings. He called himself Pierre Cline. His origin and mission were not exactly clear. He gave Ashley the name of some French unit that meant nothing to him. The name Cline didn't sound particularly French either, but he seemed pleasant enough. He was good looking guy with sleepy looking eyes that caused young frauleins to point at him, giggle, and say—"*bett zimmer augen*," bed room eyes. He had some tangible assets too: He spoke French, of course, some German and English, and, equally important, he had transportation. He would do. Ashley hired him on the spot. When team one took to the road in a two-vehicle convoy, they looked like "Cox's Army."

By most standards, the civil government operation could have been called a "boondoggle." But there were times when the strange looking group brought order out of chaos. Displaced persons (DPs), mostly from Russia and Poland, often left their American camps for disruptive adventures into the outside world. It was difficult to stop them from having fun. They had been under the iron boot of the Gestapo for a long time. But when they frequently broke into German army storage areas—and stole food and clothing earmarked for other, higher priority requirements—that was another matter. To fix the problem, Ashley's team called on the nearest American unit for help in guarding the storage sites. On one occasion ten DPs broke into a German hospital and drank rubbing alcohol. By the time team one arrived on the scene, four of the poor devils were dead and six unconscious. The team located a German doctor who quickly treated and revived the unconscious group.

The authority stamp proved to be useful in the control of Germans moving in and out of team one's area of responsibility. Ashley began to enjoy the job of being governor of the land. He seldom refused to allow movement of the civilians in and out of his area who were in search of lost family members, particularly if they were pretty frauleins.

Pierre, after a week with the group, requested a pass to his beloved Paris. Ashley obliged. Hilda, the team secretary, typed an official looking document which Ashley properly signed and stamped with the American eagle that Major Buckley had given him. Pierre promised to return within a few days with presents for all. The team wished him farewell, but never really expected to ever see him again.

"It is too bad to lose him. He has been helpful and entertaining," Ashley said, as he waved goodbye to a grinning Pierre, speeding off into the sunset. Mourning the loss of Pierre was premature. Five days later he returned.

"Lieutenant, I have returned and I have zee presents," Pierre proudly announced.

"By golly, Pierre, you did return," Ashley said. I was afraid you had left us for a beautiful *mademoiselle* in Gay Paree."

"Lieutenant, of course I come back. I brought back enough good cognac and wine for all of us to stay drunk for a week," Pierre said with a big grin on his handsome face.

"Great, Pierre, let's all have a drink to celebrate your return," Ashley suggested.

"*Bon*, I give a toast. *Vive La France! Vive La Amerique!*" Pierre said.

"Pierre, we can now say, 'General Lafayette, Americans have returned again and are now having a ball,' " O'Rourke added, as he sipped a decent cognac.

Sergeant Muller and Max had the job of delivering the daily activities reports to Major Buckley's staff at division headquarters. Normally, the report would be returned with the major's initial with an OK or good indicating that he had seen the report. But this time when Muller and Max returned in the middle of the party, they brought a more definitive note from the major:

"Lieutenant Ashley, military government specialists have arrived. They will be taking over our mission. Thank your men for me for doing a great job. Have them return to their units. I have written letters of commendation that will be forwarded through command channels to them. Please report to me here at my division office at 1000 hours in the morning." signed: Buckley, Major, AUS, G-5.

Ashley read the directive to his team, added his compliments to the major's kind words, and said his goodbyes. The next morning he reported to Major Buckley as instructed.

"Sir, Lieutenant Ashley reporting as ordered," Ashley said, rendering the customary salute from a position of attention.

"Sit down, Brett," the major responded, calling Ashley by his first name for the first time. "Say, you and your number one team did a heck of good job. You were out on your own with little help from this headquarters. I called you in because there are some things I wanted to tell you personally. The situation around here is changing pretty fast. Now, don't say anything about this. I've been told I am going to get a new job soon, a good one, and I am going to get my boys back together again. If things work out, I want you to come back on board and work for me again. How does that sound?" Major Buckley asked.

"Sounds great, Sir," Ashley said. "I could use a change. My company commanders have not been the nicest guys in the world to work for."

"Good, you will be hearing from me. By the way, your new company commander will not be much of an improvement. That is one of the reasons I have for moving you out. You have earned a break. OK, now go back to F Company! Hang in there, and this time, stay out of trouble. By the way, where did you find that Frenchman you had on your team?"

"Major, you won't believe it. He just wandered in and we took him in like you would a stray cat. He helped us out a lot. Oh, I almost forgot. Here is a fine bottle of cognac and a good bottle of wine with Pierre's best wishes. I am on my way, Sir," Ashley said, giving his old boss a goodbye salute.

23

As the war came to end, shifting of units between American, British, French, and Russian occupation zones was commonplace among the Allied Armies. The 84th Division had to be moved from the Elbe River out of the newly designated British zone to the American zone in the south. The small town of Weinheim was selected for the location of the division headquarters. Its short distance to the historic city of Heidelberg on the Neckar River was no doubt a factor its selection. The Second Battalion and its units were deployed nearby in the small villages of Ladenburg, Ilvesheim, and Heddesheim. Here they performed typical occupational functions—security, maintenance of law and order, and training. Until the war with Japan ended on 15 August 1945, the intensity and scope of training was in keeping with the anticipated redeployment of the division to the Pacific Theater of Operations.

The transition from wartime to an occupation army was not without some awkward situations. Battalion units, on orders from higher command, conducted a Nazi-type witch-hunt of every home in their assigned occupation area. Not a single suitcase or bureau was left unopened. Some GI equipment and propaganda material was discovered, but nothing of any significance.

Even though the war in Europe was over, occupation soldiers stood guard with live ammunition. Drunken soldiers, coming in late at night from local bars, were at greater risk of being shot by their own guards than by die-hard Nazi soldiers and civilians, who usually stayed home at night.

Fraternization with the local population was strictly forbidden, a rule difficult to enforce and generally ignored. American soldiers were not accustomed to seeing hungry kids crawling in garbage cans in search of food for themselves and their families. The soldiers naturally shared their food and candy with the hungry in spite of non-fraternization regulations. It was not surprising to find the locals tearfully waving goodbyes to men in units that were moved from place to place or back home for demobilization.

Lieutenant Cook took over command of F Company on the departure of Captain Tipper. Cook was Ashley's fourth rifle company commander since the Siegfried Line Campaign, the first of three campaigns. Cook, a senior first lieutenant, was with the battalion Heavy Weapons Company during the entire combat period. As a result, he failed to understand or appreciate the stubbornness and arrogance of line-company riflemen. Right from the beginning, it was an incompatible relationship between the commander and the commanded.

Cook was a very bright and intelligent officer, but he was not without personal problems. He was an excellent bridge player, but, because of his low tolerance for cheap German cognac, he seldom won.

He was also a strong advocate of non-fraternization when sober but a fraternizer when drunk. But his undoing, his real Achilles heel, was his irresistible attraction to a beautiful fraulein with large breasts and dark, seductive eyes who lived down the street from his quarters. She knowingly contributed to his problem by provocatively peeping out of the second story window of her home, as Cook and his troops marched out to drill. If the F Company had not moved from Ilvesheim to nearby Landenburg, the comely fraulein could have gotten the poor commander into serious trouble.

Travel and sports were the major recreational activities of the occupation forces. The 84th Division excelled in football, track, and swimming. It was particularly enjoyable for Ashley to see a football game when one of his classmates in his division competed with another classmate in the 100th Division, "The Sons of Bitch," as they were called for their heroics at a German town called Bitch.

But one of the most enjoyable and enlightening events of the time for Ashley and his friends was a trip to Berlin to see the 84th Division play football against the elite 82nd Airborne Division in the famous Olympic Stadium. It was in 1936 in this stadium with a capacity of over 100,000 that the black Jesse Owens won the 100 and 200-meter races. It created an embarrassing moment for Hitler, who was there to demonstrate to the world the superiority of the German race. The 82nd Airborne was also embarrassed. They lost the game by a score of 23 to 13.

Most soldiers had heard of the potential for making a dollar or two in the black-market trade with the Russians in Berlin. But what they didn't know, and even the battle hardened veterans were surprised to see, was the disreputable condition, the low morale, and the complete lack of discipline of the remnants of the once great Russian Army.

The Russian soldiers and junior officers had none of the basic American necessities—toilet articles, razors, razor blades, soap, watches, or even a change of underwear. Gonorrhea had reached epidemic proportions within the army and civilian population. There was an urgent requirement for penicillin. Little or none was available. The German whores were able to do what the German Army was unable to do in the defense of Berlin—cripple the Russian Army.

Russians routinely met Americans in the *Tiergarten*, the famous Berlin Zoo just off the *Unter Den Linden Strasse*, to buy anything the GIs had to sell. Russian soldiers came by the hundreds with pockets full of MPCs, military payment certificates (MPCs)—the same currency that GIs were paid with. It was if every Russian had been issued a money making machine. Ashley sold a loudly ticking, jewelless watch, a pistol, a carton of cigarettes, a dozen condoms, and a bottle of cheap cognac for over $1000 within an hour.

The Russians were a rumpled looking bunch who paid little or no attention to officers below the rank of colonel. A crowd gathered around an incident near the zoo center, where a Russian colonel had just shot his driver with an unforgiving American 45 caliber pistol. When asked why he killed his driver, he replied—"He raped a German woman."

"You shot your own soldier, your own driver, without a trial. Isn't that penalty a little too severe for rape?" an observer asked.

"No! It is not too severe. I didn't shoot him for rape of a German. I shot him for bringing disgrace upon the victorious Russian Army in the eyes of the Americans," the colonel replied.

Ashley left Berlin to return to his unit a little richer and a little wiser, but with much to think about. He realized he dwelt too much on the war. He had to continually remind himself that it was over—*fini!* But it wasn't easy. He recalled the comments of the young German lieutenant he had captured on the Elbe: "The Russians are nothing; they have nothing; we were winning, but we ran out of gas." The German had a point; the once proud Russian fighting force had become an uncivilized rabble of an army.

The sun began to set as Ashley's truck passed the city of Kassel, which, like Hannover, had been shelled and bombed back to the Stone Age. The sunset gave the bricks and stones a reddish tinge. It was a disquieting scene. Nothing seemed to be alive. It was as if the gates to hell had been closed and were now sealed forever.

Only a Mongol with the mentality of Genghis Khan would have enjoyed the landscape. It was Khan who said: "Man's greatest good fortune is to chase and defeat the enemy, seize his total possessions, leave his married women weeping and wailing, ride his gelding, and use the bodies of his women as a nightshirt and support."

At F Company it was the last Wednesday in August 1945. The location was Ilvesheim, Germany. If a visitor missed the road to the town, he could still find the town by following his nose. The farmers were spraying "honey bucket" collections from the town toilets on the fields, in preparation for the late planting season.

As usual, the company training schedule showed athletics, a cover meaning—take a little time off, unless you have guard duty; you have earned it. The company officers had just received their liquor ration and were gathered in the bachelor officers' quarters for the usual Wednesday afternoon bridge game. The exercise that followed, although enjoyable, was not particularly healthy. The rules of the game called for the losers of a set to pour the winners a drink from their private bottle of bourbon or scotch— winner's choice. Unfortunately, after a half dozen rubbers, there was seldom a sober player in the group.

Ashley's fortune began a turn for the better. He would see the sun rise in the morning without a headache. The company clerk interrupted the game before the first set was finished advising him to report to the battalion commander immediately.

"Ashley, you are running out on us. I had my eye on your whole bottle of Johnny Walker. Lieutenant Randolph, take the chicken-shit's place."

"Sir, I'm on my way to the Ladenburg headquarters. I may still be back in time to kick ass," Ashley said on the way out, hoping his new company commander didn't take his loose comments personally.

Not wanting to tie up a driver, Ashley drove the jeep himself. Landenburg was a larger and prettier town than Ilvesheim, a drab little village with few if any socially redeeming features. On arriving in Ladenburg, Ashley made his way to the former home of Carl Benz, founder of the Mercedes Benz automobile company. The Benz House was the finest and largest in the town. It was no wonder the battalion commander had appropriated it for his headquarters.

"The commanding officer told me to show you into his office when you arrived, Lieutenant," a polite battalion clerk greeted him.

Ashley was surprised to see Major Buckley sitting behind Carl Benz's fine antique desk. He just didn't seem to fit the picture. The position of battalion commander was a highly sought-after job of upwardly mobile, Regular Army officers. The major didn't fall into either of these categories. He was the fifth officer to command the battalion, but the first National Guard officer. It was a little irregular, particularly since the major had little formal civilian or military schooling.

But Major Buckley was a highly intelligent, versatile, and cunning individual. He was a survivor. After all, he had been the regimental S-4 under the eccentric, unpredictable Colonel Meddler, who had been relieved of his command for cause after only a couple of months in combat. Not only had the major survived with flying colors while working for Meddler, he also impressed the division commander for whom he had just finished an assignment as the division assistant G-5. Under the circumstances, he was the right man for the job. He had earned the right to sit behind the former desk of one the world's renowned industrialists.

"Ashley, we meet again," Buckley said, with his hand extended and big smile on his face. "Shut the door and have a seat. You are the new battalion S-4. When can you start?"

"Sir, you caught me a little off guard, I promised the father of my college roommate that I would try to locate his son's grave, take pictures of his burial site, and send them to him. Cal Sinclair was a great B-17 pilot. Only God knows why he 'bought the farm' sometime after the infamous Dresden raid. Through contact with another classmate in Graves Registration, Seventh Army, I have found out that he is buried at the American cemetery near Luxembourg. Major Buckley, he was a highly decorated pilot, he was among America's best and brightest. But more importantly, he was the best friend I ever had, Sir. I have to do this for him, his father and mother, whom I have known for a number of years, and also for myself."

"OK, Brett, your plea is persuasive. I will have you transferred immediately to my office. Take the S-4 jeep. It's probably the same one you had at Omaha Beach. Go to Luxembourg. Do your thing. Keep me informed. When you are through, your desk is around the corner waiting for you. You will find a room already reserved for you in the BOQ across the street on the corner."

"My God, Sir, I will never forget the favor," reaching out to shake the major's hand. (And Ashley didn't forget his friend. Many years later he stood by the grave of his old boss when he was interred at the Arlington National Cemetery).

"By the way, you are out of uniform," the major said in serious tone.

"Out of uniform?" Ashley asked, taken again by surprise.

"Here's a set of sterling silver bars, First Lieutenant, put them on. They were slow coming, but you earned them the hard way. They were mine. I saved them for a son I didn't have. So now, you got 'em," the major said.

"First Lieutenant! The Germans will call me *Herr Ober Leutnant*; I like the sound of that. Thanks again, Sir." Ashley said, with broad smile on his face. He saluted and was gone.

Ashley went back to F Company for the last time as a member of the company. He asked Lieutenant Cook, the company commander, for a favor— hopefully the last. After telling him the news of his transfer to battalion headquarters, he requested the service of Max, the runner from his now old platoon. To Ashley's surprise, Cook agreed without a hassle.

"First Sergeant, get a hold of Max from Second Platoon and have him report to the new battalion S-4," Cook ordered.

"Yes, Sir," the sergeant responded in a clipped military voice.

"Thanks, Lieutenant, I appreciate it," Ashley said.

"No sweat. You and Max have a good trip. I'm on the way to inspect the platoons. I'll see you when you get back," Cook replied.

"Hi, Max, I've got another good deal for you. You are going to drive me to Luxembourg," Ashley said.

"Luxembourg, where's that?" Max asked, taken aback at the sudden and unusual requirement.

Ashley gave Max the general plan, then the specifics: "We should leave after a good breakfast in the morning. Take my jeep, the S-4 jeep, to the motor pool; fill the gas tank and the extra can and make sure it is ready for a long trip. Pick up a couple of sleeping bags from the F Company supply sergeant and a couple of extra canteens of drinkable water. I'll get my S-4 clerk to get us some combat rations. I will also bring a couple of cartons of cigarettes and a bottle of bourbon so that, if needed, we will be able to win friends and influence people. Meet me at 0800 in the morning at my new home, the BOQ across the street from the Benz House. Please make sure I have my camera and film with me before we leave. Other than the sadness of this mission, I think we will enjoy getting away from this place again. Max, does what I said make sense? Have I overlooked anything that you can think of?" Ashley asked.

"Sir, two questions: Do you have a map? And how long did you say we would be gone?"

"I've got a map, but I don't know how good it is. We will have to watch the road signs, and check with the locals occasionally to keep from getting lost. We should be gone about four or five days," Ashley replied.

"OK, Sir, I'll be ready," Max said, and left to take care of the assigned chores.

Ashley knew he had chosen the right man to go with him. The Carolina farm boy had been at his side for the final drive from the Roer to the Elbe. He was always there when needed. His stocky body and short legs kept him a few yards behind the forward skirmish line in the attack, but he always managed to catch up. He had been Ashley's bodyguard, his helper, his runner, radio operator, and general handyman. The jeep would take them and bring them back, because Max would keep it running. Max was not much of a talker either. That in itself was an asset. It would provide both of them a time to enjoy what little beauty the war had left behind, and a time for reflection on the past and dream of the future.

There was a fall chill in the air, but a bright warm sun when Max and Ashley left the small village of Ladenberg in search of an American cemetery in a foreign land.

"Max, I looked at the map last night. I think what we will do is to follow the back roads along the Neckar River to Mannheim, cross the Rhine there and maybe pick up the autobahn west to Kaiserslautern. About 20 miles from Kaiserslautern we will turn northwest toward the Moselle River and Trier, the oldest German city. By that time, it will probably be dark and we will stop for the night. If we can't find a place to stay, we've got our sleeping bags. Who knows we might find a farmer's daughter who may think you are cute and put us up in his barn. OK?"

"Sounds good, Lieutenant. You navigate and I will drive in the direction you point me. I checked out the Jeep down at the battalion motor pool. It looks like it is in pretty good shape," Max said.

The scenery along the route was pretty much the same off of the main highways—small winding, blacktop roads framed with tall poplar trees connecting one small village after another. The old people, the war relics, walked slowly about with heads down as though in a daze. But the kids, like hungry kids anywhere, smiled, waved, and beckoned: "Chocolate?

Chewing gum?" After about an hour on the back roads, the travelers reached the point where the canal-like Neckar joined the mighty Rhine, which was not nearly as mighty or as romantic as poets and historians had written. Here they entered the sprawling, dirty, industrial city of Mannheim. It was a city that most enlightened tourists would avoid. But here they crossed the Rhine and picked up the autobahn, a four lane, first rate highway, the equal of any American interstate connector. These well designed roads were one of Hitler's few lasting legacies.

They passed Kaserslautern at noon. It was just another turnoff along the autobahn. There was no reason to stop. Like Mannheim, it had few if any interesting landmarks. Near the turnoff there was a rest stop with an inviting table and benches. Here the travelers stopped for a K-ration lunch of pressed ham and cheese crackers, not bad for combat food.

There was still an hour of sun left in the autumn sky when Ashley and Max reached their first stop, Trier, on the winding Mosselle River. As they passed through the Porta Nigra, the black gate, which dated back to the Second Century, they knew they had discovered a special town. Trier, a river valley port over 2000 years old, had been the northern headquarters of the Roman emperors. The city was a fascinating tourist haven—complete with Roman landmarks, ancient churches, and museums. Not the least in importance, Trier was the center of Germany's wine country. Ashley and Max at times had to remind themselves that their destination was Luxembourg, and their purpose was to find the grave of Lieutenant Calvin Sinclair, Jr.

"Max, are you tired?" Ashley asked.

"A little bit. How about you, Lieutenant?"

"Yeah, I think it's time to stop, find a place to

stay, and maybe get something to eat."

Max found a temporary parking spot for the jeep, but not the final, secure parking place. After wandering around for a few minutes, they found the Central Hotel, near the Porta Nigra. It was a small hotel with about 30 rooms, some with baths, and a restaurant that was being restored. The proprietor was not overly enthusiastic about renting two rooms, particularly ones with baths. But on learning that his potential guests were willing to pay their bill in military payment certificates and cigarettes, he reluctantly agreed. The restaurant was not yet open for an evening meal. After settling into their rooms, Ashley offered his host a drink of his prize Kentucky Bourbon. He accepted of course, and then suddenly remembered that there was a ratskeller on the main square that served only special guests. After another glass of bourbon, the proprietor wrote a note of introduction that guaranteed their entry into the beautifully arched cellar of a landmark fifteenth-century building.

The maitre d' was willing to accept MPCs as a favor to his friend who had sent them. On tipping the maitre d' up-front with two packs of Camels, he suggested that his newly found friends should have a Hungarian goulash soup, a wiener schnitzel with red cabbage, potatoes, and Bavarian chocolate cake for dessert, all embellished with a bottle of fine local wine.

"Lieutenant, we hit the jackpot, son of a gun. This food is great. We don't have anything like this in Andrews, North Carolina. We eat a lot of barbecue. It's good, but not this good," Max said, with a broad smile.

"Max, since you are a Bible-belt Baptist, I assume you won't be drinking your share of the Moselle. I'll be happy to finish it for you," Ashley suggested.

"Well, Lieutenant, the good Lord might forgive me of a small sin, since this Kraut's water might make me sick."

"I think you are right, Max. If I were the Lord or even the head of your church, I think I would give you a little slack. After all, as victors we are supposed to enjoy the spoils of war. Let's pay these guys the amount of the check in GI money and throw in two more packs of cigarettes for good measure. This one is on me. I owe you from way back, Max. You know that. Then we had better get back to the hotel and rest-up for the tough trip tomorrow. By the way, what about the jeep? Major Buckley would never forgive me if we let some bum steal it," Ashley reminded Max.

"No sweat, Lieutenant, when you were talking with the hotel manager about reservations, I found an off-street parking spot right behind the hotel. Then I removed the rotor from the distributor, so nobody could start it."

"Outstanding, Max, let's call it a day."

They had made a friend of the hotel owner. The next morning after they finished a warm, unaccustomed bath, a continental breakfast of black-market American coffee and rich farmer's bread with butter and jam was waiting for them. And if that were not enough, they were given a genuine farewell and an invitation to return: *"Auf wiedersehen. Haben eine gute reise. Bitte, kommt weider."*

The warmth of the morning sun continued to raise their spirits as they left the old Roman city and resumed their mission.

"Lieutenant, you sure know how to get along with these Krauts," Max said, as he headed the jeep out of the parking lot toward the Moselle River.

"Max, with enough cigarettes and booze nobody

will remember the war. OK, let's follow the Moselle on the eastern side for about an hour. Then we should see a sign that directs us across the river towards Luxembourg," Ashley answered.

"I got it, Lieutenant," Max tuned in. "What a great day to be taking a trip. The color of the trees along the river is beautiful, a lot of yellow poplars, but I don't see any deep-red maples like we have in the mountains of North Carolina this time of the year."

A long period of silence followed their initial chatter, as both men enjoyed the surroundings along the river's edge and contemplated what the day would bring. The cutoff point was pretty much in line with Ashley's estimate. They now turned to the west across the river. Road signs reminded them that Luxembourg, the little country's capital city, was next.

Germany, France, and Belgium surround Luxembourg, one of Europe's smallest countries. As such, the little country could not escape the European wars even if it tried. German forces occupied it during WWI, but the Treaty of Versailles restored its independence. It was then occupied by the Germans in WWII, liberated by American forces early in the war, but overrun again by the Germans in their final and desperate effort to win the war. Hitler's misadventure failed in the Luxembourg-Belgian Ardennes in a fight to the finish called the "Battle of the Bulge." There was severe damage in the area around Bastogne, but most of the country fared well when compared to France and Germany.

"Max, it is about noon. Let's look for a *pension*, a good spot for a bed and breakfast, for tonight," Ashley said. "We had our big fling last night in Trier. Once we get settled in, we will begin our search for the American cemetery near here—after all, that's why we are here. I have got to find the grave of my friend

Calvin Sinclair, and take some pictures for his parents.

Luxembourgers were a friendly people and appreciative of the sacrifices that Americans had made to secure their freedom once more. Max and Ashley found suitable accommodations with a local family without a problem. The host family furnished them directions to the American cemetery in the village of Hamm, three miles outside Luxembourg City.

In a few minutes, after leaving the center of Luxembourg, the travelers from Ladenburg found themselves in the cemetery chapel. They read the inscription on the outer wall of the chapel in silence:

"1941-1945. In proud remembrance of the achievements of her sons and in humble tribute to their sacrifices, this memorial has been erected by the United States of America."

The two turned from the chapel to gaze in astonishment at the sight of a slight hill with more than 5000 simple, dignified crosses and stars of David lined row after row.

"My God, Max, we will never forget this sight. It is beautiful but frightening. It is unreal! You know, this is just one of several American burial grounds like this in Europe. At Flanders, Belgium to the north of us, a poet wrote of the WWI cemetery: 'In Flanders field the poppies blow between the crosses, row on row.' Take a look around to see if you can find Sinclair's grave. I will begin taking some photographs. Signal me if you find anything. I will stop by the caretakers office to see if he has a locator."

The caretaker gave Ashley a drawing showing him the area where his college roommate and other classmates that he knew were buried. Without much delay, he found Sinclair's grave. He hoped the photograph would give his parents some relief. It was unbelievable but there it was:

Calvin Lewis Sinclair, Jr.
First Lieutenant, US Army Air Corps
California, 1945

Ashley motioned to Max. They both knelt in silent prayer. Ashley took a rumpled paper from his wallet containing a poem that he and Cal treasured. "Max, if my best friend were to speak now he would say to us:

'Do not stand at my grave and weep,
I am not there, I do not sleep,
I am a thousand winds that blow,
I am the diamond glints on snow,
I am the sunlight on ripened grain,
I am the gentle autumn's rain.
Do not stand at my grave and cry,
I am not there, I did not die.' "

With that Ashley and Max left Cal's grave and walked around the entire cemetery. In a wooded area beyond the pristine American gravesites, they discovered much to their amazement a smaller German Army cemetery. The Germans were buried by units in mass graves, under depressing gray stone markers. Stunned German visitors wandered about, as others stood staring vacantly at the graves.

"Max, I have had enough. Nobody wins in a God damned war. And no one knows it better than the Americans and Germans buried here. Let's return to Luxembourg. I have had enough of this for quite a while."

"I'm with you Lieutenant. We are out of here."
Neither looked back.

24

Ashley had planned to return through Belgium to see the spot along the La Roche-St. Vith highway that his platoon reached on 6 January 1945, cutting off the German supply and escape routes. Afterwards, he planned to visit Flanders cemetery in Belgium, and continue northward to Geleen, Holland. In Geleen he hoped to locate the family there who had graciously taken him into their home for a night and shared their meager food with him. He remembered telling the family in early November of '44 that the war would be over by Christmas. So much for the military expertise of a new lieutenant. For a brief moment, he relived one of his few happy experiences of the war.

By Ashley's calculations the trip would take him and Max more than a hundred miles out of the way—too long! That would be something special for another day. Maybe he and Kit Montague would come back together someday. That was a comforting thought. But all thoughts of his girl friend were comforting thoughts. He was also aware of the requirement to get back to work for Major Buckley as his new battalion S-4.

But first things first, he had an obligation to send the grave photographs of his college roommate to his family. What would he say to them? What could you say to a family who had lost a son? One thing he couldn't tell were some of the comments of another classmate in graves registration: "It was easy to identify Cal Sinclair's body. He wore the correct flight uniform and had his dog tags. That was not always the case. Some of these 'fly boys' were dressed in pinks and greens, wore dress shoes, and had no identification. My guys at times were so frustrated in trying to identify them that they shook their bodies and yelled, 'Why didn't you wear your dog tags?' "

Ashley eventually decided on what he would say in the letter to the Sinclair family. He also planned to send a copy of the letter to Kit Montague:

Dear Mr. and Mrs. Sinclair,

A friend of Cal's and mine was assigned to a grave registration unit after the war ended. He told me that he had personally identified Cal's body, and where he was buried. I have just returned from a visit to Cal's grave. He is buried in the American cemetery located about three miles from Luxembourg City in the small village of Hamm.

It is a beautiful area with more than 5000 graves. It was a moving and heart wrenching experience to see the neat white crosses lined up row after row as far as the eye could see. I walked the area for several hours and discovered the graves of other classmates of ours buried there. Before leaving, my driver and I knelt at Cal's grave and said a silent prayer for the best friend I ever had. Photographs of the scene are enclosed.

Kit Montague and I look forward to a visit with you all when I return home.

God bless you always.

Sincerely,

Brett

Ashley's job as the battalion supply officer became routine and even boring. The enlisted specialists in his office were able to do most of the work themselves. This left him with little to do except attend staff meetings and run errands for the battalion commander. It was *deja vu*—he was a gofer again, but this time in a much friendlier, carefree environment. There were plenty of recreational activities other than bridge, booze, and frauleins. Special service tours into Bavaria and Switzerland were frequent and cheap. He took advantage of them all. As a Southerner from the Carolina Low Country, he was overwhelmed by the beauty of the snow-capped Alps, Hitler's hideout at Berchtesgaden, Oberammergau, Garmisch Partenkirchen, and the Zugspitze, a mountain among mountains. Switzerland was an unmolested, dollhouse of a country. On first entering the little country of yodelers and cuckoo clocks, the tour guide would announce: "Gentlemen, we are now entering beautiful Switzerland, the land of milk and honey—and I don't mean the kind that comes from bees."

For a long while, Ashley managed to follow his commander's advice: "Stay out of trouble." But that was before "Fasching", the German Mardi Gras.

Lieutenant William (Wild Bill) Randolph and Ashley had a number of things in common. They both were F Company platoon leaders, both had attended military colleges before being called up, and both had early Virginia roots. They liked each other.

"Brett, I've got chance for you to lighten up and have a little fun. It's Fasching time," Randolph said, needling his friend.

"I'm already having fun. I got the hell out of that 'snake-bit' outfit you are still in. That company is bad news. You know it. I looked around at the platoon officers at the last bridge game, and realized that I was only one who had a commission when we landed at Omaha Beach. The rest of you guys came in as replacements or, like you, received a battlefield commission. So, Wild Bill, what have you got to offer this time to erase my bad memories?" Ashley said, lecturing his younger friend.

"Pretty frauliens," the smiling Randolph said, knowing that would get his friend's attention.

"Give me a break. There is a division regulation that says`no fraternizing, and no Fasching parties with Germans,' " Ashley said.

"This one's different. There is a way to go and not get caught. These beautiful girls told me that they will put us in costumes that they made themselves and no one will be able to identify us as GIs. We will go as chimney sweeps," Randolph said. What do you think?"

"Well, the risk of being caught does make it exciting. There's been little or no excitement lately. OK, but remember if the MP's come in, I never saw you. I'm out of there. I promised Major Buckley I'd stay out of trouble for a change," Ashley said, acquiescing to his friend's ridiculous plan.

Randolph was right on part of his story, the frauleins were beautiful, but the costumes were weird—dirty, black, untouchable things. Ashley's disguise was the more convincing. It came with a wig. However, even the dumbest MP could spot Randolph's short haircut. But he didn't seem to care. The "um pa pa" polka music was deafening and the beer never ceased flowing. Ashley was doing an awkward polka with his date when he saw a cocky, little MP corporal approaching their table.

"Lieutenant, I think I recognize you. Aren't you Lieutenant Randolph from F Company?" the MP asked.

"Yeah, what's your problem?" Randolph responded, upset that his caper had suddenly come to an end.

"Major Buckley, your battalion commander, is

standing over there by the door. He wants to see you, like right now. Come with me please," the MP said knowing full well he was holding all the cards.

"Lieutenant, did you think you could get by in that lousy costume?" the major said, finding it difficult to keep a straight face.

"Sir, my companion here made my suit. She convinced me I could pass as a German. Looks like she was wrong—sorry," Randolph said.

"Poor judgment, Randolph, poor judgment, even though you do have good taste in frauliens. You are confined to your quarters for one week beginning right now. Did I make myself clear about no fraternization this time?" the major growled.

"Yes Sir, sorry, Sir," Randolph responded from the position of attention.

"Who was that other slob at your table?" the major asked.

"Major, he *ist a 'cherman friend aus mir'*," Randolph's girl friend fortunately answered for him in her best broken English.

Ashley and his date found refuge in the boisterous crowd and made a hasty, fortuitous exit.

Shortly after the Fasching celebration, the division redeployed. Major Buckley never mentioned the events of the infamous evening to Ashley, leaving him wondering if Buckley really knew who the dirty, unidentified chimney sweep was. He said goodbye to the major, as the major joined the division old timers and fillers from other units going aboard their homeward bound ship. Ashley knew they someday they would meet again, and he would then ask him— "Did you give me an undeserved break again?"

The low-point military personnel remained in Germany in a variety of eclectic jobs. Ashley's next stop was with 68th Antiaircraft Battalion in the pretty village of Ludwigsburg. His assignment was again—battalion S-4, supply officer. It was another light-duty job in a pressure-free environment. His two successive battalion commanders were Regular Army lieutenant colonels who had been infantry battalion commanders in combat. They were comfortable in their temporary jobs and with themselves. They had nothing more to prove. One of them was a highly decorated officer who had been a battalion commander in the 84th Division during the entire combat period. Once he learned that Ashley had been a rifle platoon leader in the division during the same period, there was a warm relationship built on mutual respect. Ashley was the club officer and the mess officer in addition to his duties job as the battalion S-4. Even so, there was enough time for a liquor and wine procurement trip to Paris and Reims—a three-day trip in a jeep with trailer through beautiful country. There was even time for a repeat trip to Switzerland. He had gotten to know a nice Swiss family with a pretty and friendly daughter, too friendly in view of his relationship with Kit Montague—-*c'est la guerre*! Kit would understand.

But then in a month and a few weeks, the soft touch came to an end. Ashley and his supply staff, a sergeant, a corporal with an irritable dose of gonorrhea, and Junior, a thirteen-year old German orphan who was his de facto aide de camp, were left "holding the bag." The rest of the battalion left —gone, gone home until the next war. The three American adults and a German kid had been left with the job of accounting for and turning in hundreds of vehicles and antiaircraft guns. Finally, the job was complete. The sergeant and the corporal were sent home. Now only Ashley and the handsome German kid were left to fend for themselves. Except for a jeep Ashley kept for himself, there was nothing left. The two of them sat on the floor in an empty stucco building that had once housed, a battalion headquarters, billets, offices, the Officer's Club and Mess. They looked at each other and laughed.

"*Ober Leutnant*, we have no home. What we do now?" Junior asked, his laughter now turning to tears.

"Don't worry. We will stay here until I find another job. Then you will come with me. *Alles ist in ordnung*—all is Ok!" Ashley reassured Junior, as a father would a son.

25

A second lieutenant with a clipboard and the look of man with a mission entered the empty building. He was either too busy to acknowledge the presence of Ashley and Junior or he chose to ignore them. Ashley followed the intruder for a minute or two and finally decided to break the standoff.

"Lieutenant, I'm Brett Ashley, the temporary resident and owner of this building with my young friend Junior here, who has served the command nobly as a volunteer for many months. We are the only members left of the 68th Antiaircraft Battalion."

"Hi, I'm Lieutenant Jim Callahan. I'm with the Seventh Army War Crimes Detachment. We are moving into the area. I'm looking for quarters and office space," Callahan said, in an official tone that gave the impression that he had no time for social chatter.

Callahan was a big, broad shouldered young officer with a strong chin and full head of black hair. From his accent, Ashley guessed he was from the Boston area. His gold bars had never been polished— the original, lacquered finish was still intact. His uniform looked as if it had just come from the military clothing store in Heidelberg. The sizing was still in the fabric. He wore the cross pistols of the Military Police Corps.

"What's this war crimes all about, Lieutenant?" Ashley asked, determined to get Callahan to open up.

"We are a detachment of about a dozen so far, headed-up by a major, an attorney in civilian life. We have only been in the theater a couple of months. We screen the records of German Nazi internees held in US POW Camps to ferret out those who are responsible for serious crimes. We are looking for the 'big fish,' not the little weasels who joined the party to save their shops and their asses. We send prisoners to war crimes units of our allies if we find out that they have committed crimes against their people. They can do whatever they wish with them. We send the big Nazis directly to prisons in Nuremberg to be further screened and tried there for crimes against humanity by the War Crimes Tribunal at the Justice Palace," Callahan said.

"That sounds interesting, Lieutenant. By the way, you missed a nice little war. Your timing couldn't have been better," Ashley said, trying to put the new shavetail on the defensive. It didn't work, but Callahan did take notice of Ashley's higher pecking order rank, crossed rifles, and combat infantry badge.

"Sure did, Sir, I was a police officer in Boston in the Army Reserves when I was called-up for this job. Up until that time I had a waiver, because of the police job," Callahan responded testily.

"Being a war crimes investigator sounds like a great job. How do you get a position like that?" Ashley asked, in a turn of the conversation to a more serious subject. He was unemployed and needed an interesting "white collar" job to fill his time before redeployment.

"What have you got to offer?" Callahan said, smiling for the first time. He realized that he now had the upper hand in the verbal dual.

"Well, this building is still mine. I still have the paper work. I have my own jeep and easy access to an array of vehicles that I just turned in."

"Well, we could use some more help, a jeep or two, and a three quarter-ton truck. This building would make a good detachment headquarters for the major. I think we can make a deal," Callahan said.

"Good, in the meantime Junior and I need a place to eat and sleep. He usually stays near the cooks. That way he eats well and never fails to bring me my early morning coffee," Ashley said, shaking hands to seal the agreement.

"OK, this makes my life simpler. I'll have Seventh Army personnel cut transfer orders for you to our detachment in the morning," Callahan said, with a pleased look. He got needed resources with no collateral. Ashley smiled too, but for a different reason. It suddenly occurred to him that there had been a changing of the guard. The old captains had gone home to mama. The Lieutenants of the Class of '44, with a bunch of rookies who had just come over from the States, were now running the show. He liked the arrangement. Yes, he liked it very much.

Ashley, war crimes investigator, began a new— far different life than he had ever imagined. Gone were the days of killing and constant fear of being killed. He lived in a private home with two other lieutenants from the detachment. The home came with a cook, a maid, and a gardener. In addition, Ashley had Junior, his loyal follower and batman. One of the lieutenants was a much decorated, former rifle platoon leader. He introduced himself by saying that his friends called him "Kentucky", which was appropriate since he came from Kentucky. The other officer was Callahan, who had arranged for Ashley's transfer to war crimes.

Captain Ted Cooper, Ashley's immediate superior, lived across the street in a more ostentatious home with Inga Von Romanoff, a real German aristocrat. Inga had all the trappings of the aristocracy— bearing, dress, fine-featured good looks, and a gracious manner. The family had earned money the old fashioned way—they inherited it and managed it very well. They maintained homes in Germany, Spain, and the French Riviera. Inga also had a classic Mercedes Victory Coupe convertible, which she had kept hidden from the Nazis and the Americans. It was not surprising that Captain Cooper found no cause for retaining her in his war crime detachment's internee camp. He released her.

Cooper was no slouch either. He had commanded a rifle company in General Mark Clark's Fifth Army during the battles for Italy and the south of France. He was from California with movie-star good looks. He was often mistaken for Alan Ladd in size and appearance. The two made a beautiful couple driving around Ludwigsburg in Inga's convertible with the top down. Her lovely blond hair was held perfectly in place by a colorful bandana of exquisite Italian silk. Their German shepherd sat majestically in the rear jump seat, and the captain, well; he always seemed to have a smile on his face.

Ashley enjoyed Inga's company. She and her devoted captain often had breakfast with the lieutenants in their quarters. On these occasions the young officers always managed to be present, shaved and showered. Her breakfast was the same each morning: continental, plus a soft-boiled egg. The young officers were fascinated with the way she skillfully severed the upper half of the eggshell, leaving the lower half in the egg holder to be toyed with. And, she enjoyed their attention. The War Crimes investigators didn't care whether she was a Nazi or a nun. She was simply a gorgeous creature, whose smile gave them pleasure.

Inga played tennis on Wednesday afternoons, the Army's traditional recreational period. She frequently asked Ashley to play when the captain was otherwise engaged. He enjoyed the games with the beautiful Inga, but soon realized that the captain didn't care for the attention given his mistress. Ashley wisely found other things to do on Wednesdays. If nothing else, the war days in E and F Companies had taught him the art of survival.

Zuffenhausen was a small farm village within a fifteen-minute drive from Ludwigsburg. The major activity in the town in June of 1946 was the maintenance and operation of an internee prison of some one thousand upper-level Nazi officials. Infantry units were responsible for security of the facility. Ashley and his administrative group were responsible for screening and disposing of the inmates. His job was much more interesting than those whose sole functions seemed to be running the "palace guard." From his office within the compound, he became the principal enforcer of standing polices or made them up as he went along. He even became involved in seemingly trivial matters such as determining the food allowance for the sick, the active, and the inactive prisoners.

Ashley saw real Nazis for the first time, and dealt with them on a day-to-day basis. If not policy makers of the Third Reich themselves, they had served as conduits of the policies from top officials. Typical among the internees were: Herr Doctor Medicus Frank, the political advisor to the German occupational commander of Paris; Rudolph Schmidt, an operative in the Reich Chancellery with an office down the hall from *Der Fuhrer* himself; and Giller, general of the Waffen SS. Giller had the respect of the other prisoners. When a superior Russian force surrounded his division, he led a classic counterattack out of the encirclement avoiding annihilation. His action earned him the Iron Cross and the personal attention of Hitler. It was a heady experience for a young American lieutenant to see them all jump to attention when he entered the barracks. It was almost as if he were still at The Military College, when he was a cadet sergeant and fourth classmen popped to attention when he entered their room.

The Allies did not always agree on rules governing disposition of prisoners. The British played by the rules. They accepted prisoners when Ashley's team determined they had committed crimes against the English. The French were selective about whom they would accept. More often than not, they kept the prisoners for a while, removed their serviceable clothing, and returned them with unserviceable French Army clothing. The Russians made their own rules. They accepted only those prisoners known to have killed at least five Russians. They were too busy dismantling German factories and shipping them piece-by-piece to their country.

For Ashley these were small problems, and did not prevent him from enjoying the good life—the spoils of war. He had time to travel and enjoy Germany and Europe. He visited nearly a dozen countries. He rode horses in the park, skied in the German and Swiss Alps, attended his first opera, and danced in castles built for kings.

But there were some minor distractions along the way. A German policeman was seen routinely stealing gasoline at night from the vehicles parked in front of the lieutenant's quarters. Junior asked to be put on guard to catch the policeman. In essence, he wanted to play soldier without realizing the consequences. Ashley let him take the guard duty one night, armed with a pistol. Fortunately, the policeman spotted Junior and turned away. Ashley, in the light of day, realized the stupidity of putting the kid at risk. Junior's adventure with cops and robbers was put on hold.

Kentucky, the decorated combat veteran, decided to take the duty the following night from his bedroom window, armed with a shotgun loaded with bird shot. This night the policeman was not so lucky. He made the mistake of rattling the gas can as he removed it from one of the jeeps. As he turned to leave the yard, Kentucky fired a single shot, hitting the policeman in the right shoulder, spinning him around, and driving him facedown into the ground. Ashley, Kentucky, and Callahan rushed to the aid of poor devil, pulled him into the house, gave him a full glass of cognac, and picked the bird shot out of his back. The "Dodge City" episode ended with the threesome taking the police officer to the hospital for follow-up treatment. He recovered. And not a single drop of gas was stolen again.

Captain Cooper showed little concern in the police incident of the night before. The next morning at breakfast he gave Ashley an order he couldn't refuse. Actually, it was one that he would never think of refusing. It was a party, an unusual social function.

"Ashley, have you ever heard of Bastille Day?" Cooper asked, with grin on his face.

"Yes, Sir. That's a famous French holiday. It's when the French shut down everything except their bars and cafes, and go ape-shit in memory of their revolution. The Bastille was a fortress in Paris that was used as a prison. The revolutionaries stormed the Bastille on the 14th of July 1789. I think that was the year. The French, thus became free of the oppression of the Royalists. *Liberte* is a big thing with the French."

"OK, you got it. Since, next to me, you are the prettiest in the group, and I have other plans. I'm going to have you represent me at the French War Crimes Detachment celebration of Bastille Day in Strasbourg. I understand they have imported the best looking nookie they could find in Paris, and the best champagne left in Reims to drink with great Strasbourger French-German food. I don't want you to come back unless you are well fed, well hung over, and pussy-whipped. Can you handle that?" the Captain asked.

"It's a big order, Captain Cooper. It will be a tough job. But somebody has to do it. I accept the mission, Sir."

"OK, smart ass—don't push your luck. Move out!" the captain ordered.

"Yes, Sir! I'm on my way," Ashley said, remembering he was still in the Army even though this part of the Army was a route-step version of the original.

Captain Louis Marchant greeted Ashley royally, when he arrived at the Bastille Day party. The invitation said: "From 9 PM until it is finished—*de 2100 jusqui`a c'est fini.*" Since the French are not noted for timeliness, Ashley arrived 30 minutes late. It was a good call. The second round of drinks was being served. He knew it would be a long evening and he preferred to remain sober as long as possible.

"*Bonsoir, Lieutenant Ashley, bienvenu,*" said a smiling Captain Marchant.

"*Merci, Captain Marchant, pour invitation,*" Ashley responded, searching for a few words from high school French, particularly since he knew from experience, albeit limited, that it was painful for the French to speak or hear anything but French.

"Have a drink. The German soldiers are our servants for a change. They will keep your glass full.

I have told them that if they don't, I will shoot them on the spot," Marchant said in English, recognizing his guest's limitation in his language.

"Thank you, Captain," Ashley said, sensing that his host wasn't joking about shooting the German.

"Call me Louis, please," Louis Marchant said. You are my honored guest. Nothing is too good for my American friend."

Ashley found his German waiter and a glass of outstanding champagne, much better that the sparkling wine that found its way to the American troops in Germany. He was glad he had worn his dress uniform. It was a formal affair. The band and the waiters were German but the rest were French. The Parisian women were stunning and stylishly dressed. It was if they had selected models with some meat on their bones. The woman with Marchant, however, was different—not French looking at all. She had glistening, reddish-blond hair. Her eyes were light brown, appropriate for a true red head. Her freckled nose turned up, and her lips were full, both uncharacteristic of the French. Ashley assumed she was Marchant's young mistress or field spouse. He knew it was typical of German generals to carry their women with them in the field. Why not a French captain?

Ashley concluded that he should have only casual conversation with the host's beautiful companion. Then a soft female voice from behind startled him for a moment.

"Champagne, Lieutenant Ashley?" the mystery lady asked.

"*Merci, Mademoiselle*," Ashley said extending a near empty glass towards her.

"*Parlez-vous francais, Lieutenant*?" she asked.

"*Un peu, GI francais, mais pas bien*—a little GI French, but not well," Ashley responded nervously.

"*Bien, speak some GI francais, si'l vous plait,*" she said, mixing French and English.

"*Voulez-vous coucher avec moi? Mademoiselle,* will you go to bed with me, Miss?" Ashley said haltingly.

"*Oui,* yes, of course. Call me Simone," she said.

Ashley belatedly realized that he had asked the wrong question, and had gotten an answer he wished, under the circumstances, he hadn't heard. He turned to a lighter topic, and in English this time.

"What is your sport?" he asked. It was a topical subject, since young Europeans normally participate in one or more sports.

"Gymnastics," she said.

Fortunately, Captain Marchant announced that dinner was ready. The first round with the irresistible Simone was over. Ashley was saved by the bell— the dinner bell.

Ashley was given a seat of honor at the opposite end of the large table from the host. The main entree was wild boar in a sauerbraten like sauce with every imaginable vegetable, fruit, and pastry accompaniment. Champagne was now replaced with wines, fine whites from Bourgogne and excellent dry reds from Bordeaux. Customary toasts were made first by Captain Marchant. He again welcomed his American guest, praised the courageous American fighting men, and saluted President Harry Truman. Ashley appropriately reciprocated with thanks to his gracious host, praise for the French people, and kind words for General Charles de Gaulle.

By then the captain's glass was nearly empty. In keeping with his ultimatum, he summoned his personal waiter, pulled his pistol and shot him. The young German soldier fell to his knees. Marchant spared him at least for the night. He purposely fired through the extended sole of the German's hob-nailed boot. The soldier, discovering that he was still alive, snapped to attention and filled the captain's glass. The guest smiled and continued as though it was part of some customary ritual. The band never missed a beat.

Exactly at twelve midnight, the band stopped playing and the captain stood up and announced: "Ladies and gentlemen, we will now proceed to the parade field for the evening's entertainment."

The ten-minute walk to the parade field and adjoining barracks was a needed breath of smoke-free fresh air. When the group came to within 50 feet of the entrance gate and guardhouse, they were surrounded by paramilitary personnel armed with submachine guns. The uniformed, rough looking individuals slithered down ropes like monkeys from trees on cither side of the gate. Marchant identified his personally trained security guard as Polish DPs, who obviously had no love for Germans. He then ordered the Poles to stand aside. They saluted and the guests passed into the VIP section of the stands of a brightly lit former athletic field, capable of seating at least 10,000 spectators. A sole German Army trumpeter stood in the middle of the field and sounded "assembly."

The show began. Three battalions of an elite paratroop regiment, nearly two thousand strong, made their entrance in perfect cadence to martial music that only the Germans can play. Suddenly, the field was a mass of gray uniforms aligned abreast by battalion behind their officers wearing perfectly shined, black knee-length boots. Captain Marchant motioned to Ashley and said: "*Apres vous, si'l vous plait.* We will take the review to honor those who gave their lives at the Bastille so that we can enjoy *liberte* today." The other guests stood in the stands as Ashley and Marchant took their positions on the reviewing line.

In keeping with international military protocol, Ashley stood to the left of the captain. He remembered how disappointed his class was when they went off to the war, and General Pealot did not allow them to take the review of the Corps of Cadets. How things had changed in two years, he thought, a whole elite German regiment was roused out of bed in the middle of night so that he could have the honor of taking the review.

The German commanding officer called his regiment to attention and saluted Marchant, who returned his salute. The commander then ordered the regiment to the position of "present arms" and motioned to the band to begin. It played a stirring version of *La Marseillaise*, the French national anthem, as the French tricolor flag was lowered. The German then turned from the flag to Marchant and reported that the regiment was formed and all were present and accounted for. Marchant then ordered them to "pass in review." Pass they did—in full goose-step. This time Ashley joined the captain in returning the salute of the German regimental and battalion commanders as they gave "eyes right" orders to their units when they passed the reviewing stand.

With the show over, the celebrants returned to the party for continued eating, drinking, and dancing. It was after a few late drinks that Marchant confided his frustration in the inability of his detachment or any other allied war crimes unit to locate the notorious Nazi, Martin Borman. Marchant felt that it was his karma to find Borman, and to bring the little weasel to justice before he could escape to Argentina with other influential Nazis. He reasoned that

Bormann, a fanatic Hitler loyalist, knew of the last moments of Hitler's life. He was known to be one of the last to say goodbye to Hitler in Berlin on 30 April 1945, when Der Fuhrer entered his bunker under the Reich chancellery and shot himself.

It was 3 AM when Ashley said *bonne nuit* to the Captain and Simone, who he assumed was the Captain's mistress and hostess for the most unusual and unreal party he had ever attended. He staggered to his assigned room, and immediately fell across the bed and went to sleep. At sunrise, he was wakened by Simone, standing completely nude in front of him.

"Wake up, Lieutenant, it is a beautiful day. It is time to get up." Whereupon she did a cartwheel followed by a backhand stand against the door, Ashley's only escape route. He initially thought he was in the middle of an insane dream. But he knew he wasn't. His head was killing him, and he found himself buck-naked without any idea of where his clothes were.

"Simone, I have an awful thought that what I see and feel is real. Where are my clothes? Any moment your lover will be coming through that door you are upside down against and kill us both. I saw him shoot that German in the foot, and I have a good idea where he is going to shoot me," Ashley said, with a sheet pulled up under his chin.

"*Mon ami Lieutenant*, I undressed you last night, so you could sleep well. Since I didn't want you to get cold, I got in bed with you to keep you warm. You were *magnifique*," Simone said. "You called me Kit, just like a kitten. That was nice."

"*C'est tres bien.* I'm glad I was, but we are going to get killed. My head is splitting open, and my mouth tastes like a platoon of Russian WACs bivouacked there last night. If I don't get a cup of coffee soon, I'm going to die anyway. Where are my clothes?" Ashley said.

"*Attention, attention, Lieutenant*, your clothes are here in the *armoire*. The Captain is my father, not my lover. He told me to take care of you. I hope I did.

"Here is a wet cloth. Now wipe your head. I will be back in minute. You can get dressed if you like," she said, leaving Ashley to sort it all out. She returned in a few minutes with coffee and a continental breakfast of orange juice, butter, jelly, and fresh French rolls. She was dressed.

"Simone, you are very nice. *Merci beaucoup*. But I have to tell your father goodbye and go back to Ludwigsburg, Germany where I came from. I will give you my address. Maybe you can visit me sometime," Ashley said.

"You need not rush. My father left early. He said to tell you goodbye, and that he had a lead on the whereabouts of Martin Bormann. He thought you would understand."

"Yes, I do. I will remember you and this weekend for a long time. But I'd better leave now," Ashley said, with a sigh of relief. He kissed Simone for the first time.

"Simone Marchant, that's something I wanted to do since we first met," Ashley said mindful of his unstated mission to maintain good relations with the unpredictable French. "You really are *tres belle, tres magnifique*." Ashley turned toward his waiting jeep. She held his hand and pulled him toward her as they walked together.

"*Au revoir, mon ami*, Brett Ashley."

"*Au revoir*, goodbye, lovely Simone Marchant."

She waved until he was out of sight. Ashley turned his jeep north along the romantic Rhine. He thought of the mission Captain Cooper had given him the day before. He laughed out loud. The captain, not realizing it, had done him a big favor.

It was after midnight when Ashley arrived at his quarters in Ludwigsburg. The next morning, he was awakened by a military policeman knocking on his bedroom door, too loud even without a hangover.

"Lieutenant Ashley, Military Police," the intruder called out, without regard for the condition of the occupant.

"Yeah, what is it?" Ashley responded.

"You had better get up, Lieutenant, a friend of yours is in trouble," the MP said.

"OK, be out in a minute."

"Last night, we picked up a German kid north of Heidelberg in a little village called Schwetzingen. He said he worked for you. He was about 14 years old, good looking kid. He was driving one of your detachment jeeps. We impounded the jeep. You can pick it up whenever you want at our police station. We put the kid in the German jail here in town. You will have to go to court get him out. We questioned the kid for about an hour. He is an honest kid. I think he told us the truth all the way," the MP said.

"Schwetzingen, eh? That's the asparagus center for the whole country, maybe even the whole world. Tender white asparagus. It's delicious! The farmers grow it in mounded rows, you know. When the tips show just above the soil, it is ready for harvest. There is nothing else much there except a beautiful 18th century palace," Ashley said, reminiscing.

"Lieutenant, it was not asparagus the kid was after."

"What was he doing there? I was in Strasbourg last night on business, didn't get back in until after midnight," Ashley said.

"He had a young girl friend with him, a local

farmer's daughter," the MP answered.

"I'll be damned. I did the same thing when I was 13. I stole my dad's new car. Drove it 50 miles, one-way, to see my girl friend. She was impressed. But my dad wasn't. He grounded me for a week and threatened to put me in jail. Strange turn of events, isn't it? OK, I'll pick up the jeep today and get the kid out as soon as I can. Thanks very much for getting a hold of me," Ashley said, his thoughts still with Simone in Strasbourg.

Ashley had no difficulty retrieving the detachment jeep. But getting poor Junior out of German jail was another matter. Not only was there German paper work involved, but American as well. Since Germany was still under martial law, Ashley had to petition an American Military Court for Junior's release. Ashley didn't visit Junior at the city jail for a couple of days. He thought two days would teach him a good lesson. It was a very bad call. Junior was a pitiful sight. He was thin, drawn, and dirty from head to toe. His eyes were red from crying and lack of sleep.

"*Leutnant*, I sorry I took jeep. I don't think you care. I miss you. I need your help. Look at my hands—all blisters! The 'sonsabitch' make me dig holes all day. They feed me nothing but bread and water," Junior said, finally crying.

"Junior, don't worry. In a couple of days, I will see the American judge. Maybe he can help us."

Ashley's next step was to go with Junior back to his cell and then get hold of a prison guard or the chief warden, if necessary.

"*Wachter, sprechen sie Englisch?*" Ashley growled, in a tone that got an instant response from the arrogant German guard.

"*Jawohl, Herr Ober Leutenant*," the guard

sounded-off, clicking his heels as he came to attention.

"*Gut*, now I want you to listen. That boy is an orphan. He is a good young man. He has no one else but me to help him. All of his family was killed by American bombers during the war. It is my duty, my obligation to take care of him. I am going to see the American judge tomorrow to get him out. I don't want him abused anymore. I want him to be fed good food and be allowed to bathe. If not, I'm going to have your ass kicked and put in solitary confinement. *Est das klar?*" Ashley yelled.

"*Jawohl, jawohl Herr Ober Leutnant. Ich verstehe,*" the nervous guard said.

Ashley returned to the jail that night with food and clean clothes for Junior. He had now had a bath and was out of solitary confinement. The next day Ashley went to the JAG office and persuaded the executive officer to move Junior to the top of the docket for the following day's trial. The judge was moved by his sincere petition on Junior's behalf, and released him to Ashley as temporary guardian.

It was a temporary fix. Ashley knew he would be leaving soon. A dark cloud was always in his inner thoughts—what would the kid do when he went home? Who would take care of him? He knew that he lacked the wherewithal to take him to the States and take care of him. His profession would be student for several years.

Ashley didn't want to bother Captain Cooper with his personal problems concerning Junior. The captain had problems of his own. He needed money to support his girl Inga in the manner she had been accustomed to. He and Inga concocted a wild export-import scheme that they thought would bring them instant riches. They first studied the economic situation in Portugal—rich in food but poor in coal. The post war situation in Germany was the opposite. The plan seemed simple enough. They would arrange, as a start, the exchange of Portuguese sardines for German coal, and garner a sizable fee for themselves. Their immediate requirement was for working capital. Inga's family money was being held in a Swiss bank account until proper identification could be arranged.

MPCs, the allied currency, were of little or no value outside of the occupied areas. Therefore, Cooper and his partner began an all-out conversion effort, the exchange of their MPCs and personal property for hard currency, preferably American dollars. Ashley gladly parted with a US 50-dollar bill for $350 in MPCs, which allowed him to cover local incidental expenses.

The export-plan went well initially for the twosome. But then they became reckless. They decided to smuggle their sizable cache through Switzerland, France, Spain and into Portugal. The plan was brilliant, but not without risk. They removed the steel fenders from Inga's Mercedes coupe and replaced them with look-alike fenders made of platinum, worth a fortune on the black market. There was speculation that when Inga and the captain crossed into Switzerland, they were arrested by Swiss border guards on smuggling charges, and were being held by the Swiss authorities pending arrangements with the US Government for their disposition. But no one in the detachment knew of their whereabouts or heard from them again.

26

"Lieutenant Ashley, I just got back from Seventh Army personnel. I've got some good news for you. You are going home," Lieutenant Callahan said.

"When?" Ashley asked.

"Here is a copy of your orders. You have to be at the port of Bremerhaven no later than 2400, 31 July 1946 for in processing. You will probably get out in a couple of days. Looks like your ship is the US Army transport ship 'Seaflyer,' " Callahan said happily.

"By God, you are right. They don't give you much notice, do they? I hope it doesn't take as long as it did on the *E. B. Alexander*, the one I came over on. That one took 12 days, but then we were escorted by navy ships through a picket line of German submarines. One of my college classmates was on a ship that was sunk in the English Channel. All aboard were lost," Ashley said, staring into space.

"Hey, the orders are good news," Callahan said. "You don't seem to be happy about it at all."

"Well, Jim, I got a problem—Junior! How can I leave him? You know he has no family, and how he depends on me. What am I going to do with him? I grew up as a teenager without a father, that was bad enough—but this kid doesn't know where any of his family is."

"I'm probably going to be around here for another year. I'll take care of him. Besides, I like my coffee delivered to me at a reasonable hour in the morning too. And since I'm now a first lieutenant like you, I am entitled to a handy man," the upbeat Callahan said.

"Thanks, my friend. That's a weight off my shoulders. I'll break the news to Junior whenever I can muster the courage. They say that one way to legally miss the boat, and not be court-martialed is to buy a dog at the last minute. They won't allow you aboard until the dog has had his shots, and goes through an appropriate period of quarantine. If you see me come through your door with a boxer in the middle of August, you will know I couldn't leave," Ashley said, now in a better frame of mind.

"I've heard you talk about the beautiful Kit Montague waiting for you. You won't miss the boat."

"You are right. You've made it easier for me. Which reminds me, I have to write my family and Kit and let them know that I will be home soon. Jim, I'll never forget your help. Thanks," Ashley replied.

Dear Kit,

Good news—I think. I will be leaving on or about the first of August on a ship called the Seaflyer. If it lives up to its name, I should be in New York about the 11th of August.

Life this past year has been a ball, particularly the past few months as a war crimes investigator. I've tried to do exactly what Cal Sinclair told both of us to do in his last and portentous letter to forget the war, move on, and enjoy life! Of late, I have been following Cal's advice.

I've seen something of twelve countries but not enough. I have lunched frequently at the beautiful Von Zeppelin Hotel in Stuttgart as the personal guest of a friend and manager. Also saw Mozart's Marriage of Figaro at the opera house there. I rode horses for the first time since being thrown from a racehorse as a kid, learned to ski at a black

*forest resort, and then went on to ski in the Swiss
and German Alps. If that wasn't enough, I danced
in former castles of kings.*

*Despite all of the good times, I miss not hav-
ing seen you in nearly two years. Since then the
whole world has changed. I'm afraid that those
of us who helped change it may never be the same.
That may not be all bad.*

Stay safe in God's hands until I see you again.
Brett.

Callahan volunteered himself and Junior to
take Ashley to the port of Bremerhaven. Their good-
natured cook prepared a tremendous picnic lunch
for the three of them to break up their long journey.
Ashley said goodbye to the family-like house staff and
tipped them generously. Thanks to Ashley's barter-
ing success, he was a lot better off now than he was
when he came ashore on the French coast.

The travelers arrived well within the estimated
drive of about five hours. During the last half of the
trip, they passed through the picturesque seascape
of northern Germany. But the beautiful scenery did
not detract from Ashley's lingering, unpleasant
thought, the difficulty in saying goodbye to Junior.
He knew he had to make it as unemotional as possible for both their sakes.

"Jim, again I can't thank you enough for what
you have done for me. Let's keep in touch please,"
Ashley said, keeping his cool so far. Then he turned
to Junior.

"Junior, I want you to take care of Lieutenant
Callahan as well as you have done for me. You have
been like a son to me these many months. Grow up
to be a good man. Oh, by the way here is 100 dollars
for transportation to your girl friend's home in
Swetzingen. Next time you won't have to walk off

with a lieutenant's jeep." He hugged Junior, and then tried to make a quick exit.'

"*Leutenant*, I will miss you much. You have tears in your eyes. When I came out of prison, I had tears in eyes but I had blisters on hands. You have no blister on hands. Why you cry?" Junior asked in all innocence.

"Junior, I have blisters inside, painful blisters. You can't see them, but they are there. I will miss you son, more than you will ever know. Goodbye. God bless you," Ashley said finally.

He then embraced Callahan and turned quickly toward the processing center. The ship stood waiting in the harbor. The next day he would be on it.

Early morning on the second of August, the ship slipped quietly through the North Sea into the Atlantic. It was then that the captain made his presence known:

"*Attention, all passengers aboard the Seaflyer, this is the Captain speaking. Welcome to the now peaceful Atlantic. We anticipate good weather all the way to New York. Our estimated time of arrival is 0900, 11 August 1946. We will keep you posted from time to time should there be any significant changes. I speak for myself and the crew in thanking you for the contribution you have made to our country. I hope you will enjoy your voyage home.*"

The captain was correct in predicting good weather and smooth sailing. What he could not forecast, however, was a disturbance in the overheated galley below deck. A half dozen GI malcontents, who had been in the theater less than a year and never strayed forward of division rear, decided to test the system. There were some reported communist cells that had infiltrated the American military. They were thought to be partly responsible for the wanna-go-home protesters who demonstrated in front of the Supreme Allied Command headquarters in early summer.

For whatever reason, the rebellious group refused to clear the enlisted mess after dinner so that the cooks and helpers could clean the area for the usual showing of the evening movie. They refused to obey the orders of Ashley, the mess officer, and a major, the designated commander of troops. The ship's first mate suggested that the rebellious group be arrested, placed in the brig in the hottest hole in the ship, and fed bread and water until making land in New York. He reminded the army officers in the chain of command that the master of a vessel had the authority to take the action under the provisions of the Uniform Code of Military Justice. Ashley and the army troop commander were in favor of less severe measures. They proposed the formation of an intra-command police force of Regular Army Military Police to restore good order and discipline. The troop commander reminded the first mate and his officers that to do otherwise could lead to delayed debarkation and an extensive investigation of the incident. The net result could be delayed release of the principals from active duty. The argument carried the day.

Within an hour, a volunteer police force armed with "billy clubs" was stationed at the exits from the mess. The protesters, seeing they were now imprisoned, began a slow retreat. As they left, the MPs announced to the waiting, restless movie crowd that due to the disruption of the six individuals now leaving the mess that there would no showing of the evening movie. The action taken proved to be successful. Six men with black eyes and split lips appeared at sick bay the next morning.

The ship arrived in New York within two hours

of the captain's estimated arrival time. There were no delays in troop departures from the ship for out-processing posts. The "mutiny" aboard the *Seaflyer* had failed.

Ashley lugged his duffel bag and suitcase down the gangplank and hailed a cab. It took him over 30 minutes to get a cab. The dock was swarming with a crowd of GIs in rumpled uniforms, all in search of transportation. Most were headed for Penn Station. Ashley had other ideas.

"Where you wanna go, Lieutenant," the cabbie asked, in a typically careless tone.

"Hotel New Yorker," Ashley responded, without a lot of small talk.

The New Yorker looked about the same to Ashley as it had in September 1944, nearly two years older and a little seedier. He remembered the inviting bar off to the left and the unpretentious coffee shop to the right of the entrance lobby. It was noon by the time he checked into his room. His first move was to the coffee shop to satisfy an urgent need for food and drink uncommon to Army mess halls and European cafes.

"What would you like, Sir?" the coffee-shop waiter asked.

"A dry gin martini with an olive, straight-up, a cold bottle of Bud, and a BLT on white toast," Ashley responded.

"All at the same time?" asked the waiter.

"Yep, all at the same time ASAP!"

"Anything else, Sir?" the waiter asked, surprised even for an unflappable New Yorker at how quickly the lieutenant had cleared his plate and emptied his glasses.

"Delicious, delicious. Check please," Ashley said.

"Your check has been taken care of by a very attractive young lady. She asks if you would like to join her," the waiter said smiling.

"Did you say attractive?" Ashley said, paying attention to the waiter for the first time. He was lost in his thoughts of the last time he was here—September 1944 at the same table with two other rifle platoon leaders from the division. They were dead now. One killed in the Siegfried line and the other in the Bulge. Why them and not me? he wondered. The unanswered questions would remain with him and haunt him the rest of his life.

"Yes, Sir, I said attractive. I would even say—beautiful," the waiter said.

"In that case, where is she?" Ashley said laughing.

"In the third booth off to the left. You can't see her from here but she is there."

"Thanks, here is something extra for you," Ashley said while moving towards his benefactor.

"Oh no, Kit Montague! It can't be? How could you find me? You are really a psychic after all," Ashley said, giving her a lingering kiss.

"This was an easy puzzle to solve. You told me the name of your ship and the approximate date of arrival. Friends in the military department at school gave me some particulars, such as when you were required to be at Fort Dix, New Jersey for your discharge. I knew you were an incorrigible romantic. My vibes did the rest. I felt you would come back to the exact place you started from. So here I am. If I missed you here, I would go over to Fort Dix and catch you there. Besides I missed you so much, I couldn't wait any longer," she said.

"Miss Montague, you are something special," Brett whispered, as the waiter delivered Irish coffees.

"Drink your coffee. There's enough raw Irish whiskey in that coffee to make you think I'm beautiful. If you don't say that I am, I will cancel reservations for the dinner in the Rainbow Room at the top of the RCA building, and a late show that I've made for us tonight."

"You are beautiful! You are! Wow, and you do have a lot of confidence in your gift as a prophesier. You made those reservations assured you would find me here. That's self confidence."

"Brett, let's go up to your room and think about how we are going visit the Sinclairs in California, visit your family, and get you back into school in less than three weeks. By the way, I have the air tickets with me that Cal's dad got for us."

"OK, let's go to the room, rest a minute, and then decide how we can beat the time restrictions," Brett said.

"Brett, wake up, wake up. I've got an idea how we can solve the problem."

"Kit, kiss me again and I'll wake up."

"Not until you stand up. You are not totally focused on real business in the prone position," she reminded him.

"OK, I'm awake."

"While you nodded-off, I thought of a solution to our California problem. Hear me out. We will make tentative reservations now for a flight out of New York to Los Angeles, allowing two days to clear Fort Dix. We will rent a car at Los Angeles, and drive to the home of the Sinclairs at Newport Beach. That would put us in there about three days from now. I will call for air reservations now. As soon as I get something firm, you can call the Sinclairs. How does that sound?" Kit elaborated.

"Brilliant, you plan like a military commander.

Some of that military college stuff must have rubbed off on you. You even delegated the tough job to me," Brett said, surprised at how workable Kit's plan seemed.

Kit successfully completed her phase of the task. Ashley had a warm and pleased response from the Sinclairs. The trip was all set.

"Kit, you won't believe what Mr. Sinclair just told me. He sounded excited about our coming. He will have his chauffeur pick us at the Los Angeles airport when we arrive and take us to their home. Then the bombshell. He plans to make a donation of several million to a separate college educational fund in memory of Cal. And get this, as a separate action he wants to build a monument to the Class of '44. He wants us to think about the proposition while we are in route and give him our thoughts on the subject," Brett said.

The long and tiring trip from New York to Los Angeles gave Brett and Kit ample time to analyze the senior Sinclair's philanthropic plan and prepare a reasonable response to his search for ideas on how to implement the plan. They both agreed that Brett should present the response, and as a woman of the period, Kit would do what women were supposed to do—look pretty and be supportive. However, if asked an opinion, it did not preclude her from displaying some of her considerable intelligence.

Brett passed along information that Cal had told him over the years about his parent's background and life style: They lived among the rich and famous in a mansion built on a high bluff with an unobstructed view of the Pacific. It didn't start out that way. It was built in sections, simple at first but grandiose in the end, in keeping with the continuing rise in their wealth. The elder Sinclair was a prominent

California lawyer turned venture capitalist. He followed the money trail wherever it led him. A few of his most affluent clients were associated with the mafia. Sinclair was instrumental in getting them out of illegal businesses into legal, flourishing enterprises. Just as boats at his yacht club rose with the tide, his fortune rose with the tide of the good fortune of his clients. Cal said that his mother was a beautiful woman, a one-time model who found small parts in B movies.

The flight to Los Angeles was an hour late. But Sinclair's faithful chauffeur waited patiently and gave them a warm greeting on arrival. The short drive to the mansion was exciting. The chauffeur acted in the role of both driver and tour guide, frequently adding spice to his stories with inside information about Hollywood stars.

27

The arrival at the Sinclairs was near ceremonial, like a Hollywood production, except the actor and actress were real, loving people. The butler met them at the door and escorted them into the library to "rest for a brief moment until I fetch the hosts." He then instructed the driver to take the luggage to specific, preassigned rooms.

Kit and Brett were wide-eyed as their handsome hosts came into the room with arms open and embraced them for a seemingly indefinite time. All eyes were moistened by uninhibited display of joy. A maid circulated with champagne and hors d'oeuvres and ever so soft classical music played in the background.

"You know Calvin. I'm Elizabeth Sinclair. I can't tell you how much it means to us to have close friends of Cal's visit us. He was so fond of both of you. We will talk, cry, and laugh a lot together while you are here. It will be a time of healing for us all. Don't ever forget, this is always your second home. Now I know you are exhausted from your long trip. Why not go to your rooms and rest for about an hour. You will find bathing suits waiting for you in your rooms. We will take a dip when you are rested, after that we will have cocktails and then dinner. How does that sound?" It was clear she was the lady of the house.

"Wonderful," the two overwhelmed guests said.

Sinclair echoed his wife's welcome. A rare visit for Kit and Ashley with the rich and famous had begun.

The Sinclair garden, like the rest of their home, was like a movie set. The gardener puttered around in a distant corner of the garden as Kit and Brett followed their hosts down a half dozen marble steps from the house patio on to a walkway. Tropical and semi-tropical flowers, plants, and trees, tall stately palms and orange and grapefruit trees nearly over-burdened with luscious fruit surrounded the walk.

The large pool area was in a Roman motif. Marble columns and imported Italian statues were professionally located around the pool. Waterfalls flowed gracefully into an oval-shaped pool where the temperature was carefully maintained at 82 degrees Fahrenheit winter and summer. A steaming Roman bath, or one the Romans would have liked, was con-nected to the pool. Arched gates framed the entrance and exit areas. The Sinclair coat of arms was carved on the inside of the arch of the entrance gate. The motto of the arms was *carpe diem*—seize the day. It was an appropriate one for the elder Sinclair. It would be obvious to any guest, friend or foe, that he was a man who seized the best of each day that passed.

"Pinch me, Mr. Ashley, to make sure this is not a dream," Kit said for laughs and to break the ten-sion.

"It's not a dream," Elizabeth Sinclair said. "It is yours to enjoy as long as you like."

"I wish we could stay for a long time, but in a few days I have to get back to the world of a student," Brett said, allowing some flexibility for the selection of a reasonable departure time.

The cocktails and dinner that followed the swim were perfect. At the end of the dinner, Sinclair of-fered an entertainment schedule.

"While you folks are here, there are a couple of

things you ought to see. I suggest George, my chauffeur, give you a tour of Newport Beach, the city and the beach tomorrow. When you finish your tour, come on back here for lunch and hang out around the pool and enjoy yourselves. Tomorrow night we will go over to the yacht club for dinner. It is a nice setting, and the grilled seafood is first class. I think you will enjoy it. Then the next day I'll have George take you in to Los Angeles for a couple of days. I'll put you up at the Hollywood Roosevelt, a modest little hotel where a few stars show up sometimes. While you are there, George can give you a city tour including the homes of the stars. I will also arrange for you to visit one of the Paramount movie sets where you will be able to see a production in progress. The guy in charge is a friend of mine.

"As I remember, your tickets call for you to fly home out of San Francisco. I have made reservations for you at the Mark Hopkins Hotel. Stay as long as you like. George will drive you to the city and drop you off at the Hopkins. This will allow you two to have some time to yourselves before you return home. You will enjoy the bar on the top floor, great panoramic view of the entire city. It's a must! I will also give you the names of a couple of good San Francisco restaurants although most all of them are excellent. Your mission, Lieutenant, and mine, is to see to it that you and your lovely partner enjoy yourselves. Now, how does that sound?" Sinclair asked.

"Absolutely wonderful," Kit answered for the both of them.

After the yacht club dinner, Sinclair suggested that Brett join him in the library for a brandy and a cigar while the ladies enjoyed an aperitif and fresh air in the garden.

"Brett, what do you think of the idea that I

mentioned to you about setting up some sort of flex-
ible trust fund for the benefit of the college in memory
of Cal? Think in terms of about five million plus whatever it takes to build a monument to the Class of
'44," Sinclair said not wasting any time getting to the
point. His decisiveness was no doubt a factor in his
enormous success.

"Sir, it's an excellent idea and a generous
amount. General Pealot, the strong president that
he is, would have to be involved from the beginning.
I would give him a million for his unrestricted use for
the college. This should win him over to your side in
any showdown that might arise with the Board of Visitors. Then I would use the remaining four million to
set-up three, four-year scholarships each year. Each
of the three departments, academic, athletic, and
military would be allowed one nomination and one
scholarship each per year. The department heads
would submit the names and resumes to you or your
agent for final approval each year.

"I particularly like your idea of building a monument to the class. No other class contributed more
to the war effort. General Pealot warned us that we
would be in the thick of it. He was right! I picture a
life-size figure of a combat platoon leader moving forward in the attack pausing for a moment to observe a
sky filled with allied aircraft enroute to strike the
enemy's heartland. It is a vivid picture because it
would be a reenactment of an actual scene on Christmas Day 1944 when the skies cleared for the first
time in a long time. Cal was flying his B-17 that day,
and I was on the ground with my rifle platoon. I waved
and cheered like hell hoping he would see me, even
though I knew he couldn't. Sir, It really happened in
the frozen Ardennes. Churchill called it the Bulge.

"Kit Montague will be your right arm. She was

born on the campus. She is the daughter of the registrar, and knows all of the principals in the departments, closet skeletons and all. Kit has the right academic credentials too. She's phi beta kappa, with a masters degree in psychology," Brett said, ending his contribution while still ahead.

"Brett, those are some good ideas. I will put together a legal document covering the specifics you have given me and I will send you a copy when it's complete. Using Kit's connections, I want you to get me an appointment with the general so that we can discuss the proposal with him and his advisors. Now one important point. I want you to be my agent on location, and as such make decisions on my behalf. On matters of major importance, you can get in touch with me. Your job will be like that of an executor of an estate. It may come as a surprise to some of the elders at the college that you have the part time job because of your age. That's their problem. Cal trusted you and so do I. You won't have to work pro bono either. You will receive an annual stipend equal to one tenth of one percent of the principal each year based on the value of the trust on 31 December of each year. Does what I suggest sound OK to you?" Sinclair asked.

"More than OK, Sir," Brett said. "Sounds great."

Brett and Kit enjoyed every day of their visit with the Sinclairs. George proved to be an excellent escort and knowledgeable tour guide. He made sure they saw the city's best tourist attractions. He took them to a nightclub frequented by the stars. They even caught glimpses of John Wayne, Lana Turner, Red Skelton, and Rita Hayworth. After a couple of days in Los Angeles, they returned to Newport Beach to say goodbye to the Sinclairs and packed for their final trip to San Francisco and home. Kit and Brett found new, compatible friends in the Sinclairs and friends never more generous. Sinclair reminded Brett that he would be hearing more from him on the college trust fund, and to check with him on employment prospects and plans as graduation neared. And that the two of them might consider working with him in California.

George took them on a beautiful drive from Newport Beach back through Los Angeles and along the ocean to San Francisco. He dropped the two off at the opulent Mark Hopkins near the top of one of the city's many windy hills.

"Thanks, George, for the wonderful time you have shown us. We wish you the best of everything in the future," they both said.

"It has been enjoyable being with you both. I've got the feeling you will be back. I saw the way the Sinclairs looked at you and you at them. Their son Cal was a warm and wonderful young man. Their lives have been empty since he left them. You two could easily help fill that void," George said in all sincerity.

"Goodbye, George, take care of yourself until we meet again," Brett said as he tipped him as much as he could afford and said a final goodbye.

Kit and Brett were now on their own for a while. They decided to spend three nights at the hotel which would give them a chance to take in the sights, smells, and sounds of one America's most beautiful cities. They planned to spend their last evening at the prize— the Top of the Mark.

And what a sight it was to see the sun set over the bay and the lights coming alive over the sprawling city. They sat by a window sipping a Manhattan, still believing they were temporary visitors in a fantasy world.

"Kit, you pinch me this time to make sure I'm here and what we saw and heard this week was real. I can't believe how wonderful and generous the Sinclairs were to us. Do you remember when Mr. Sinclair took me into his library that second evening that we were there, and you and Mrs. Sinclair went to the garden?" Brett asked.

"Yes, I remember it well," Kit answered.

"Kit, he asked for my thoughts on his planned gifts to the college. I gave him the ideas that you and I came up with. He liked our plan, all of it. He wants to implement it soon. The gift turns out to be five million dollars, which comes as no surprise. But the shocker is, he wants me to be his agent. I will have nearly complete control in handling of the trust. My annual salary as the agent or executor will be one tenth of one percent of the five million. It just occurred to me how much that is—five thousand dollars. Let's have another Manhattan. Can I afford it?" Brett asked, suddenly realizing their good fortune.

"I think you can. That is a lot of money! That's more than my dad makes as the college registrar, and he has been there a lifetime. I think we had better give you a values check to see if you still have both feet on the ground. OK, here are the questions from your psychology professor: What are the three most important things to you at this stage of your life?" she asked seriously, too seriously Brett thought.

"Well, I will have to think about the question, I assume you mean things other than God, country, and family. So in that case I have to say—The RING, the bonding symbol of the Corps; the ARMY with all of its faults; and last but not least, YOU, who are without fault," He said, pleased with himself at the eloquence of his response.

"Brett, as your self appointed shrink, I grade

you A+ on your answer! Now, I have one more final question for you. Will you marry me?" she asked.

"Yes! Why did you wait so long to ask? But one word of warning, so that you can change your mind later if you want to. I'm not the 16-year-old kid you greeted as the acting college registrar in 1940. Or the boy-lieutenant you kissed goodbye on the dock in New York in September 1944 just before the ship sailed into the unknown. I carry a sense of guilt for being alive when others aren't. I jump at the sound of loud noises. I cry easily for many things—the sight of starving children, or men dying for some politician's war."

"I'll take my chances. Meet me in the cadet chapel the first week in June," she said as she kissed him. And she found out that he could cry about happy things too—things over which he had some control.

"Kit, I had a dream last night that I had finished my final year at TMC with your help, and we left the Carolina Low Country. We were married as planned. Then, after a big reception at the Dock Street Theater, we packed our few worldly possessions and turned the convertible that Cal gave me northeast— northeast to New England. I have heard that it is a beautiful place, a place where the rich colors of the leaves of the maples, oak, and birch in September are God's gift to the people. I have heard too that snow begins in November and continues until April. And the air is clear and crisp and easy to breath.

"I could teach you to ski. I learned quickly in the German and Swiss Alps. I would attend whatever state graduate school that would accept me. You could continue to work toward your PhD or teach. Then the dream continues. I would take a year off and write a book about you and me and the war. About how we survived and others didn't. It would have to tell the painful truth. It may offend some of my old military commanders and classmates. Some will hate me the rest of their lives. But it is a story that has to be told," Brett said staring out from The Top of the Mark over the light-drenched city of San Francisco.

"Brett, let's do it! Let's follow your dream. We are still young. We have a long life ahead of us. Your military friends may or may not like what you have to say. So what? That life is behind you. Forget it. Your classmates? I think they will forgive you, for they will know from your book that you have earned the right to wear the Ring.

EPILOGUE

Ashley never understood completely why old soldiers wallowed in the nostalgia of war. Yet as time pasted, he found himself wondering about what happened to those with whom he had served. There were many, some he had forgotten, and some he couldn't forget. From the landing at Omaha Beach on 1 November 1944 until V-E Day 8 May 1945, Ashley had served under two regimental commanders, five battalion commanders, and four company commanders. He had commanded two rifle platoons in three campaigns. Through contact with division veterans at reunions and correspondence, he was able to find out something about the early post-war years of the principals:

Colonel Meddler was the first commander of the regiment. He was a demanding, hard driving Regular Army officer with little command experience and limited military and civilian college training. He was over 50 years old. It was no surprise that the physical and mental stress of the battlefield took its toll on Meddler early in the war. He was relieved of his command for cause, and was never selected for an important assignment again. He was passed over for promotion to brigadier general.

Major Thompson was the second commander of the battalion. The first commander was relieved of command shortly after landing at Omaha Beach. Ashley served as Thompson's battalion S-4 for a few days before asking for and receiving a transfer to E Company. Major Thompson was a Regular Army officer, and distinguished ROTC graduate. He was severely wounded leading the battalion in the Battle of the Bulge. He recovered, but not soon enough to return to the battalion before the war ended. The major retired with rank of colonel after serving many years in the Pentagon and other staff and command assignments. His last known service was to God as a priest.

Major Okie, the peripatetic battalion executive officer, was a descendant of a heroic Cherokee Chief. But unlike his antecedent, Okie was more eccentric than heroic. His dependence on alcohol made him an unreliable and a dangerous member of the command. He was Ashley's major nemesis throughout the war. Major Okie was returned to inactive status with the Oklahoma National Guard. His last known residence was on an Indian reservation in Oklahoma.

Lieutenant Colonel Norwell succeeded Major Thompson as the third commander of the Second Battalion. Ashley was favorably impressed with this new commanding officer—a tall handsome man with thick, graying black hair and a strong profile. Ashley saw him for the first time during the battle for Hannover. It was only the second time that he had seen an officer above the rank of captain at the front. However, within an hour after congratulating Ashley and his platoon on the success of his platoon's attack on Hannover, he too was relieved of command. Failure to aggressively pursue the attack was reported as the cause for the relief action. However, the incident did not have a significant bearing on Norwell's distinguished career. He was favored with many successful assignments, decorations and promotion to colonel. He retired in California.

Major Bill Buckley was Ashley's best friend and sponsor in the chain of command. Ashley had the good fortune to work for him for a few weeks at Camp Claiborne and as his battalion S-4 for a few months when he was the last commander of the Second Bat-

talion. As a National Guard officer with limited schooling and active duty service, Buckley's concern was
not so much about being promoted, but whether or
not he would be able to retain his present rank and
stay on active duty. He had the misfortune of being
caught in the major demobilization of the military at
the end of the war. James Forrestal, President
Truman's first Secretary of Defense committed suicide, leaving the thankless job of reducing the military to Louis Johnson, Forrestal's successor. To be
riffed or to be reduced in grade was to be
"Johnsonized". This meant that reserve component
officers, except junior officers who for obvious reasons were in short supply, could be expected to be
released from active duty or serve in enlisted grades.
Regular officers were selectively reduced in rank by
one grade or retired. Major Buckley was a survivor.
He had two things going for him—an excellent performance record and the respect of the division commander. When the general was assigned to the Pentagon as Army G-2, Buckley served him faithfully for
several years as the G-2 logistics officer. Following
this assignment, Major Buckley commanded reserve
component units in Florida where he retired as a lieutenant colonel. Ashley maintained contact with him
over the years.

Captain Tipper was the commander of F Company during most of the time Ashley was with the
company. Tipper was one of the first officers to return home after the war. He was plagued with number of physical problems as a result of the harsh conditions experienced in the Battle of the Bulge. He
was welcomed by members of his old company at one
of the first division reunions, but attended few if any
of subsequent gatherings. They say he worked for
the railroad. A friend spotted him on the Chicago to

New Orleans train, and on other occasions enjoying the fine food and drink at great New Orleans watering holes.

First Lieutenant Fortner, the F Company executive officer, and back-up commander of F and G Companies, was the most mysterious and least understood member of the command. Some believed that his problem stemmed from a threat of court-martial by a senior officer while on Louisiana maneuvers. Fortner went out of his way to be discourteous to Ashley and members of his platoon. But it never diminished Ashley's belief that he was one of the most competent company commanders in the battalion. He never attended a division reunion or maintained contact with division members. He is believed to be in Texas, address unknown.

Sergeant First Class Fisk was Ashley's platoon sergeant during the last two campaigns of the war. By the time Ashley joined Fisk in F Company from E Company they both had seen their share of mayhem. They made a good pair doing a difficult job. They had learned the survivor's war—do all that is asked of you but no stupid heroics. This way they figured they could make it. They did. Fisk returned to Texas and did well in the oil distribution business.

Sergeant Muller was the squad leader of the First Squad. He was a corporal in Ashley's platoon during the Bulge. He was a good field soldier—cool and unflappable under fire. He was one of the few from the platoon to survive the Bulge. Ashley got him the Silver Star for his courage at the battle of Dulken in the final drive to Berlin. Muller returned home to Illinois, studied auto mechanics under the GI Bill, and eventually ran his own auto repair shop.

Sergeant Murtha commanded the Second Squad. A former University of Michigan football player, Murtha was the strongest and toughest man in the platoon. He was also a strong squad leader when sober. He returned to the university, played varsity football again, and earned a degree in physical education.

Sergeant O'Rourke had the Third Squad. At 28 years, he was the old man in the platoon, and the only one with a college degree. He liked his 21-year old lieutenant, if for no other reason, he thought he was experienced enough to keep him alive. The respect was mutual. O'Rourke returned to his beloved Kentucky to fulfill his dream—open a bar-restaurant and make enough money to own a stable of thoroughbreds. He succeeded.

Max, the platoon runner and Ashley's special friend, went home to North Carolina and ran the family farm. He refused come to the division reunions. He told Ashley that he never again wanted to be reminded of the sorrows of war, particularly after seeing the 5000 white crosses at the American cemetery at Luxembourg.

Corporal Murph, the entertaining platoon scout, also did well. He reduced his consumption of red wine from excessive to moderate, and found a temporary home in the Army—he applied for reenlistment, and surprisingly enough the Army took him in. Murph was frequently seen at division reunions, surrounded by a laughing group, listening to the story of his experience in the French whorehouse in beautiful Paris.

After graduating from TMC, Brett Ashley and Kit Montague began a perfect marriage. Ashley received early acceptance from several New England universities, allowing them to combine their honeymoon with campus visits. They got as far as the University of New Hampshire, and looked no further. They were both not only accepted in the graduate programs but also as well-paid graduate fellows. They concluded that their selection was not because of Ashley's academic record, but that there was some secret quota system requiring the recipient to be an Infantry veteran, a Southerner with an Anglo-Saxon name, and married to a beautiful French Huguenot. For whatever reason, they knew that they continued to be blessed. With the income from Ashley's GI bill, their pay as graduate fellows, and the annual fee that Ashley would receive as executor of the Sinclair Foundation they made more money than department heads. They rented an entire house, not the normal room with a faculty member. So began their first-class life style in academia.

After a long hiatus, Kit and Brett resumed contact with their old friends. In a letter form Liz Rutledge, Kit found out that Liz married an Ivy acquaintance—her mother's choice—very soon after she learned that Cal Sinclair had been killed in a flight over German lines. Liz said she would be spending most of her time in Boston, but would also maintain a small place in Charleston to escape the "awful New England winters."

Ashley also received a letter of many surprises from Jim Callahan, dated 4 July 1948. It had been a year since he had said a sad good-bye to Jim and Junior. Callahan reported that all was well in the War Crimes Detachment, that he had been promoted to first lieutenant and was now the detachment commander. He figured he was lucky to have gotten promoted in view of the reduction in force throughout Europe. Promotions were frozen.

"By the way," he continued. "A big surprise. Our old boss, Captain Ted Cooper, turns out to have been a CIA plant in our operation with the job of keeping the Agency apprised of the Nazi trials in

Nuremberg. All the stuff we heard about him and Inga being picked up by Swiss police at the border was just CIA cover. Apparently, Cooper was a well-trained intelligence officer. He even made a mint for himself and Inga, in a legitimate deal by selling the platinum finders he put on her Mercedes Coupe. He played it straight—paid the import tax, etc. He surfaced in Bern. He was really a major. He took over the job as the Military Attaché' with the embassy there. That guy is some smooth cookie. He got it all. When he is not making some deal he is in bed with one of the wealthiest, best looking Kraut blue-bloods in all of Europe. Yeah, she did crack the Swiss bank account of her deceased family—with Cooper's help. Inga is now worth millions. I think old Ted will retire early. Wouldn't you?

"A final bit of news. I attended the Bastille celebration for you this year. Captain Louis Marchant is still chasing that Nazi bastard—Martin Borman. And that lovely Simone that was hot on your trail, asked me to send you her love. No wonder you returned to us with a smile on your face. She recently married Charles De Gaulle's aide-de-camp—she's in high cotton now.

"By the way, I'll be returning to Boston in early September. I start back with my old police lieutenant's job in Boston. I will give you a call as soon as I get settled in. We have got to get together soonest. I have another surprise for you. Junior sends his regards. He is doing fine. Give my love to Kit. Best Wishes. Jim."

Kit used her TMC military connections to find out when Jim Callahan's ship would arrive in New York. She and Brett met the ship. It was the end of the first week in September. There had been a few cold nights, which helped the leaves display their breathtaking colors for their new guest. It was a perfect day when the old transport made its turn past the Statue of Liberty into port.

There were surprises on both sides. Jim Callahan did not expect to be met. And Brett was equally shocked to see the guest that Jim brought with him. There was a handsome kid with him carrying his and Jim's bags like a stevedore.

"Can that be Junior," Brett mumbled to himself. "My God it is!" He said to Kit as he made a dash toward exit gangplank. Kit followed quickly. She was also caught up in the excitement of the moment.

Brett gave Jim a high sign as he passed him toward Junior. They embraced each other for a long silent minute.

"I missed you, Ober *Leutenant.* I had to see you again," Junior finally said.

"Yeah, I missed you too—a lot," Brett said holding on to the kid.

Jim and Kit watched the two, crying tears of happiness. They both knew when they saw a spark come to the sad, dark eyes of the young man that the two would never be separated again.

About the author

Colonel John (Jack) Cobb USA(ret.) has been a soldier, scientist, pilot, parachutist, war crimes investigator (Nazi hunter), writer and publisher. He has 32 years experience in the subject from the foxhole to the office of the Joint Chiefs of Staff. He led a rifle platoon in the three final and decisive campaigns in Germany and Belgium and commanded a battalion in Vietnam during the Tet Offensive of 1968. He was inducted into the Infantry Officer Candidate Hall of Fame at Fort Benning, Georgia in 1970.

The author of War Class has written numerous scientific studies and reports, edited literature and film, and prepared position papers and speeches for industry and government leaders. In addition to the novel War Class, he has written/published six other titles.

He has been a guest on the New York television show Chance of a Lifetime. He was also selected to present one of his books on Wordsmith, a VHS presentation for use by Virginia state libraries for information and education.

Cobb graduated from The Citadel and earned a masters degree from the University of New Hampshire as a graduate fellow. He is also a graduate of the Army's Command General Staff College, the Armed Forces Staff College and the Industrial College of the Armed Forces.

He and his wife Bettie Tillitt Cobb have lived in Alexandria, Virginia, since his retirement from the Army in 1974. They have three children: Katharine. an attorney, Patricia, an accountant and Edward, an engineer. Notable additions include six grandchildren.